MOTHERBORN

Motherborn

—

Nada Holland

LENDAL PRESS

First published in 2021 by Lendal Press
Woodend, The Crescent, Scarborough, YO11 2PW
an imprint of Valley Press · lendalpress.com

ISBN 978-1-912436-97-2
Catalogue no. LP0001

Cover design by Paige Henderson, Lindsey Tyson,
Jamie McGarry and Peter Barnfather
Cover illustration by Tanor
Text design by Peter Barnfather
Edited by Paige Henderson

Printed and bound in Great Britain by
Imprint Digital, Upton Pyne, Exeter

Contents

Part One: Today   11

Part Two: −1968   31

Part Three: 1968–2002   91

Part Four: 2002–   201

Part Five: Today   263

I've always been fascinated by water: by its vitality in the way that it changes. When I was at school, we used to have to go for walks on Sundays, and we could choose where we wanted to go. There was one place where the river Char will run into the Isis, and you were on a kind of island, and it was almost like the underworld, very glady and dark, with water all around you. I used to watch that for hours and hours.

It made me wonder what all those creation myths meant. How could everything come out of water? What did it mean, that the world was without form and void, and that the spirit of God moved upon the face of the waters, and divided them?

(Jill Purce, *More Ways Than One: The Mystic Spiral*, BBC Documentary, 1974)

PART ONE: TODAY

By the pool in Ubud, Bali, surrounded by rice fields—
green, crickets, cool breeze—Tamara kisses her first older
woman. Though Elektra isn't old. The woman is fierce.
Lean, yoga-athletic, Elektra de Kock is the most furious
50-year-old white lady Tamara has seen.

They're drinking coconut water, from real coconuts,
laced with Tamara's stash of Jamaican rum.

Smile, says Tamara, taking a picture to send to grey old
Cambridge, to Elektra's daughter, who 'studies mushrooms'. Tamara's own Android is in her room, she's
holding Elektra's device. A series 5iPhone which has seen
better days—Elektra directs her furious passion at people
these days, not things.

Just as the shutter clicks, the phone rings.

ගු

This virus is cracking the 'travelling salesman problem', eighteen-year-old Biology student Chinna de Kock thinks. She's in Medan, Indonesia—same country, but far from Bali. Water runs down her fevered face, sweat streaming like tears, like Jill Purce's rivers Isis and Char, but hot—not cold.

Sweat pools below her sharp little bones, in the hollow of her clavicles. The travelling salesman problem is one of the hardest nuts to crack, too: Chinna spends a good chunk of her Cambridge days obsessing over it.

On her own in her virtual lab, or in the real-world lab, with her very real, very flesh and blood young professor— all iridescent eyes, dimples, and curls—watching fungal roots, *mycelium*, at the same job. Comparing fungal behaviour to her own computer circuit boards. Neither fungi —the flesh, the blood, the professor—nor circuits, are ever far from her thoughts.

Even here, between her grandmother's four walls, in this infernal heat, watching Jill's decidedly analogue BBC documentary on her phone.

The travelling salesman problem is what programmers like her call a nondeterministic, polynomial-hard problem. The deceptively simple question Amazon faces, and anyone with business in several places: the optimal routes between many cities. It's near-impossible to solve perfectly, because the number of potential solutions increases exponentially as new cities are added.

Solving mazes and complex routing problems is what mycelial fungi have evolved to do, Merlin had explained—the bright-eyed professor, always a goldish flush of *psilocybin*, magic mushroom, about him.

Chinna has watched *mycelium*, the root network that forms the body of the fruit we think of as mushrooms, grow its way through a model of Britain in the lab. Colonised blocks of wood representing cities, from Ipswich to Bath. Each block was the starting point for a separate fungal colony, just like urban populations in reality. Chinna has watched fungi, finding the fastest ways from A to B, reinvent the wheel, recreate the nation's actual motorway network: M5, M4, M1, M6.

All by themselves.

Now she's waiting to see the virus raise the stakes, capture the entire globe. Unlike the fungus, the virus starts in one single city, branching out. Which brings the calculation within Chinna's favourite realm: evolutionary algorithm. How many ways are there to spread to cities 360 degrees in the round: in every direction?

The reason even computers have trouble with this question is that the number is near-infinite, astronomical, which is where Chinna's brain has built itself an odd kind of niche, a rarefied little shelter of mathematical tranquillity and peace.

The virus, needing a host to replicate, lacks life by most definitions, let alone a brain. But it's using human travel to deliver itself to every address on earth, like a Mastermind, monster Amazon. It's bound to arrive even here, in the back of the world, in this hotter-than-hell-itself room. If it isn't already here. Chinna needs to think about this, the virus, the travelling salesman problem, logic gates, computational biology, or she'll go insane. If she thinks about what she is really thinking—flames, *burning*, flesh of her flesh—she is lost. She's pretty much lost as it is.

Love.

Watching Jill Purce—*her professor, Merlin's mum!*—on her phone in her grandmother's room.

With her own mum hundreds of miles from here, her grandmother Sophia wailing away outside the door. Chinna has sparsely a word of Indonesian. But even she gets this. *Anak*, child—that's her.

Anak mau mati! Mau mati!

The child is dying!

౧

Day 41 in the life of God's newest creation, in what a Swiss scientist calls life's 'biological arms race against bio-technologists'.

Biotechnology, with its own agenda of beating Nature in the form of antibiotics, has given rise to ever more clever counter-inventions: bacteria with not one but several ways of getting rid of the antibiotic arsenal aimed at them.

Some can even feed on it.

Horizontal gene transfer, combined with human travel, spreads such innovations throughout the world within weeks. In his book of changes, *Arrival of the Fittest*, the Swiss scientist explains how proteins called efflux pumps force antibiotics out of the cell 'like some rescue squad pumping toxic gas out of a contaminated house.'

And so. COVID-Z. Born in rural China, this viral little fucker beats them all.

ᨈ

Day 41, and much of China is down with the flu, the rest of the world stockpiling useless stuff, while in Wuhan, a traveller sets out bearing gifts. It's a simple toy, a wooden spin top. Bought for a very distant relative, someone's great-great niece's grandchild—distant genes, distant place: a new baby born to a woman herself born in a horned long-house, in equatorial Sumatra in Indonesia, at zero degrees latitude, by a volcano crater lake. The traveller is an old man. He had consulted the Book of Changes, *I Ching*, China's ancient oracle, which promised an auspicious trip.

Good fortune! No blame!

Though borders across Asia, and in the west, glare fire-engine-red alerts, masked workers checking every entrant to every airport, even by Day 41 Indonesian guards find not a single case.

A Harvard computer model, its algorithm predicting the number of cases per country relative to incoming flight routes and traffic volume, singles out Indonesia as the world's one anomaly, the vortex of divergence. The one place where the airport checks must be about as water-tight as a Moses basket.

The Indonesian president, insulted, cites instead his country's piety, as compared to the West, and God's resulting great mercy on the Indonesian people. Travellers from Italy and Iran, South Korea, all the viral hotbeds, have long been banned, he says. Funnily enough, the Chinese are still free to come and go, as it has to be said: they do carry more than their fair share of the economical load. The president fails to comment on this, as well as on claims that, although the country vigilantly checks all travellers, Chinese or not, it does not in fact possess the technology to spot the *virus* in those checks.

So much for Jakarta, Day 41.

Meanwhile, the Chinese traveller has left Bejing. The spin top for the baby, a gorgeous nipper called Aafiyah, ten months old and trying to walk, is underway.

៣

Chinna de Kock, British—but by pure chance, like Baby Aafiyah's mother, also conceived by that volcano crater lake, between those ancient echoing jungle walls, cool and perfumed with cinnamon trees, fiddlehead ferns, screeching with capuchin monkeys—is stuck between four arid, scorching walls elsewhere in Sumatra: in a clear-felled development just outside Medan, four hundred miles north, where the sun beats down on the corrugated iron roof. The room crackles. Toast.

Chinna is dying, she can't help it. She's lost a third of her body weight. Her shape is concave.

Outside her door, inches from her wailing grandmother, her Dad Nova, Indonesian, is on the phone with Elektra, who is in a Bali spa. With her gorgeous black, queer girlfriend, Tamara.

Chinna grimaces. Mum *would* be.

More accurately, Elektra and Tamara are in a co-living community, called Roam. A boutique hotel-style, more yoga-minded, luxury version, Chinna imagines, of her own Cambridge University halls.

Chinna is still on her phone, watching *More Ways Than One*, Jill's quaint documentary on YouTube. *How could everything come out of water? What did it mean, that the world was without form and void?*

Jill Purce has the longest, lushest, blondest hair Chinna has ever seen. She can't take her eyes away. Well, '74: being longhaired, of course, was a thing. Still. *This* long?

Jill, twenty something, blue-eyed, walks on, along the river Isis, in what are possibly also the widest flares Chinna has come across, as well as the biggest, longest, weirdest-ass poncho. Fashion aside, Chinna is mesmerised.

All that hair.

Brown—not blond—and a mass of unruly curls on her son, Chinna's young professor. Her tutor. Merlin Sheldrake. Same blue eyes though.

Love.

No.

Computers are the microscopes of the twenty first century, Chinna reminds herself. Data is our new lens on nature. Mycology professor Merlin, like Jill Purce, his mum, is old school, analogue. Slicing up specimens, boiling them down, dying or irradiating and pressing between plates. It's Chinna who has been serving as his modern-day microscope, writing algorithms, crunching data—who's been helping his blue eyes see his fungi, alive. His *mycelium*.

But she's not watching Jill Purce just for traces of Merlin's gaze.

There's something hidden in the documentary, something deeper, cool as water, an undersong—soothing Chinna's flesh—flesh of her flesh—Merlin?—love—her *burning* body—

In Jill's voice, in her words, there's the peace, the enduring hum of Chinna's own astronomical numbers, her hyper-dimensional realm. Algorithm.

Chinna can smell it, taste it, feel it, even in this dementing heat, sweat gathering in the concave space of her belly. Her hollow drum filling up, like the watery world Jill describes. The river Char running into the Isis, a glady and dark underworld, cupped between Chinna's jutting hipbones, her sharp pelvis. Or like one of Darwin's own 'warm shallow pools', for life to self-originate, all over again, as Chinna is sure is happening in one form or another this very instant: microbes feeding on moulds in her belly button, fungal hyphae snaking in and out of her epidermis; her biome, her virome, inside and out, sweltering, exalted by all the fresh, fecund bio-matter, the teeming tropical banquet, pulsing with life, all over her own starving flesh.

Dying.

She turns up the volume, to listen to Jill—*any initial impulse gives rise to form*—and to override the wails of her grandmother lamenting outside.

ʊ

Any initial impulse gives rise to form. Any input.

Evolution follows an algorithm, so simple a computer can do it. Alter a virus' DNA, and you give rise to its altered form.

It's as simple as zero or one. If the mutation gives rise to a better form: select and keep. Mutate again. Select. Repeat.

It's the working mode of Chinna's brain.

ひ

Reprogrammable circuits are her domain. Zeros and ones. Circuits are sets of logic gates, each asking its input one simple question, always resulting in either a yes or a no. Together, these simple yes or nos answer the circuit's exact string, or DNA, of basic questions.

Output, in direct relation to what went into the circuit's configuration, or DNA, of its logic gates, is a circuit's function.

It follows, of course, that the DNA determines that function —though the opposite isn't necessarily true. *More Ways Than One*, Jill's documentary is called. And just as there are more ways than one for the virus to reach any one city, just as both 2×6 and 3×4 make 12, there are more ways than one to wire a circuit and get the same result.

In reprogrammable circuits, each logic gate can be changed. Each part of the circuit can be rewired—or mutated, to change its DNA.

You don't even need any real wires. Or any real-world circuits. To study circuits, and how they mutate, how changes in their DNA give rise to their form, Chinna has built an entire lab of virtual circuits, simply in code.

In the real-world lab, meanwhile, with the very real tutor, she's been working on the travelling salesman problem with fungi. Together with a researcher named Adam, who's developing a biocomputer.

Mycelium is a network of long, microscopic tubes, which can split and fuse again, a dense fabric which can spread in all dimensions, over large areas. Adam researches how electric pulses coordinate the network's activity, just like our own neural networks—like a spread-out, body-wide brain. Or, as Adam prefers to think, like logic gates.

Mycelial networks 'compute' data encoded in electrical spikes, Adam likes to say. *Once we can quantify and standardise how the network responds to any given stimulus*, he'll sip his coffee in the lab, tapping his keyboard with a meaningless QWERTY, just for something to type, *it becomes a living logic circuit.*

Stimulating the mycelium, using a chemical or a flame, we could input data into the fungal computer.

Flame—burning—

Chinna will go insane.

Slicing, boiling, dying, squashing between plates—

Chinna lies on the lurid, 3D-printed sheet of her grandmother's bed, sweating, watching Jill, and returning again to thoughts about travelling salesmen, viromes. Circuits. Her virtual lab, her virtual world.

Where her computer is her microscope:

More Ways Than One. Circuits solve the travelling sales-man problem in more than one way. But Chinna can't find the words to explain—

The same thing occurs in the way they mutate. Their DNA, too, the way the circuits rewire—changing each logical gate, each gene of their DNA, *while keeping their functions*—it's the travelling salesman problem, but in the round, in the, in the hyper…—

It's the fastest routes to 'cities' 360 degrees in the round, and that again in the round, 10 to the 46 times, but that doesn't begin to describe it—nor the leaps and bounds, the *speed*—

Let alone how—*how do they do it?*—

There isn't the words, there's barely the *thoughts*.

Chinna can't eat, can't speak. Words. What do they *mean*?

In the face of everything—

Not just the beauty, the speed, but the heat, her inflamed brain—cataclysm—pandemic—burning—

She stares at Jill Purce on her phone, darts a look at the clock on her grandmother's wall—ornate, Arab script—black, quivering hands saying quarter to twelve, nearly noon, but it's really *a minute to midnight*—

QWERTY

24

Chinna has fallen between the words. Her grandmother wailing, Dad on the phone, extinction, climate catastrophe, free fall—what does it all mean?

What Chinna is thinking, watching Jill Purce through her own black eyes bloodshot with heat and lack of food and sleep, is *how*—

How her domain—the hyper-dimensional, astronomical numbers of her pet circuits, left behind to breed on her Cambridge hard drive—are mutating at warp speed, with quantum leaps—

The way the virus is.

ʊ

You have to come, Nova says on the phone. Gatwick yesterday had been all stiff upper lip, not a face mask in the entire airport. As it is for most ordinary, preoccupied people today, Day 41, the virus to Nova is still something happening elsewhere in the world. Even Jakarta International had been tranquil, almost sleepy. Indonesia has a clean bill of health. Not a single case. Himself not one to overdramatise, the whole thing is well under Nova's radar. He has bigger problems. *The college sent her home. Either that or they'd section her. She won't speak, lost a third of her body weight, hasn't eaten in weeks—*

He listens to his ex. *I couldn't look after her in London*, he says. *I just got her on the first plane, Elektra. She has diarrhoea, flu, can't walk, she needs a bed, to sleep with family, eat. She's too weak to move. My mother can cook. And she knows how to bring down fever...*

Sophia's home sits in a barren development of identical rows miles from the nearest road, in a stripped zone the size of the Hiroshima bomb site, about half an hour's drive from Medan. Her house is one room, which also holds the tiny tiled concrete bench that forms her kitchen. It has a walled off section with a door, a tiled basin and a hole in the floor: the bathroom. Plus four more walls. The one bedroom. The room Chinna is in.

The one bed.

Which sleeps Sophia's entire family.

Nova waits for his ex-wife Elektra—in her Bali, poolside, co-living spa, designer landscaped, al fresco bathrooms with orchids growing on walls, each airy room fragrant with ylang-lang, frangipani, dimpled with shade—to respond.

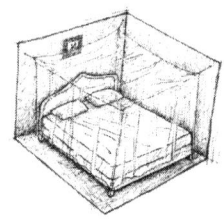

And the Arab clock on the wall reads a minute to midnight. And Elektra curses her husband, and howls. And waters part, and rivers break, and Elektra howls, and heaven and earth shake.

And you howl, Elektra, and your howls, your wails overtake Sophia's. And your wails overtake Sophia's, wailing outside the door.

And you howl and curse your husband. And strike, claw, bite at his face.

And the room shakes.

And outside the door, Sophia wails, and calls upon Allah, and inside Elektra calls upon the Great Mother.

And we are not Allah, nor the Great Mother, nor are we

God, we are none of your human forms. You lie in Sophia's room, Elektra, lie on the bed and strike your husband's face, screaming murder and rape, and cursing Creation.

And you scream, you plea to us in your own imagined forms, Ishtar, Isis, Inana, all your Great Mothers of heaven and earth.

And you echo words we hear through the ages, Elektra, and your words are the words of ages, and your pleas are the pleas of ages.

And we are not Ishstar, Isis, Inanna. Yet you plead, and beg and call upon us, and echo the High Priestess of Ur. And yet you beg, to turn dark into dawn. And yet you plead, *to run*, to escape.

And yet you echo the words of the High Priestess of Ur: *My body has experienced your great punishment, Inanna, bitter lament keeps me awake.*

And ever since the Priestess of Ur set her words in stone, we've heard your cries for mercy, compassion, care for yourselves.

And since your chorus could speak, Elektra, since the High Priestess set her words in stone, we've heard your pleas for a plague, a pestilence on your assaulters.

Mercy, compassion, care, lenience are yours, Inanna, and to cause flood storms, to open hard ground and to turn darkness into light.

And you plead and curse and look at the clock, Elektra.

And the clock reads a minute to midnight. And you imbue the black hands of your clock with meaning.

And the hands go around in circles, in spirals with no beginning nor end, like us, the ones you call gods. The ones who see all. And we are neither here nor there, Elektra, and we are not then and not now.

Where is your girl, Chinna, that is all you want to know.

And we cannot tell you, Elektra. We bring mercy, compassion, lenience. And yet you are deaf with fever, and are blind with rage.

You will break. Before your clock strikes twelve, your time will come. And you will rupture, and your skin and tissues will sunder, no matter how much you curse your assaulter, your husband, and curse your fever, and curse your world. And only the blood and the flesh of your daughter, Chinna, flesh of your flesh, can save you.

Blood of your blood.

And all we can do is hold back your black hands and your time and turn beginning to end and end to beginning. And turn back your clock.

PART TWO: −1968

[Jill Purce, an artist in her early twenties, walks the green and blue ribbon of Oxford, along the banks where the river Char meets the Isis. Jill's voice, high, received pronunciation, sounds very young. It's 1970s celluloid footage, with a brown-and-green and flared-denim palette, sepia tones. A stone lands in the river, leaving concentric rings]

You can't see the forms in water, until you disturb it.

[Water roils]

Any initial impulse, like this flow rushing into calmer waters, gives rise to form. For the resistance causes the flow to turn back on itself, creating a kind of inverted shape.

[Jill's longhaired silhouette against the turbulent river]

When water flows past something that resists it, like a stone or a post sticking out of the water, forms are created, like this rhythmic chain of vortices.

[Calmer water, flowing and swirling and passing along]

Each spiralling vortex is an entity independent from the flow, with its own characteristics of rhythm and speed. And yet if you see it in the wider context, it's not separate from the flow.

It can only return to it.

Chanting is a healing art, Jill Purce will say later, *a communal tuning in to what lies beyond what we can see. Everything that we know of in this world is made of vibrations.*

As Jill Purce will tell Chinna, more than 50 years after making the documentary, when Jill is a voice healer and family therapist: *a child is a shape, a form, born to a family constellation.*

I, Chinna, trying to conceive, am listening with intent. The ghosts of my dead ancestors, with their cataclysmic pasts, clamouring in my head. Jill, old now, still blond, goes silent. Her voice, that formidable gong, lingering for another moment among her Hampstead curtains, then truly absorbed into the heavy velvet, as Jill returns to the flow of her own thoughts. Rivers, waters, spirals of thought, oracular now, in their prescience.

And I, Chinna, Chronicler, dreaming of becoming a

mother myself. Murmuring, whispering origin stories, to lure my own child, still softly churning in dreamtime, into this world. Chanting, under my breath, the vibrations of her first ever shape, a name. *Poppet*.

Family constellations. The pattern, the story of how she will come to be. And like any Chronicler, I start at the source. With a hum, a word like a comma, a spiral, with its big belly—I imagine pointing at Poppet's own—and a little tail at the end: ℧

Motherborn.

In her own future world, Poppet draws the shape, the circle of *mother*, the downward little coil of *born*.

In the beginning, there was the word. Chroniclers, timekeepers, organise, I tell her: summarise, drawing tables and timelines. Words fill our natural histories. Timekeepers fill libraries with our hypotheses, with our conflicting stories and accounts.

Chronicles, fact-finding tomes. Seeking the astounding clarity and simplicity—which in turn organise complexity: the infinite variation underlying even the most basic mutations in nature. In our own bodies and genomes.

Even some of the smallest chemical reactions required for natural selection to favour a newly formed molecule, if left to pure chance, might take longer than the history of the universe itself, to occur.

Now I have her attention.

So how shall I ever come to life? How does it work?

But I'm going too fast, I'm running ahead, I'm in the future instead of the past. It's a minute to midnight, and young Chinna has fallen between the words, into the vortex, a wordless, eternal realm of timeless and unchanging forms.

The beginning, around fourteen billion years ago, is darkness, single-pointed heat, then the first ever flash, and there was light. But the universe is never a thing; it's always a verb, a song, a harmony, as much as a shape. A self-organising vibration, much older than natural selection or life itself. Atoms emit or absorb radiation, according to their forms, which combine in molecules with yet different wavelengths, yet different hums. These waves shape themselves into spiral arms, the gravitational waves of galaxies, pushing atoms so close together they fuse: matter into stars, and those into systems.

Stars implode, casting out choirs of inorganic drones, trills and chimes like helium, nitrogen, phosphorus and gold. Clouds of interstellar gas join in with a polyphony of organic voices, organic structures, organic molecules. They're also thick with life-giving water and other vital elements.

Around five billion years ago, our own Milky Way becomes an armed spiral, forcing matter into a gravitational pull strong enough to cause our own nuclear fission. The scale of the blast, outwards, counters the inward, gravitational pressure of the spiralling waves, and becomes the self-perpetuating helium explosion that is our sun.

Rapidly, Earth's proto-disk forms. Earth and moon both appear, around 4.5 billion years ago. Meteorites and comets bombard us soon after—3.8 billion years BC. Bringing down ten times more water than all our modern oceans combined, showering us with a thousand times more gases than today's atmosphere holds, and bringing many of life's key components. From the amino acids living things use to build the proteins that make up our DNA, to carbon—at least ten times more than the total carbon spiralling its way through every living cell of our planet today.

(Newly arrived in Cambridge, only seventeen, Chinna, like Earth's parched little disk, hungers for all of this. Having grown up in an East London tower block, Chinna has been plugged into her Mac from age six, has maths and algorithm at her fingertips—but she's starved for natural history, anything sap-soaked and verdant. Earth swallows those biblical showers. She soaks up her professors' words.)

Light carbon, the kind photosynthesising cells like to eat, with a wavelength her own instruments can still hear today, gets trapped soon after the deadly bombardments. The meteor showers kill any possible previous life on earth—but listen to this.

—In Cambridge, young Chinna pricks up. In her unborn world, the tiny coil of my future daughter quivers, alert—

In 2015, Elizabeth Bell, a young California researcher, turns everything we think we know about our earliest planet upside down. Even before the bombardments, she claims, some hardy bit of green feeds on that plant-favoured carbon. It fossilises into graphite, which in turn finds itself trapped in zirconium, around 4.1 billion years

BC—a mere four-hundred million years after Earth's own birth. Her team find it in Jack Hills in Australia.

Life on Earth starts almost the instant the planet itself does. It might take a few hundred million years to get cracking with photosynthesis, but instead of the boiling sea of lava we think of as Earth before the shower of water from the meteorites, it's a much greener place, already teeming with photosynthesising bacteria. Blue-green algae or forever lost metabolisms—extremophiles thriving on heat, carbon and light—that we can't even imagine.

(Like little Chinna herself, in her childhood room, wired to her Mac, but brimming with life on the inside.)

The universe's very earliest tune, its drones and trills, combine with its organic voices, almost instantly bursting into the polyphonic choir of life's early molecules. That choir is not an isolated entity created in some singular location, some earthbound solo aria, like Mozart's *Don Giovani*. It's the universe's very form, its self-frequency, its undersong. It choruses through space, it choruses on Earth, wherever catalysts like iron sulphide and zinc sulphide zing, such as Earth's hot, volcanic, oceanic vortexes and vents. It choruses in lightning and gases and water.

And it soon starts spiralling further inward, curling up into itself, creating the self-sustaining, self-repeating rhythms we think of as life itself.

(*Polyphony*.

It's a term young Chinna's professor uses to compare an African song, 'Women Gathering Mushrooms', to mycelium.

Oh, to see him do it! *There's no leader, no soloist...*

His eyes will light up. *When I soften my hearing, something happens.*

The many melodies coalesce to make one melody that doesn't exist in any one of the voices alone. I can't find it by unravelling the music into the separate strands.

It's an emergent song.)

↺

Motherborn, she will lure the little shape of my comma, with her clever lullaby, her murmurs, her knowledge. *Yes* —she has my attention.

In my own future world, I draw the shape, the circle of *mother*, the downward little tail of *born*. Even drifting, floating out here in dreamtime, in my proto-world of probabilities and possibility, before life on Earth, I'm not dumb.

I hum back, turning my slow turns in deep space, murmur in return. *So how does it work?*

↺

Listen, I respond. Poppet. Listen, and see.

We're myopic, and hard of hearing. We think of life as resembling ourselves, genotypes with DNA, we think of metabolisms as resembling our own—solo *Don Giovannis*, lone, complex peaks in the universe's undersong.

But the citric acid cycle, a network of ten chemical reactions, uses carbon as building blocks, and feeds on inorganic molecules and energy-rich nutrients to spontaneously replicate itself without any nucleus or RNA, possibly forming life's earliest autocatalyst, self-replicating metabolism.

The cycle, again, is not an entity, but a harmony, a network of reactions. In the process it produces, as it still does in our own bodies and those of all our ancestors, molecules that are the ingredients for many of the sixty-odd building blocks of life today, such as sugars, amino acids, DNA nucleotides, plus the lipids that will complete the spiral of earliest life. As you'll see.

Each of these products spiral off in their own directions, involving yet more elements, binding to themselves yet more processes, creating enough complexity for natural selection to start kicking in, saving the best to keep proliferating.

Mutate, select, repeat.

But life does not begin with genes. Nor, clearly, does natural selection.

Earth's volcanic, hydrothermal vents rich in iron sulphide and zinc sulphide seethe with clay minerals, which twirl parts of RNA into long strings of nucleotides without any other help at all. All natural selection needs is a container. With the help of the same clay minerals, some of those lipids produced in the citric acid cycle will, when in water, spontaneously curl up in a circle, creating a tiny blast, a membrane, a womb, the earliest cell: an echo chamber, holding a metabolism's melody together, perpetuating its song, to repeat and innovate, to riff on infinite variations.

The membrane, with its feeling, sensing skin, also forms our first brain.

How does it work?

Once nature has created its first metabolisms, and the twirling RNA replicators, plus the lipid membranes to hold it all together, life as we like to think of it is underway. Lifeless membranes will replicate even without DNA, spontaneously forming droplets, copies of themselves, containing their RNA contents. How these earliest cells fall into step though, how their RNA vibrates to the precise hum of the enclosing membrane, is still a mystery. If the RNA would grow faster than its membrane, the cell would explode. Any slower and the RNA would be too diluted to fill each new droplet as it forms, leaving its offspring lifeless, void.

It's the essential ratio, that universal, eternal tone, the *om* within the undersong.

The exact rate of expansion, which prevents the universe from either exploding or imploding—

Earth's life-bringing distance to the sun—

The golden mean which rules the speed of growth of the logarithmic spiral itself—found everywhere from the spinning arms of galaxies to the sea's nautilus shell—

As it is, little Poppet, in your own dreamtime comma, your little belly, and tail.

Perhaps this underlying rhythm is just the universe's oldest, most enduring habit, formed at the very beginning, a routine engrained so deeply, so solidly, that it grounds, sustains and pervades everything else.

It's a harmonising force profound enough to carry all the teeming innovation, all the passionate involvement of every conceivable process with everything else, creating the baffling complexity of even the simplest genetic mutations, of the fusions and mergers, the symbiotic exchanges found in every single phenotype today. From the photosynthetic chloroplasts with their own DNA settled snugly inside the membranes of plants, and their distant relations, the mitochondria, likewise with their discrete genome, living within our own cells—to the bacteria, fungi, archaea, microbiomes and viromes that make up each living being including ourselves.

(Involution, not evolution, Merlin Sheldrake, young Chinna's professor, will call it, this rolling inward, not out, involving everything on our path in innovation and exchange.)

From the start, this rolling-in habit of sustenance keeps running deeper, evolving. Long before Elektra or Chinna are born, their patterns form. Membranes protect, feel, sense exactly what to let in and what to keep out.

Self-organisation forms Earth's oceans and crust. Compressional tectonics yield the Ur supercontinent. Around the time it breaks up, bacteria start photosynthesising, eating carbon and producing oxygen. The continental plates start drifting.

As Earth changes, environments change, and metabolisms become more complex. Various bacteria can survive radiation and corrosive acid, boiling water, ice, seawater of more than thirty percent salt, live on the bottom of oceans so deep the pressure would crush us. On the most hellish sources of fuel, bacteria create every single one of those sixty building blocks: including the twenty amino acids used for nucleid proteins, DNA, of which we can make only twelve. The hardiest ones thrive on an entire catalogue of things that would kill us.

Their metabolisms evolve exponentially. At least three billion years before we appear, proteins take over RNA's job in expressing our genes. Proteins have twenty different amino acids—RNA only four. For a string of ten characters, the number of combinations goes from RNA's four-letter alphabet, around a million different types, to protein's twenty-lettered alphabet: ten trillion possible genotypes. As protein strings grow longer and longer, the number of possible genotypes increases to astronomical heights.

(*Astronomical heights.*

Young Chinna's world, her still little niche, the place

where genotypes grow exponentially, at quantum speeds: her timeless, hyper-dimensional realm of pure maths—beauty and peace—has arrived.)

ʊ

A metabolism that can survive in more than one environment needs to get more robust, and thus needs more chemical reactions, becoming more complex. Life's complexity and robustness increase with environmental change. And as complexity grows, so does the number of possible genotypes: a self-organised, spiralling network of creation and innovability, growing, like everything else favoured by nature, at that mystic, life-enhancing, deeply habitual and ingrained logarithmic rate.

Family constellations, Chinna repeats, calling out to me. The pattern, the story of how I will come to be. She hums the other word, my form, the comma, the spiral, with its big belly—she imagines pointing at my own—and the little swirl at the end.

I feel myself taking shape, my tiny taillet lifting. Listening.

520 million years ago, almost to the day, an early crustacean, little Fuxia, swims along the sandy ocean floor with her young in tow. The four tiny shrimp stay close to her tail, exploring the rich sand, teeming with arachea, plankton. But Fuxia doesn't let the nippers out of her sight.

The hologenome of the coral reproduce themselves more or less wholesale, the plankton around Fuxia too replicate without much ado. Her other fellow parents, of the myriad species roaming the ocean floor, simply trail blobs of eggs for a while before swimming off—some early fish, worst parents of all, can't tell the difference and turn round, feed on their own young.

But Fuxia doesn't only carry her eggs full term, she protects and cares for her children till they're grown. Her innovation will further deepen the habit, the pattern, the rolling inward of nature, rolling out mammals like us later, into infinity.

Even if it won't save Fuxia's own young. On they swim, the four tiny shrimplets, barely a few millimetres long, sticking close to eight-centimetre-tall Mum. Before the whole group is buried in fine sediment.

The first known mother, four little ones in tow. The first individual who's not just a solo entity, not even within her own species. She has a fully inheritable,

ian trait, extending herself beyond her own boundaries, beyond the scales of her body, circling the network of her own species' environment, a virtual membrane embracing her young.

Their remains were found in the Chiungchussu Formation, a fossil site near Lake Fuxian in South China, dating back to the early Cambrian period when the oceans held mostly soft-bodied animals. The ephemeral, fragile bodies of most other beings at the time, hairline, single-celled filaments of fungi—*mycorrhiza*, life's earliest roots—involving, enrolling in and entangling all life, have rarely survived.

(Filaments have been found suggesting fungi have been around for about two and half billion years, but undisputed evidence starts 600 million years ago, Merlin will teach.

Young Chinna, starved for green, will read his lips.

Read my lips, she'll hear him say. *Six-hundred million years.)*

Adorable, our youngest selves, so gullible. My dear Poppet.

Mycorrhizal relationships will later appear independently more than 60 times on land, in separate fungal lineages, so surely they first evolve, over and over, underwater: early rhizomes fusing and merging with their extended biomes, networks of archaea, microbes and bacteria, a polyphonic choir. Fusing in particular with the abundant blue green algae they're metabolically so compatible with, and that will shape life—grass, flesh—*love!*—as we know it. As Merlin will put it, plants are 'fungi farming algae'.

Fungi appear underwater, privately, barely leaving a trace, forming symbiotic lichens, plants, billions of years before ever growing into the entities we call mushrooms today.

(Polyphony, again, that term Merlin likes. *Polyphony*, he will say, talking about fungi, and shivers run down Chinna's spine.

Hyphal tips are like voices, each exploring a soundscape for themselves. No voice surrenders its own identity. Nor does anyone steal the show. Each sings her own melody, no two are alike. Each is free to wander, but their wandering can't be seen as separate from the others, the whole. There is no centre or command. Nonetheless, form emerges.

Mycelium, his face will dimple as he'll spread his hands, as if caressing some intangible cheek, or lip, or curve, *is polyphony in bodily form*.)

ও

All flesh is grass, the ancient Old Testament chronicler, Isiah, says. The fungi-algae symbiosis—plants—the resulting Cambrian green boom, extract so much carbon from the air, they produce the Cambrian Explosion. Land animals flourish, from dinosaurs to birds and mice and everything in between. As Chinna's tutor will wonder out loud, bringing Chinna to such heights of feeling, plunging her into the vortex, causing her to stop eating, stop sleeping: *If all grass is fungus, and all flesh is grass—does that mean all flesh is fungus?*

It will be Day 15 of the virus, a Sunday, and Chinna is still in Cambridge, weeks before she'll be carted off by her father to Medan. Chinna will be at Merlin's door, still bearing her full body weight, and wait. Half lost in her tutor's gaze.

Taking a flame to a mushroom, to measure strain, Chinna will think, studying Merlin's face for some recognition, affirmation that what she's feeling in her body—searing, cringing *pain*—is real.

If all flesh is fungus, is this fellow man, this flesh that she loves, *loves*, this fellow fungus, who can stand right across from her and explain how fungi feel pain—is this flesh apparently feeling no pain—this man whom she loves— loves!—

—Is this *love*?

What would Isiah say?

Back alone in her own Cambridge room that night, she'll wish she could ask her mum, all the way in Bali, in volatile, volcanic Indonesia. She almost says it out loud.

Mum?

ᘉ

Motherborn, she'll say instead, so much later, luring the little shape of my comma. *Yes*. I'm paying attention.

But there's still no human mothers in our constellation, no sign of Chinna, nor Merlin, nor even of the Old Testament, or Sophocles, the Greek playwright who created Electra, after whom Chinna's mother is named. Nor of Electra's chorus, the Women of Mycenae—not in a long while.

Still, our habits, our patterns evolve, and endure. It's the

Cambrian era, and in Indonesia, on Sumatra, Mount Toba erupts, an explosion reverberating throughout space, preserved in the radiation record today. Still life soldiers on. From fungus grows grass, and from grass grows flesh: animals grow more complex. The more complex we get, the longer we take to build and live, and the longer our generations, the more hampered by slowing evolution we become. We animals are on the slow track to innovation. Bacteria, in and out, on top of this intergenerational speed, allowing entire populations to mutate in the evolutionary blink of an eye, more or less have sex sideways, casually swapping DNA, the horizontal transfer involved in lateral genetics—as opposed to our vertical transfer from generation to generation.

But this sideways transfer also happens between classic 'branches' of the Tree of Life, fusing and merging the branches back together at points: the fateful lateral genetics. The lifeless viruses are masters of this, simply reprogramming a host cell to copy the viral genome.

(Yes, in Chinna's day we've arrived in Medan, Day 42, and the virus is breaking the travelling salesman problem. It's about to dismantle the world as she knows it. It is fateful.)

But in humans, retroviruses contribute around 8 percent of our total DNA. And at no point more fatefully so—for Chinna and Elektra, and every other being, as the Old Testament will have it, from woman born—than, more than 25 million years ago, when a retrovirus enters our closest ancestors, apes.

It becomes a syncytin, which is a cell with double DNA,

containing both the host and the viral genome. Just as certain bacteria merged into the cells of multicellular beings much earlier as mitochondria, this double DNA is now part of our own biont, with stunning results. It forms synctiotrophoblasts, tightly strung bubbles making a protective layer in the placenta, allowing the foetus to draw nourishment from the mother's blood—while still maintaining its own genome. Without this viral DNA, simply living on, side-by-side with our own—this sideways innovation—*none* of us will be born.

ひ

All that remains to our constellation is my cradle, that Sumatra crater lake, and how it comes to be at the centre of the world.

From pre-Hadean times, the continents keep drifting—though that might not be the word. Tectonics are brutal. Tibet soars up from Antarctica, South, arriving all the way in China, North. In the planet's most cataclysmic crunch, Antarctic New Guinea gets pushed towards the rest of current Indonesia, on the tropical Sunda plate, in turn forced all the way down from the opposite, Northern end, today's Arctic pole, Siberia.

Between them, the two oceanic plates, plus their combined continental ones, create an inverted shape, a spiralling vortex, tearing off land masses, squeezing them into the ribbonlike, 180 degree Sumatran swirl on the equator (where, at zero degrees, between its ancient volcanoes, both Chinna and Elektra will, billions of years later, find themselves lost in a mountain market maze.)

The spiral tears the fist of prehistoric Sunda into the archipelago's slender, radiating fingers—As its heart, the Sunda vortex, keeps sinking and spiralling inwards—Its volatile shocks and pressures creating, quaking, inundating with tsunamis—Bali, Lombok, Aceh—

—Radiating out all around the Pacific—

—Laying the Ring of Fire, the fault lines of earthquakes, volcanos and biblical floods, encircling the globe—

Nowhere quite as violently as in that volcanic hotbed, Indonesia.

Poppet holds still.

Sunda, I whisper.

Not only my cradle, but the heart of our Chronicles, our natural geohistory: the human story, within all that primordial cataclysm and violence, from big bang through nuclear fission to vortex.

Three million years ago, early hominoids appear, start their trek out of Africa, into Europe and Asia, where Java man appears around a million years ago. The Sunda Arc still being squeezed between plates.

Sumatran Mount Marapi explodes, creating a fertile plateau: the little Minangkabau market town of Bukittinggi, high up in the mountains, mothered by volcanic ranges—a protective membrane, all around. The maze.

By Day 42, the virus will be making its way even here.

But three hundred thousand years ago, homo sapiens finally emerge in Africa, in turn dispersing around the globe, like the virus, towards Sumatra, at just the same time that Mt Maninjau, Marapi's sister volcano, erupts, leaving a crater—a cradle—for Baby Aafiyah's mother, Lia, in the Minangkabau longhouse by the lake all those years later.

The cradle for me.

Around 70,000 years ago, Java Man and Chinese Neanderthals called Denisovians, plus Homo Erectus, still interbreed around here. But imagine this.

Yes. I am here.

Modern humans not only exist, but already make their first ever art—in an Indonesian cave, right at the heart of the Sunda vortex. Chronicling not themselves, as we, their myopic descendants will—we and our selfies, from Genesis to the Insta-sphere—but their networked, pan-biotic world: sticks with birds' heads, bison, and the adorable dwarf swine still found here today.

Depicting not just themselves, but their proportion, their life-bringing ratio to everything else.

Other sustenance than this joyful art is also making its way. Again, from China. About 2000 BC, the Austronesian expansion begins, bringing rice from the Yangtze valley. Austronesians cross the oceans in boats, carrying with them their viromes, as they still will today—the little spin top, Baby Aafiyah. But also that mythical animal, especially for the future Minangkabau, the mountain people who will name themselves after it: the water buffalo. The Carabao.

Rice grows, and on the Sumatran equator, the Minangkabau rice goddess emerges, Saning Sari, blessing that cradle for me, in the crater lake, between steep jungle walls peopled by capuchin monkeys, and the lake's native orchids and ferns, lichens, lianas, all entangling the great mahoganies and fragrant cinnamon trees.

Now for the word. In Sumeria, just three hundred years earlier, princess Enheduanna, daughter of King Sargon of Akkad, is made High Priestess of Ur. She becomes my first named predecessor.

The first named Chronicler in history, long before the Old Testament, long before Isaiah, when she writes her Hymn to Inanna.

To run, to escape, to quiet and to pacify are yours, Inanna. To rove around, to rush, to rise up, to fall down are yours, Inanna.

My body has experienced your great punishment. Bitter lament keeps me awake.

Mercy, compassion, lenience are yours, and to cause flood storms,
to open hard ground and to turn darkness into light.

The first known poet. The first known woman's words.

.

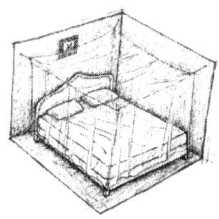

In the beginning, there was the word. And the earth was without form, and darkness and void. And there was neither life nor death. Neither time, nor space. In the beginning, you were none, Elektra, yet it is the beginning and we are here. And you were none, Elektra, yet we are all. We are the word. The alpha and omega. Beginning and end, the circle.

And you are the becoming, Elektra, the expiring. You are the rise and the fall, the peaked line, the dying. In the beginning, there was the word. And the earth was void, and there was neither time nor life. And there was no seeking.

And yet you seek. And yet you quest. You quest your origins, the origins of life. A mirage, Elektra, a mirror. The beginning of life is the beginning of death.

With every breath you take, you lose an eon.

Every word you say parts you from the very thing you are trying to name.

And yet you hold on, with everything that you've got, to the last breath, the dying word. And yet you plead. Struggle and fight, and you curse heaven and hell, Elektra.

Your clock on the wall, your black hands read quarter to midnight. We have set back your hands. We try to soothe you, *it is not yet your time*, yet you are immune to our ministrations. You rage at your husband's touch, and refuse to know him. Your body explodes and revolts.

It is not yet your time, we sing yet again.

And you, Elektra, are deaf yet again.

Again, yet again.

You fight him off, you struggle, tussle—have words. He holds you down, you lash out an arm. And you let go a white-knuckled fist.

A first strike in the face. Perplexed, he withdraws, you jump up, he pushes you back down, and you strike again and you bite and you claw.

We are not Inanna. We are not God. We are not the Women of Mycenae, your Chorus. And yet we sing, and echo their words. And yet we sing your Chorus's words back to you.

O Electra, among all mortal beings,
you are not the only one, my child,
visited by grief, but you show less restraint.
You must be brave, my child, and not fear.
Leave that excessive rage of yours.
Do not take your anger at your enemies
to an extreme.
Do you not see
how by your own actions you plunge yourself,
to your great shame, in self-inflicted ills?
Out of kindness, we advise you,
like a mother, do not add
more grief to what you face already.

And yet you rage, Elektra, yet again, and yet you stare at your black hands, your clock, as it turns and revolts, closer, twelve, ten, and now five, and now three, and now one, minute to midnight.

[Jill Purce, tall, blonde, statuesque in her naturalness, walks past a playground. Children in flared denim run around]

Our growth from childhood is like a spiral. We explore the world around us in ever increasing windings, as our confidence grows: slowly transforming the unknown.

Chaos into cosmos.

Chaos into cosmos. Black clouds, black puffs of smoke, into clear skies. Once women write words, from the Hymn to Inanna to today, words too form habits of nature, self-organising, rolling in, entangling everything. As Virginia Woolf does on the page, opening the floodgates, the minds of Elektra's characters are linked as they watch the same objects, the same black clouds, black puffs of smoke and pinpoints of light move through the same sky. Watch the same tempestuous tempers on the horizon, the same mighty rulers, with their inky moods, the same smoking guns—tack tack tack—fade to black. In Chinna's time, it's still Day 42. She has woken in Medan alone, without her mum.

Elektra had been kissing Tamara by the pool, when her husband called. *You have to come.*

She's an inspirational podcaster, with her Oxbridge daughter and aged-hipster look, who once made a brief, tenuous name blogging about the genesis of archetypes in books. Now she does roughly the same in *Elektric Ladyland*, a mildly successful podcast. From Sophocles' Electra, through Mary—what happened to rage?—to Portia, Emma, Beyonce. That type of thing. It's sponsored by Oprah and Kylie Minogue. Straight out of pocket, too, no suits or record company intermediaries. She'll tell the story someday.

Elektric Ladyland starts with Electra of course, written 400 BC. The Women of Mycenae, the Chorus: *Oh Electra, you're not the only one. But you show less restraint—that excessive rage—self-inflicted ills...*

Unlike chroniclers, Elektra is free in her associations, not bound by timelines, by chronology. The podcast is an alchemy of fact, fable, and Elektra's quest to make sense of her own life, her own wayward flesh. *How deep, how wide, can a woman be*, Elektric Ladyland asks. Are we bound by the four walls of the familial sitting room, by the immediate and intimately personal, like Austen and her Emma, Rooney's Normal People—or do we enter Virginia Woolf's Room of One's Own: do we expand to embody The Handmaiden's speculative world, our own planet *Shikasta*'s spiralling history in Lessing, the *Earthsea* galaxy of Ursula Le Guin? Are we one body, or a constellation, a sum—of world-building, of myth-making, of our archetypal heroines? From Inanna to Electra to Bey: body to body to body.

Elektra hops from bible to YouTube, from gossip to Gospel, a starburst of female emergence, a fever dream of convergence.

Or so she likes to think. If she were thinking.

Before Nova calls, Elektra is sharing a poolside pina colada in the shade, and telling Tamara about Tamar, her biblical namesake, an archetype from Genesis itself, written by the author known to Elektra only as J. She pulls up the episode, on her battered series 5 iPhone.

J is the granddaughter of King David, a lady at the court of David's son, wise King Solomon—her own voice rings as she presses play.

It's Harold Bloom, actually, Elektra thinks, now that she does think. Who wrote The Book of J. About the politics at the time. What was that all about, again? David's great kingdom falls apart under the rule of his idiot grandson, whatsisname.

She watches Tamara listen. Crickets.

Though J never mentions the old king, her grandfather, if that's who he is—we're filling in J's details for her, there's no record—King David, Jesus' direct ancestor, is the star on J's horizon. The later Star of Bethlehem.

Well…, poolside Elektra nods along to her own podcast voice. J's vision of Kingdom on Earth sure is more enlightened than J's heavenly ruler, Yahwe himself. With his black, lightning moods. Of course, J never sat down to write a holy book. She made her God up, including his temper, which is closer to that of J's cousin, the idiot king. Her characters, Rachel, Tamar, all burst with life.

The pool, Tamara, go still as the podcast goes on. Rice fields whisper. In the distance, a bare-kneed farmer pees from a dyke. Brown snake, hissing, then nestling again. Celestial skies.

J's innovation is to chronicle, from the beginning of time, not the Gods, but a family constellation, along her own family line. With at its heart, each spiralling time, a child. J's Creator himself, Yahweh, is not exactly an afterthought, but he's never the star of the story, and certainly not the most memorable character.

No biggie, he was never meant to be. He's an extra, a convention of the day. The real star is Tamar. Tamar is E.'s wife. Well, to begin with. Tamar has a few goes at this whole family constellation thing.

Tamar is J's opposite: born far from the court, a peasant girl when she marries into blue-blooded Judah's lineage. E. is Judah's eldest son, a nobleman, descended straight from Abram.

But Tamar's fresh husband is a drinker and philanderer and Yahwe strikes him dead before Tamar can conceive.

Conception. There is always something Elektra is thinking about, when she isn't thinking, or there's something she's trying to not think about, when she is. Her own daughter, in Cambridge, the black hole Chinna has left on the twenty-first floor. Empty skies, barren flat. Walls. It's why Elektra is in this pool at all, with a woman, she's a refugee from her own body, on the run, from the sore, empty sack of her womb and that's quite enough of that

—Elektric Ladies, please. Tamar. Babies.

As is the custom, Judah's next son in line, her husband's *brother*, marries her.

Yet the inauspiciously named Onan is worse. Convinced —don't ask why, J doesn't explain, perhaps it's another convention of the time?—that his offspring won't count as his own, but instead as his dead brother's, Onan refuses to impregnate Tamar.

Yes, they do do the deed, but he famously scatters his seed. Odious boy.

So it is: whenever he enters the arms of his wife, he spills it to the ground.

No joy for Tamar. All she wants is her right as a person, a woman, in J's universe, even a lowborn one. A flipping *child*.

Nova—Elektra has the one, fleeting thought, a premonition perhaps, of sorts—glancing towards her podcasting voice, her phone. But he's in London, of course. O, her daughter—Her underlying, buried thought. But Chinna has fledged, flown, is out of her hands.

'Settle in as a widow in your father's house,' says Judah to Tamar, his daughter-in-law. 'Stay there while Shelah, my son, grows up.'

Old Judah has only the one son, Shelah, left. More feeble than Onan, truth be told. *Judah thinks: Heaven forbid death touches him too, like his brothers.*

Judah stalls and stalls, and Tamar sits in her father's house, as a widow, waiting for Shelah to grow the heck up. Growing old.

Until one night she is told that old Judah himself has been spotted near a crossing. She parks herself by the road, disguised with a veil, flashing some tactical bit of flesh.

'Entertain me', he said, 'In your arms. I wish to enter there.'

'What will you pay me, if I take you in?'

They haggle a bit, until he leaves her his seal, and ring, and stick, all to be exchanged for a goat the next day. Judah's choicest one, a kid.

When Judah arranges to send the anonymous lady the kid, the woman has disappeared.

The local people reported: 'No holy lady ever stood there.'

There's the small matter of Judah's staff, the seal, the ring. The people have seen the goat, they know their king is up to something. Let her keep those things, Judah says. *Heaven forbid we are taken for fools here.*

Wisely shy of being known as a whoremonger, Judah lets matters rest.

So it was: About three months pass when Judah was abruptly informed. 'Your daughter in law has played the whore, and look: now she is pregnant by prostitution.'

At least this time, things are straightforward. *'Take her away,' judged Judah, 'To be set afire.'*

As the torching squad arrives, Tamar, with her neat little bump, simply sends her father-in-law his deposits back. Plus a note. Yes, I got knocked up, by a John who left me this ring, seal and stick. Please look into it.

Judah recognised his own. 'She is a truer judge than I, I failed to marry her to Shelah, my son.'

Tamar has won.

Yet he would linger from entering her arms again.

Portia, two-thousand years later, give or take, tricks the dark clouds of male moods in the same spirit. As life becomes more complex, Elektric Ladyland concludes, fictional creations mutate, their details, their genotypes change, to survive in multiple settings. But their under-song, their characters live on, no matter how many changes they go through. Characters are robust. It's not just because their forms resonate, become habits, arche-types—it's because we resonate with *them*.

J's creation, her habits, her bold-as-brass forms, created *us*.

It's what sparks Elektra's phantasmagoric chimeras, her furious, celestial bursts of bodies, made up of many. Oprah loves the idea, just as much as she loves reading itself. Kylie is nothing if not a celestial burst of body herself.

They don't know the idea belongs to rotund Shakespeare scholar Harold Bloom, with his own tempest moods—who reportedly tried to enter the arms of his most famous student, feminist icon Camille Paglia, author of *Sexual Personae*, on which much of Elektra's own thought is based. Oprah and Kylie just pay.

Elektra chronicles on.

From Genesis through Mary, Mother of God, through the medieval witch hunts and onwards—to me.

Yes—before Nova's phone call, in the pool, on the run, in blindness and light, my child self is on her mind.

I, Chronicler, listen, my daughter—a Kylie-fan before being born—already rapt in her proto-world.

So how do we come to be?

500 years after J's own time, 400 BC, The Bible is cobbled together. J's wit is redacted out of Genesis, her Yahwe is preened and propped up to resemble something worth believing in. By some truly divine intervention, bolshy Tamar somehow escapes the cutting room floor. And then Tamar's most famous descendant is born. David's spiritual son. The year is zero AD, or thereabouts. Three Wise Men, Bethlehem, and then the Holy Mother, losing her son, but not before imprinting the world with her form: the golden-haloed circle of mother-and-child. A becoming, a cycle, stubbornly undermining the straightedged Trinity of Father, Spirit and Son.

Even when western women, under the smoke-filled skies of the Reformation, disappear altogether. Fires everywhere, women on stakes. Here, the podcast traces Elektra's own bones, searching for single cells in the dark age of her own lineage, across the Seven Seas: her father Boy de Kock's blue-blooded ancestor, Baron de Kock, and her grandmother, Agnes de Vries.

It's the sixteen-hundreds, and the ever-seafaring Dutchmen, devoutly Protestant, sail to Java, chasing coffee, the bark of the cinnamon tree. They plant their flags in Batavia, their churches and steeples, and in an attempt to cut corners, sea-wise, and find a shorter way to the Indies, land on the other side of the world, founding New Amsterdam.

Still believing they're in the Indies, they plan fresh plantations. Sit down to buy the land from the 'Indians'.

The Elders, the great mothers and fathers of the Americas, are baffled. *Where are your women*, they ask.

The Dutchmen sell their hustled, manhandled land to their British counterparts, and sail back to the East Indies, in a straight line this time.

Under Baron De Kock at last arrive among the cinnamon trees of the Minangkabau. In the Minang's Sumatra mountain kampungs, their villages and hamlets, ruled by a curious mix of Islam and traditional *ardat*, Minang law.

The Minangkabau, who name themselves after that great, life-giving animal, the Carabao, will have nothing to do with either straight-edged sharia, or the bible-bashing of the Dutch. They live communally, sing, dance and chant in houses built like the water buffalo itself, a curved horn on either end of the roof, lifting it into the sky, like dancer's arms. Sons join their prospective wives, in the women's maternal homes under the horned rafters.

The land, the horned longhouses high up in the hills belong to mothers and daughters.

Within weeks, De Kock reaches the top of a peak cupped by volcanic ranges, mount Marapi and her sisters. High mountain, it's called, *Bukit Tinggi.*

A fit place for a fort, thinks De Kock.

Again, the elders are perplexed. The wooden walk of the white men, their inability to sing or to dance, their crass voices, their steepled cocks built from stone, and square little dwellings: all that, they could find merely amusing—but there's one thing they can't understand. To be fair, from the Minangkabau point of view, it's a bit hard to fathom.

Where are your women?

ʊ

And still, Tamar survives. By 1942, a Chinese woman, Mei Ling, lives with her husband in Chinatown, just under Fort de Kock on that volcanic plateau, the mountain market town of Bukittinggi, West Sumatra. Elektric Ladyland continues her story.

Mei Ling has a neighbour called Kartina. All Kartina wishes, like Tamar, is a child of her own. Her husband, a spendthrift like Onan, fails to provide.

While next-door Mei Ling conceives, there's a strange constellation in the sky, and a mutation occurs.

But it's the second world war, and a lot is going on. The Dutch are fighting the Japanese, the Japanese fight the Indonesians, both fight the Dutch. Soon, the first Independent Republic of Indonesia will be proclaimed by one of the town's native sons.

It's all a moot point for Mei Ling, who will never find out who wins, or what happened to her mutation. Mei Ling dies in childbirth. The Chinese father, believing the infant is cursed, refuses to raise her.

Again, things are straightforward. *'Take her away,' judged he, 'To be set afire.'* The father leaves the baby to die.

It's the neighbour, Minangkabau Kartina, who removes her ankle length gown, her veil, and sleeps with him. Once, and then twice, until he relents, and gives her the child.

The infant, with her queer, hidden genes, moves into Kartina's little house on the corner, just opposite the turquoise mosque in the mountain town's deep, low little Chinatown main street, which lies under Fort de Kock, at the bottom of a stepped alley, steep stairs in fact, which lead up to the maze of the market on top.

Kartina names the child after herself, Baby Kartini.

Four years old, Kartini sells cigarettes high up on the square by the town's famous clock tower, built by the Dutch. With its Dutch little steeple on top. The small girl watches as in front of the clock, the Japanese raise their rifles at a small line of Indonesian rebels. *Tack tack tack*, the tiniest plumes, black black black, one by one rise to the sky, as Kartini follows them with her eyes. Where they drift once again, twenty years later, 1965, as Kartini herself will be chased down these streets, a bundle of baby clothes on her back, a child strapped to her chest. Marching bands, murder, in the air. Smoke rising from the houses among her.

Black plumes, turning to black sheets of cloud, reverting to black clouds on the horizon for Elektra's grandmother, Agnes de Vries, back in the second world war.

Like Tamar, Agnes has a few goes, at the family thing. Boneheaded boyfriends (blindered, overblown, entitled) all bite the dust. Agnes is a Dutch-Sundanese teacher in Batavia, a champion swimmer and rower, when she finally marries her Dutch-Javanese husband, Louis de Kock, and they settle in Surabaya. By '45, she has a young son, Elektra's future father Boy, conceived just before Louis is interred by the Japanese.

By then, both De Vries and De Kock families have lived in the colony for six generations, part of the large *Indo* community of Eurasians, the half-million strong mixed-race group, many of whom have never been outside the Dutch Indies.

After the great mushroom cloud of Hiroshima, the Japanese capitulation, Indonesian revolutionaries declare Independence. The Dutch army have retreated, and there's a void, a formlessness vibrating throughout the country. Death, black, is in the air, and in the sounds. Instead of the singing and chanting, marching bands drum. Skies change their undersong. The wireless broadcasts the dark, viral form of the word, the slogan.

In his radio speeches, Surabaya revolutionary leader Sutomo sets his slogans on the Indos. On 15 October 1945, he proclaims from the mic, *Torture them to death, destroy those bloodhounds of colonialism to the root. The immortal spirits of your ancestors demand of you: revenge, bloody revenge!*

It's the evening of 'Black Monday'. That night, Dutch and Eurasians are rounded up all over Surabaya, jailed and shot, knifed, set afire.

Twenty thousand die in the violence nationwide in the coming weeks. They are burned alive, or cleaved with machetes, thrown straight into rivers, which darken with blood.

Of the surviving Indos, most disperse, to countries they've never set foot, where they have neither relatives nor roots. Westwards, to the Netherlands, or east to Australia, out to the Pacific along the Sunda vortex's fault lines, the Ring of Fire. The De Kock family scatter around the globe, Agnes and Louis to The Hague (where Elektra will be conceived over twenty years later, to the Ronettes' *Be My Little Baby*), the rest of between Canada and California, between Hawaï and Melbourne and New Zealand, where Elektra's only cousins in the world—all second, third—will be born, never to meet in person.

As Jill Purce will say to Chinna (more than 80 years later, when today's whole virus is long in the past, over with, done, when they sit and rock—oh those dimples, those curls!—Chinna's own little girl): *a shape, a form, a family constellation is born.*

Family constellations, I, Chronicler, Chinna de Kock, will whisper to my girl, still unformed, in her dreamtime world. Listen how you came into being!

Out in deep space, her shrimplet takes shape, with its tiny tail.

Listening.

Back to chronology.

Natural history starts with your great-great-grandmother Agnes' ancestor Hugo de Vries. In 1859, Darwin writes *On the Origins of Species*, his own Chronicle, the timeline of life, how change comes to be. *Natural selection*: the survival of the fittest. Evolution, as simple as zero or one. If the mutation gives rise to a better form: select and keep. Mutate again. Select. Repeat.

But within forty years of Darwin's treatise, another Dutchman sailing against the wind, the botanist Hugo de Vries, rephrases the question. Natural selection, he claims, can only preserve what has already changed. It cannot explain *how change happens in the first place*.

Even Darwin had been aware of this. Mutations, he said, as scientists all over the world still claim today, happen by 'random chance'. Which, as Darwin is the first to admit, is another way of saying *we don't have a clue* how we change.

Hugo de Vries calls the problem not the survival, but the *Arrival* of the Fittest.

It will take a Swiss scientist, an eponymous book of changes, and a full third of young Chinna's body weight, to answer the question of *how we mutate in the first place*.

(A hint: *robustness*, those bacteria who could live on both corrosive acid and acetone. As complexity grows, so does the number of possible genotypes. To astronomical heights—young Chinna's realm of platonic form, of pure maths, which can't be seen until the twenty-first century microscope, the clustered computer, arrives.)

But Hugo de Vries is the first to ask the question, back in the 1890s.

Fifty-odd years later, the second world war on the horizon, the Chinese woman, Mei Ling, is about to find out. She carries the gene for two healthy hands. Conceiving her first child, a mutation occurs. As the foetus grows within the warm hum of her womb, outside clouds of strife rise, battle cries sound. Mei Ling never does find out what happened to her genes, she dies in childbirth, it's Tamar's spiritual descendant, Kartina, who raises Kartini.

Who carries the gene, that day, twenty years later again— 1965, when The Ronettes are banned, replaced by murderous drums, slogans, when the first president of Independence is being ousted—she carries her own child in the sarong. Burning streets, as once more, order turns to chaos around her—

Young Kartini and her mother Kartina, the Women's League dance group leader, are walking fast up towards Fort de Kock in Bukittinggi, away from the main street below. Black smoke overhangs Chinatown. The stench of corpses is thick in the air. Speeches, marching bands, sound from transistor speakers.

Kartini carries a bundle of baby clothes on her back, the child strapped to her chest.

A young man in flares follows at a distance.

The women walk very fast. Faster yet. Kartini trips with the baby. Her mother dives, lands under her, just in time to break the infant's fall. They get up, continue to walk, dusting off. On the circular road at the bottom of the hill, ahead, a gang of teenage boys can be heard, revving their mopeds.

Behind Kartini, the young man in the flares is approaching. He starts shouting to the boys on their bikes, indicating the two women.

A thin lady with a missing front tooth comes out of an alley, pulls them in. Old Kartina signals to her daughter, and they follow the woman into a house. Kartini has never seen the woman before, but her mother returns her greeting.

They can hear the mopeds disappearing in the distance. Smell parts of Chinatown burning around them. The women nod at Kartini. Who looks away.

Please, the other two say. …He'll be safer with his father.

Slowly, she untucks the sarong in her neck, unties the baby. Hands him over. The woman with the missing tooth takes the infant, leads Kartini and her mother through the house. Lets them out the back door.

It's only after they're running up the stairs, on towards Fort de Kock, the emptiness at her chest stinging, that Kartini notes the baby's clothes, still in her bag. She wants to stop, to run back, to return to the woman with the missing tooth to give her the baby's things, his little socks, his pants, all the things she has sewn for him herself—

But there is no time. They have to run. She can smell the smoke, the mopeds, hears the engines revving.

They cross the road to the fort, and descend on the other end, make it to Bantolaweh, a village at the foot of the hill, where they stay in hiding at a Women's League friend's house for twelve nights. Without her baby, Kartini's breasts leak uncontrollably. She squats in the woman's kitchen, on the tiles, unable to bring herself to enter the main room, so scared is she her chest will simply burst at the sight of the woman's children. But she can't stop their young voices carrying back into the kitchen. For twelve days, twelve nights, she sits on the tiles, bent over her throbbing chest as hot tears of milk stream down her rib cage.

On the twelfth morning, the young man who had chased them before is outside the house, wearing the same pair of flares. They escape out the back door once more, run through a maze of back-alleys, deeper and deeper into the *kampung*, the village.

They come to the house of a former local area-chief. The chief, a woman, lies dead in her front room, the corpse abandoned, the house empty and half burned-out. Kartini and her adoptive mother huddle into the roofless bathroom together, lock the door. The bathroom had also served as the family's kitchen. Dirty dishes and mouldy meat pots still line the floor from the day the woman was murdered. There is no other food in the house, and after two days they scrape the rotten rice from a pot, eat it with tap water for sauce.

That night they climb over the wall, out on the neighbours' corrugated roof, and down again, into a narrow lane.

Kartini watches a gang of youths burn down another house down the road.

The Bukittinggi Police too, are standing by, watching the glow. A marching band sounds from the radio.

Inside the burning house, she now hears women screaming. A child runs out, its hair on fire.

Kartini starts running towards the child, then stops in her tracks and starts running in the opposite direction, back into the alley. She hears old Kartina echo her own footsteps, two feet behind. Then it's the young men again, the gang, who she hears: harder, faster footfalls, chasing after the two of them.

Ahead is the blind wall of the house she just came from. Kartini turns around to see her mother being stabbed in the neck and fall to the ground without resistance, a ghost of herself already, instantly dead.

Kartini rushes on still but there's only the blind wall to run into. In the corner, she starts passing out as she's kicked, beaten. For some reason, the kicking suddenly stops. She comes to, opens her eyes. Finally. The police have arrived.

As she tries to get up, her vision goes dark, she falls into a hole, a vortex, soundless, without feature or shape. Fading to black. Back in England, from that same void, young Jill emerges, a decade or so before, fully shaped, it appears, even as a newborn, with the express wish to figure out sound, emergence, form. She goes off to Headington school in Oxford, on those watery Sunday walks. Where the Isis meets the Char, and all is glady and wet, and she stares at the water for hours.

What does it mean, that in the beginning the earth was darkness and void?

How does change arrive? How does form emerge from nothing?

In the darkness, the void, Kartini watches her life pass by before her: her younger self selling wares on the street in front of the tower—batik, pastries, anything that can bring her cash. Saving up in the back room of her adoptive mother, Kartina, on the corner of the stairs in Chinatown, under Fort de Kock. Kartina, the mother, teaches her Minangkabau ways: the singing and dancing, the chants, championed by the first president, the left-leaning Bung Karno—with his Women's Leagues, his dancing and chanting, his subsidised bricks and mortar. In the ten years between, as the CIA sets its sights on that damn Red, Bung Karno, young Kartini builds a room of her own, a little ways up the stairs, with her own hands. Adds another, plus another, a big arching roof. Brick by brick. Singing, humming. Pasting mortar. As her mind's eye, in the darkness, the void, arrives at the present day, the baby she just gave away, to the toothless woman, her bursting breasts, it goes black again. Black stacks of smoke in the street, the long black hair of teenage boys chasing after her.

Fade back from black, Poppet, take shape, your own form emerging from nothing but chance, from the vortex of future and past. Black black black. The tiniest star. Black tunnel. Black sheets of rain, black veil of tears, as back in England teen boy Rupert Sheldrake, Merlin's future dad, like Jill Purce goes off to boarding school. Six years, away from the world of women. Black sheet of tears, as he arrives. Darkness and void.

Before his parents drive home, there's the headmaster's speech in the Hall. *Now I will tell you parents something I know. In the next weeks you'll receive letters from your child, begging to come home. Tell him that you did not raise him to remain a boy.*

The first year is hard, ladies, especially for you, mothers, who will miss your sons. But I'm asking you this. Give me your son for a year. I want your boy to know the pleasure of returning home a different person. A young man of academic rigour, a young man who has been trained to think as a scientist, a young man who is ready to return here and complete a first class education, an unrivalled preparation for the very best universities in the world.

The first week, Rupert's form is made to do push ups on the old oak dormitory boards. A classmate, too exhausted to turn away, throws up on him. Rupert starts crying again. Black sheets of rain. In collective penance, the boys all have to roll around, until there's no vomit left on the floor.

He survives. Arrives, as promised by that headmaster. In Cambridge, reading Biology. Some small voice of wonder, left alive. Sets out to become a botanist in India.

His question, watching the labia of orchids, their incredible shapes, is the same as young Jill's. *How does this world with its complexity, these astonishing forms, come into being?*

Jill's mother is a concert pianist, her father a surgeon, turned GP. But old man Purce has not lost his wild hairs, his passions for his artistic wife, during the long hours spent at the practice, listening to stomach complaints, ailments big and small. Holidays do not consist, as for Jill's peers, of trips to some sticky Georgian seaside pier. On a wild September day, Purce loads his children aboard a dinghy to a remote island off the Irish West Coast. The only other people in the small boat are the old women of the island returning home.

Almost immediately, as they leave the shallows and hit the black Irish sea, the sky clouds over. Cumulus clouds, a deep, midnight slate with their watery weight, start pressing down their load. Then break. As the heavens descend to the waters, the waters rise up, great dark waves overtaking the boat.

Blacks sheets, again.

It's clear they will sink, it's clear, even to Purce with his beautiful wife, his artistic mind, that his children will drown.

In the back, the old women, dressed in black, strike up a roar. They wail, a three toned note, from the rear of the boat, a single three-voiced howl.

Black wall of sound.

Wall of Sound, Phil Spector, The Ronettes, all disappear from the Indonesian airwaves, replaced by the marching music of war: while in Washington Bob Dylan sings *Rainy Day Women*, the CIA works with the Indonesian murder squads, army and police, to remove that upstart Bung Karno, eradicate the Reds, the commie Women's League. Death is in the air, and everywhere. As women are stoned, cleaved with machetes, set afire, Kartini wakes from her vortex of sleep, her coma in the street, gets up, stumbles towards the officer who saved her.

He kicks and pulls, pushes her down the road, to an abandoned school. The windows are coated black. Blood stains the tiles of the entrance. Inside, screams echo in the hall.

Kartini is pushed into a former classroom. Inside, ten women are crammed together. There is no furniture, no desks, no chairs, no beds, just stained, bloodied mats on the floor. Each mat has one or more women squatting or lying down. Shrieks resound from the next room. Some of the mats are empty. One in the middle holds nothing but a wrapped-up baby. It looks barely a week old. The women on the mats around it all sit up facing it, in a circle. No one moves, no one speaks. Someone waves Kartini over to share her mat. She sits down. They all listen to the howling next door. Heavy objects fall. They sit or squat with their ears pricked up. Another bump. Each sound makes them wince. Only their attention, it seems, can protect the mother next door, shield the child in here. They're all so absorbed in the noise, so keenly, for so long, they don't notice the baby has fallen asleep.

Finally, the mother is carried into the room. Left on the mat, beside the baby, her bloodied face to the floor, a sarung clumsily tied around her. But there's no time to think, let alone speak, because Kartini is being kicked into the hall and pushed next door. The room is small, thick with smoke. The walls are spattered with blood. Eight men sit and stand around. Women lie on the floor, some unconscious, all covered in bruises and cuts, all naked. Electric cord is attached to a young girl's genitals. The black smoke in the room comes off a different woman on the floor, whose pubic hair is burning.

Chanting is a healing art, Jill Purce will say later, a communal tuning in to what lies beyond what we can see.

Everything that we know of in this world is made of vibrations.

We tune into that vibratory universe through the circuit of our hearing and our voice.

The Chinese and the Greeks said quite explicitly that if we don't sustain this tuning, if we don't make the right sounds—then the world will fall apart. Light turns to darkness—form to void.

But that will be much later. For Jill, it's that wild Irish September day still, in the boat, with the deep black sea overtaking them all. The three old women striking up their three-voiced howl.

A three-voiced note.

The women sing on, a song deeper, older than even the sea. A wail, a strange, unearthly chant that out-sings even the waves.

The children in the boat, young Jill, feel their fear dissolve, their own bodies humming in response. Black terror turns to bliss.

The wind subsides. The storm abates.

Chaos to cosmos, again.

Once women write words, from the Hymn to Inanna, on to today, words too form habits of nature, self-organising, rolling in, entangling everything. Chronicles, family constellations, along our own lines. With at its heart, each spiralling time, a child.

Not far North from the Indonesian cataclysm, the killing of a million peasants and women, young botanist Rupert in India—perhaps already half in love with his future wife, though he doesn't know it—makes do with exotic flowers for now, a few choice specimens of the 28,000 strong family of *Orchidaceae*.

Elektra sees the light in a Dutch hospital, lands in a sterile little glass bassinet. It's The Hague, where many Indos have fled after the war—though Elektra's mum is Frisian, blonde. It's the end of the Sixties, The Ronettes on Dutch radio, Bob Dylan singing *Blowing In The Wind*.

Everything about Holland is little, still. A breeze wafts the net curtains on the ward, strung in front of the modernist little window panes, in their cream painted frames, between wooden shutters open to the sun—the same Dutch little curtains, shutters and frames as sat shaking across the world, in Bukittinggi, and in the longhouses around the crater lake in Maninjau, all also preparing for regeneration and birth.

In Banda Aceh, on the most northern tip of Sumatra lies Sophia, in a tiny wooden house close to the beach.

Within thirty years or so, she will be grandmother to Chinna. Here, now, she births and holds her firstborn. A beautiful son.

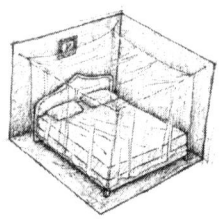

In the beginning, there was the word. And now we've turned back the hands of your clock, Elektra.

And so it is: your black hands say eleven hours and a half. And you have yet time. And yet you listen not to us.

You walk around in circles, alone, in the small room of your mother in law, though there is not yet room to walk. Though there is only the strip of tiles, between the bed and the walls. And you pace around the strip of tiles like a trapped animal.

And yet you pace around in circles, stamping around, frightened, butting into the walls, into the door, you pace hot with fever, without rudder.

And all you will think of is your daughter. Three streams of blood from her neck. And you are bitter with rage.

All you see, delirious, is not her face, as you've seen it in your dream, but her headless neck, and three rivers of blood.

And we chant, and soothe you, we hum, for the wind in your sails to subside, the winds of your fright, of your rage, for your storms to abate.

And yet you pace. And so it is: we show you her face, as it was in your dream, your daughter Chinnamasta, as a young girl. And we show her wearing a smile.

And yet it soothes you not. And all your body will recall is your pain.

And we are neither here nor there, Elektra, beginning nor end, we are not then and not now. Yet you dwell, and recall, and you cannot hear our hum, as we sing it to you, and yet you hear not our undersong.

And you pace in circles on the tiles, and fight, and you hit the wall and the door, and you are trapped in your mind, Elektra, are being cleaved head to toe. And you are cleaved all over again, as you were as a child, as you will be again, come midnight.

And yet there is time!

And yet you are delirious, and violent, a wild animal, trapped in pain from the past, and yet you clench up your opening, close it, hard as a rock, and recall the pain of being held down and entered by force.

And then your black hands, your clock on the wall read quarter to twelve.

And the time has arrived and your husband enters the room.

PART THREE: 1968–2002

In his German bed, Jill Purce makes violent love to Karl-heinz Stockhausen, the Young-Turk composer, in a sublime whirl of starburst, thunderbolt and noise. The two are halfway completing his famous *Alphabet for Liege*: mystic chanting, *Om*, overtone singing, a revolution in sound. They are it, the revolution: their young, solid bodies, entwined, their movements and percolations a whole new universe, a Big Bang in itself.

Oblivious to the tumult, next door in Holland little Elektra plays in the playground, sitting inside a plastic tree that fits her dark body like a glove. She too is enchanted, safely held, like a shell. Day after day, she crawls into her little shell in the tree. Bliss.

Until, age six, she gets too big.

In an English playground, girls and boys her own age, in

flared denim, play a spiral game. A BBC camera on their trail.

Meanwhile, twenty-something Rupert Sheldrake, still soulfully single, is tripping on acid with mushroom guru Terence McKenna in California. With them is fellow botanist and magic mushroom enthusiast, Fred. Fred is Dutch, has the longest, most fungal beard in their crowd, which is saying something, and bakes their daily sourdough bread.

McKenna is author of the *Magic Mushroom Growers Guide*. For McKenna, 'armed with little more than jars and a pressure cooker', as Rupert's son Merlin will put it, 'serving up unlimited quantities of psychedelics is only a little more complicated than making jam'. Or, as Terrence himself says, they're 'neck deep in alchemical gold'.

(Later, in the 1990's, Fred will spot a loophole in Dutch law, which will allow him to flog shrooms the way the famous Dutch coffeeshops peddle their skunk. The industry booms. First in Amsterdam, then online. Spores and grow-kits will sell like cakes. Psilocybin, as Merlin will imply, will be on the same evolutionary road as his fungi, who in order to become plants, started farming algae.

Magic mushrooms will be farming the Dutch.

The humble little shroom will grow from its obscure Colombian origins into a worldwide, mastermind influencer, rewiring brains all over the e-market place, 'dope-slapping people out of their stories', as one researcher will put it: dissolving ego, creating wholeness and generations of peace and love-loving teens, including Merlin and

Chinna themselves. As it turns out, there are 'few environments where psilocybin mushrooms won't thrive'. As Merlin will go on to note, they tend to 'occur in abundance wherever mycologists abound'.)

But there's no sign yet of Merlin. It's 1974, and nights are spent man-to-mushroom, mushroom-to-man. Terrence is still asserting the mushroom's might, happily serving as a conduit, claiming a sufficiently large dose will allow psilocybin to speak plainly and clearly, talking 'eloquently of itself in the cool night of the mind.' Until every person on earth has been dope-slapped into submission, Terrence claims, he can translate, speaking English for fungi, spreading their message to the world.

It is time—one might observe, Poppet, quite objectively—for a good woman, to enter the scene.

Back in England, Jill Purce, gorgeous and blonde, walks past the children playing their spiral game in the playground, the cameras on her. In her brown flares, her poncho. She's being filmed for a BBC documentary, to talk about logarithmic spirals—shells, the golden mean. Its proportion, its rate of growth is divine. Not too slow and cramped, not too fast and wide.

She holds up a fossil, an ammonite. The spiral was too tight, she explains, *it didn't survive.*

[Closeup of Jill Purce in a red antique chair in her studio. Precipitously slanting stacks in the background. Jill, long blonde hair loose and parted in the middle, no makeup, large eyes, strong jaw and nose, talks, oblivious to the jumble behind her]

In the geometry of the spiral, there are basically two kinds. One is the Archimedean spiral, and the other is the logarithmic. The difference is in the speed. One is constant, like this…

[Draws circles in the air with her finger]

…Like coiled rope, and the other is dynamic and increasing, like this…

[Motions fast]

What determines the kind of spiral is the speed with which

this point moves out, and the speed with which it revolves.

[Camera zooms out and the stacks behind Jill are dis-ordered shelves haphazardly heaped with paper and folders and a small pink box, more cardboard boxes and a type-writer. Her desk towered with books, Jill, in a cream smock and brown velvet cloak, holds a crayon and draws on paper]

With the Archimedean one, these two speeds are constant.

[Draws tightly coiled spiral]

With a logarithmic spiral, the speed of the point of the pen increases with its distance from the centre.

[Draws fast widening, fast opening swirl]

We see it in the growth of shells…

[Reaches behind her for the shelves. Her cloak falls open and the smock contorts, winding round her braless chest. She turns back to the camera, and holds out a shell, cross-cut to expose its inner coil]

…Like the Nautilus shell. And it seems that in nature there is one speed of growth, which we find in the galax-ies, and in shells and in plants.

[Holds up a fossil of a tight little coil. She has clean, long nails, silver rings on her fingers]

This is an ammonite, which a similar family to the Nautilus, but it grows at a rate much, much, much slower.

And it's as if it were too slow to survive…

[Gazes at the little coil, wonder and pity in her voice. Looks back up]

…And it became extinct.

In Maninjau, the crater lake, the cradle, in a tiny Minangkabau longhouse, imposing, curved horns on either end, baby Lia is born in her mother's bed. It's a rare, stormy day, black sheets of rain. Tack tack tack on the lake. Lia is Hati's thirteenth child. Here, as in Elektra's Dutch hospital ward years before, little net half-curtains waft between tiny cream shutters. The boards of the small room's wall are painted pink. But for the thirteen children, not all is safety and bliss, as it was for Elektra in her playground shell.

The children lie under little stones, scattered outside, around the house. Each stone holds a potted plant. A stalk of bougainvillea, an aloe vera, an orchid. Hati, betrothed at twelve, married a year later, is still in her early thirties. Her surviving daughters, five, will live in the house with her, and their husbands and children, as is the custom, until Hati dies. They will inherit the house. Her sons, the two remaining ones, already sleep over in the mosque, and will do so until they marry into the homes of their wives.

O, her daughters! Good girls, they will make precious wives, Inshallah, all five. Little Lia, the infant, her prettiest yet. Good girls, yes, her own flesh, her very skin, they'll rub along among these walls, embrace her, fold her in, God willing, stay till the end of her days.

The boys, like the clouds in the sky, already drifting away.

Wind blows. Hati glances out the window. The house sits alone. Paddies.

The surrounding longhouses in the crater village are a notch bigger, wealthier, the women better connected than she. Hati hasn't been able to keep up with their celebrations, the ritual exchanges of rice and gifts—with her children falling ill, with buying syrups and pills. O she worries. Penicillin, new brands and names, boxes half covered in *Inggris*, English, as fresh fevers and coughs keep hitting the village.

What she cannot know, Poppet, is that outdated American antibiotics, banned domestically, have—since the CIA-assisted coup, the removal of that commie Bung—been dumped in Indonesia. Where they've given rise to new adaptations in microbes. The ones in the village have little pumps that flush out the meds, plus an innovation that allows them to use hosts' cell walls for themselves.

Evolution: an algorithm so simple a computer could do it. Poppet.

Mutate, select, repeat.

But listen. Not like this.

Like us. *Mother to daughter.*

Like Jill, holding up her ammonite: *Its coil was too tight... it could not survive.*

Knowledge obliges. Not being dumb. You, in your dreamtime world, already perking up in your coil, your sweet little swirl:

Mum?

There. Raising your voice.

Polyphony.

Privilege.

ʊ

In Aceh, more clouds. Family gather around Sophia's bed in her room, the men washed and groomed, in black caps and white shirts and stiff, pressed sarongs. All dressed up, all ready to go to the mosque.

Sophia remains on the bed in her yellow housedress.

The men, in their checkered sarongs, whisper, *Time to go.*

She holds the cold bundle in her lap, the women around her, the men pleading. Sits on the bed, the men repeating, again, *It is time.*

Sophia doesn't get up, in her crumpled robe, sits and holds and rocks her still little son, barely two years old, her firstborn, her body spiralled around him. Will not let go.

ʊ

In Chinatown, Kartini is back in the house on the stairs, that she built with her own hands. She repairs the damage, brick by brick. All the damage she can. Tries not to think of what is beyond repair, beyond salvaging, beyond pasting back together with mortar. Keeps selling anything she can sell, in front of the tower. Builds extra rooms, to rent out to boarders. A little pink ensuite bathroom, with a water basin and a squatting loo.

She has lost her firstborn—but he's alive! Strong! Handsome.

The child is being raised by his father, who has left Kartini, pregnant with child number two, for a younger woman. His new bride is a girl who is not tainted, not Chinese—thus probably communist—like Kartini herself. A proper, muslim, Minangkabau girl. Religious.

Within months, Kartini's second son Afin is born. Precious boy! Try what she might, with her two little sacks, drooping from her chest, still tired from running, she cannot nurse him.

Milk simply won't come.

Evolution, Poppet. Remember your great-great-great ancestor Hugo, the botanist. Darwin explains preservation of change: select, repeat. But Darwin says nothing, about how we mutate.

Arrival, not just survival of the fittest. De Vries: how do we change in the first place?

As baby Afin turns first one week, then two weeks old, Kartini's birthmother Mei Ling's mutation—remember that gene for two healthy hands—at last arrives. The new gene, skipping a generation, comes to the fore. Either that, or it's formula, marketed aggressively by Nestle, also outdated and dumped.

Baby Afin's little hand will not grow.

[Jill holds up the crosscut of the shell, in her other hand, which has stacks of gemstone rings on each finger]

…Whereas the Nautilus, it's dynamic, it grows fast. Not only is this a logarithmic spiral, but it's based on a very special speed, a very special proportion, which has been recognised since Pythagoras, since the Greeks, and it's called the golden mean, or the golden section.

[Looks up from the shell, cheeks flushed, wide-eyed. Voice young, measured, perfectly intoned]

And it's called by Pythagoras divine.

Elektra outgrows her shell in the plastic tree in the playground, her small body grows and grows, yes it does!

And then one day it does not.

She is short.

The Sex Pistols have come and gone, in England, but to her, in her small Dutch town, they're still pretty hot stuff.

Botanist Fred has been there, done that with Rupert and Terrence, packed up his pressure cooker, his jars, and moved back to Holland. Dutch law: Fred will become an expert one day—already is, in some ways.

Elektra too had packed up her stuff—*Never Mind The Bollocks* on tape, a walkman, the first two singles by *Wham!*, Duran Duran—and, fourteen years old, left home. Here she goes, into an alley leading to an abandoned factory, god knows what they used to make here, the towns are full of these dark looming things. Ghost mills. Textiles, probably, trade long disappeared to China, after the Dutch found oil in the North Sea in the Seventies, or something. Dutch Disease. What's left is this, rows of millworker cottages, broken up by red-brick monsters, useless chimneys threatening to come crashing down. Most just sit on the streets like inverted bomb sites, half-upright, half blackened, stinking of kiddie pyromania and piss. The safest thing, perhaps, is what the council allows youngsters like her to do, which is to simply move in, nail some bedspreads in the remaining windows, board up the rest, lay a mangy Persian rug over the floorboards. Lie low for 24 hours, and pronto. Proof of habitation, which gives them the right, under Dutch law, to call the property home.

Inside, in the gloom, Fred boils water for tea. Some hippie noise record is playing, Stockhausen probably, Fred plays Stockhausen more than a bit, Fred and Karlheinz are friends, or was it Sun Ra, she can't always tell the difference.

Sun, hippie noise, it all sounds pretty gloomy to her.

Elektra, he grins, taking his kettle off the hob. He has pots and pans too, that pressure cooker, all black with stratified grease but functioning, if Fred had the sense to buy meat. But their squat's vibe is definitely vegan, because of Fred, the owner, if squats can have owners. He makes tea and sits down in the corner, on a banged-up leather sofa. That's the problem with good squats like these, she thinks, they've all been squatted donkey's years ago, by hippies.

Fred has a beard, doesn't wash, and also doesn't normally speak. He scares her, with his bony fingers, his fallen-in cheeks. His silence, interrupted by manic giggles, and sometimes a long rant about gods or the universe or his time with McKenna in California, tripping on mushrooms and acid. Now he's a hermit in this crumbling mill. Darkness and grime. But fuck knows the man can provide. See? As always, some day-old sourdough sits on the coffee table, a rind of goat cheese, a jar of shroom jam or whatever these hippies eat. Her mouth waters.

She nods at Fred, sits on the other end of the sofa. Cuts a chunk of bread, spreads it with jam. The walls are lined with books. Mostly botany and esoteric shit. Dark science. She pours tea and eats. Fred is still on the other side of the sofa, reading a heavy, cloth-bound volume, black with a yin and yang symbol on the cover. *The Book of Changes*, he says. Reads on. Again she shudders a bit, glancing at him. It's okay for kids like her to live in places without women, but there's something nameless and alarming about it to her in a grown man. Dirty. Long, blackened nails on his hands. She never, not once, has felt creeped out by any of the other squatters, still sleeping around them in their makeshift rooms, misfits and punks her own age.

Know the I Ching? he looks up.

She shrugs.

It's an ancient Chinese oracle. You can ask it questions.

How?

Throw three coins. Six times. Heads are two, tails are three, you tally each score. Even numbers give a broken line, odd numbers a straight one. The six lines make up one of the 64 hexagrams in the book. You look them up.

She shrugs again. She wears a mohawk, safety pins in her nose, all very tough, but she's impressed. Tries to sound heavy, but tweets, like a bird, *Cool.*

You know Jung?

Not really, she shrugs once more. *Like Freud?* She snorts. *Penis envy?*

Nah, says Fred. *I don't think Jung was too hung up on his dick, he was hip to the whole peace and love thing.*

But how does it work? How can a book know what I'm thinking?

It's called synchronicity. When things happen at the same time, and they're significantly related, but there's no discernible cause and effect. Here, read the introduction. By Jung.

She takes the heavy tome.

It really is pretty cool. She reads the intro, enthralled. Jung himself throws the coins! And he asks the book a pretty cool question. What does it, the *I Ching*, mean for the world?

Jung throws sixes and nines, which apparently means important lines, or something, in any case, the hexagram is 50, the Spice Pot, and the notable line, the second, says that the pot carries food, but that people are jealous and sort of ignorant and arrogant about it, and the *I Ching* says the world should pay attention or else, anyway, that's how Elektra, squatting, going hungry when she's meant to grow, reads it. A spice pot is just what she needs.

Also, this synchronicity thing makes sense to her. She's always confused between what she sees as reality—you know: her thoughts, the stuff she is thinking and reading and talking about, on the one hand, like this whole synchronicity thing in the first place, *wow!*—And then on the other, that strange disconnect: the unruly realm of, errm, for lack of a better word, *reality*, her rumbling tummy, her feet, always cold in the squat, her body with its insistent infections and sores. All the stuff she's actually *living*.

Her body, small, a little dark skinned from Dad's Indonesian heritage, just doesn't fit. No matter how much she tries to starve it, it won't fit her *thoughts* about reality: her tall, blonde mother, or the leggy pictures in teen magazines.

...It's called the divine proportion, because it runs through nature, from the galaxies through shells, plants, and everything we see around us.

[Wide, rosy, confident lips, a dimple in her cheek]

And you can derive this proportion, if you draw a line...

[Holds up both hands, still holding the shell]

...And you divide it.

[Brings hands closer together]

And you divide it so that the smaller part of the line...

[Demonstrates golden mean]

...Is as the larger part of the line, to the whole line. It's very simple, but it's very special, and nobody knows why this is so…

[Cheeks, ivory skin flush more rose, as her lips form the word]

…*Perfect*. It's beautiful.

It takes eons, in the end, for Rupert to reach the conclusions Jill Purce arrives at through instinct—since her teens, or perhaps from birth, simply through staring at glady rivers, through walking and watching and thinking a bit. Or so she will feel. Rupert, with his meticulous education, his curls still somehow retaining their neat prep school shapes, faint echoes of the headmaster's words still clinging about him. *Give me your son for a year, and I'll give him the pleasure of scientific thought, of being a man of academic rigour.*

Rupert of course is on the same quest as Jill—if from opposite ends.

Bound to collide, at some point. *How does form come into being?*

Or as Rupert, with his classic education, his nomenclature, will have it: how does morphogenesis—the genesis of *morphe*, form—*work*?

In India, and through his communication with the psilocybin world, with the mighty mushroom—as translated by Terrence McKenna—Rupert is formulating his own theory of morphogenesis.

Received wisdom holds, of course, that this happens individually, through genes. Each new individual needs to go through the process on its own.

But Rupert observes some very strange things. Crystals, for instance. They're famously hard to get to actually crystallise into their typical grids, in the lab. But once they have, then in labs all over the planet, quite separately, they will start forming, spontaneously, the same grids.

Scientists attribute this to their beards, believing they somehow carry crystals in their facial hair from lab to lab, like seeds.

Rupert raises a polite, Clare College eyebrow at this.

And what about the brain. We like to think our brain is unique, since we're the only species on earth to have quite so much of it, compared to the rest of our bodies, and to have it so marvellously encased. That sculpted skull. Beautiful.

It makes us individuals. We consider the brain our personal computer, the seat of memory, consciousness and agency, made of unique material that gives us these properties.

Yet Rupert observes something else. When one of us, like the crystals, learns something new, it becomes easier for everyone else. IQ tests, for instance, become increasingly easier to do, not because we gain in IQ, but because of some collective process he's trying to name. *Nomenclature*, he thinks—is it him? Or is it just his brain, trained, drilled, flogged, forced to roll through vomit for simply feeling—yes, he thinks, it's a habit—memory—this naming of names—

Not even his own habit, but one he picked up from the ether—headmaster—scientific rigour—all those grand men naming things before him—

What if memory is not a thing, but a verb? Not an entity, but an emergent property, like magnetism or electricity? Or almost anything else for that matter, consciousness, the universe itself, the distinct hum of the various atoms, the cosmos?

There. A theory of the brain. It's a receptor, he believes, of the vibrations of the universe. Not the source of our thinking, but closer to an antennae.

Genes, proteins, those large, folding and spiralling molecules, vibrating keys: same thing. Genes too tune in, transmit, are actions, rather than nouns. Like the brain, they receive and transmit information, aren't simply entities, or stuff.

In *A New Science of Life*, he gets it all down: the *habits* of nature, those self-organising patterns, the spirals of galaxies and shells, are what rule our world, rather than natural *laws.* The oldest, deepest, most ingrained patterns, reson-ate most. *Morphic resonance,* is his term. The habits form nature's memory banks, which generate form, through *morphogenetic fields.*

On the other end of the spectrum, Jill Purce, no longer sleeping with Karlheinz, too tries to bridge the gap between materialism and the new science of life. She juggles overtone chanting, Tibetan lamas in the Himalayas, with her work on the spiral structure of DNA as a research fellow at the Department of Biophysics at King's College, teamed up with Nobel laureate Maurice Wilkins.

Om is one of the most ancient mantras, and when you use a sound which has been used for sacred purposes for thousands of years, you tune into the attainment of all the great yogis and saints who have chanted it before, and their attainment becomes available to you too. It's the principle of all prayer and ritual and mantra. Everything that's learned becomes a natural memory, and the more people who've learned, the easier it is for everyone else in the morphogentic field.

—Morphic resonance—

There you have it.

Jill is thinking Rupert's thoughts.

Their minds, on a collision course for so long, had to meet.

Of course.

୭

But now that they have, what's next? Will they crash and burn, like Jill and Karlheinz before—or flow together: fuse and merge, like the hyphal tips of fungi, like mycelium, connecting rock to air, heaven to earth?

They decide to get betrothed, just for now—see how it goes.

But it's still not that easy.

First, an Irish mystic, a lady, a seeker named Melangell, would have to cross the Irish sea, centuries before. To a great wild forest, on the Welsh coast, remoter even than the island young Jill had tried to reach in the boat, in the storm.

The woman, young Melangell, in the ancient green realm would save a hare from a Welsh hunter, a prince. The hare found refuge in her skirts. In her long dress, her dropped waist, her mystic skirt, she'd be portrayed in stone, an effigy in an overgrown, misty little chapel erected in her name, deep in the remotest woods on the Welsh coast.

When Rupert and Jill cross the forest hundreds of years later, to exchange vows, they find the effigies of Melangell and her Welsh Knight waiting, side by side, a great rib connecting the two. By pure chance, Jill's own betrothal skirt too is wide and dropped and long, the same shape of the mystic skirt that saved the hare. The rib that connects Rupert and her is the question they've each asked for years, *how does form come into being?*

The rib, more accurately, perhaps, is the answer—*morphic resonance*—they've both arrived at, each in their own way.

Rupert, Clare College educated: slow as the hunter, aiming his bow at his audience, proposing his theory in his elegant, meticulous way, rigorously argued and articulated.

Jill moment to moment to moment, quick as lightning, both the hare and the arrow, all contained in her skirt's mystic folds.

By December they are married.

Family constellations, she'll say (in late middle age, when she's a voice healer and family therapist, when we're with her in the room, I, Chinnamasta, Chronicler, and you: first turning your slow turns in deep space, in your morphic field—now being rocked on Jill's knee), *are forms resonating from earlier generations.*

Here, she's still only thinking the thoughts, as Rupert puts the ring on her finger. *Constellations are habits, memory, morphic fields made flesh.*

Within years, little Baby Cosmo Sheldrake will not just hum, but sing overtones. Just months later, Merlin is born, all dimples and curls, with that golden flush of psilocybin, that resonant aura, that he's had since before the womb.

ʊ

In Maninjau, the surviving children in Hati's longhouse, under her proud carabao roof, survive.

Lia turns six, still in her mother's bed, in her mother's house, which she won't have to spend a night away from as long as she lives. Behind the half-curtains, the cream shutters, she will always find food in her mother's pot, will never have to expose her fine little limbs, not even her shapely ankles or wrists, to anyone's gaze. If her family's poor, Lia never feels less than secure. Her future, her birth right is here, she outright owns the room she is in, the land it's built on, teeming with green, tomatoes, chilli, beans in the garden, avocados, papaya, mangoes in the trees; rice in the paddies, her watery fields.

She will never, for anything or anyone—least of all food, a roof or husband—have to leave.

ʊ

In Holland, lunchtime, Elektra, in her safety pin piercings and mohawk, wanders the street, past the chippy—she has no money—past the little bakery, where she glances at the fresh-baked baguettes. They sit in a basket by the counter, rarely has anything looked that good, but she walks on. She's meant to grow, small enough as it is, nothing like her blonde, Frisian mum. Every Indo cell of her being reaching for the sun, furiously, aching to stretch, hungry like the wolf.

Back home, the squat sounds deserted, the dusty bedspreads nailed to the windows, the coffee table, all silent. Everyone still sleeps, beyond the wall with its shelves of dusty hippie books, where her friends have all improvised rooms from curtains and hardboard, built platform beds. You can hear them, her sleeping peers, smell them, even here.

Elektra makes for Fred's sourdough bread, a newish chunk left on the coffee table.

Fred comes out to make tea. Sits beside her on the sofa, pours her a mug.

You know about Kali, the Hindu goddess of creation and destruction? You'll like Kali, she's fierce, reminds me of you, he gets up, takes a tome from the shelf. Sits back beside her.

Elektra leans in. *I'm named after a Greek character in a play.*

Of course. Here, this is Kali.

The Hindu Goddess looks fearsome, but cool.

Fred flips through the pages, *Here, this is even better for you, Tibetan Buddhist, a dakini. Look*, he points at the picture. *A secret syllable*, he says. *Vajrayogini's mantra,* BAM.

In the full-colour plate, a woman's body is blood-red, her hair stands on end. She dances, naked, in a ring of flames. A knife, a huge blade, raised above her head.

Fred points, *That's fifty human skulls, chained round her neck.*

Fifty skulls is pretty punk, and sure beats a mohawk, safety pins. Or Wham, bam, I am a man... *But what is she,* Elektra says. *What's a... daquiri?*

A dakini.

Right.

A sky-dancer, says Fred.

...Like a demon?

No, not that at all. Closer to a goddess.

An angel?

Not exactly, sighs Fred. *Angels are kind of... angelic. But a dakini can be a person.*

You mean a real one?

Well, that's the idea. That she sort of... emanates as real people. Women. Who are messengers, closer to the mystery than we, y'-know, they hear the music of the spheres, they read a secret, twilight language, like pure maths, the essence of things, like Plato's Cave.

...Sure. Elektra nods, vaguely, not much the wiser, but she's probably just being fat brained.

The dakini is holding a skull cup, she now sees, filled with blood.

Wait, no, this one is you. Chinnamasta, my own personal fave, Fred turns the page. *Fiery little Chinna.*

A new plate.

She's basically Vajrayogini, but like you, in a state of rage.

Chinnamasta, like the dakini, dances in a circle of flames —but she has no head. It dangles from her hand. Her headless body dances on, scarlet.

Three crimson streams, three rivers, curved and deepest, darkest, bloodiest red, spurt out from her neck. A gruesome fountain. Knife still in her hand.

She cut off her head, Fred whistles.

Eek! Elektra feels sick, her stomach turns. She feels sourdough bread coming back up, and tea.

And then Fred is pushing at her. His little thing, pricking at her. Searching.

She freezes, clenches up. Straining, every cell, every fibre of her growing little body resisting, reversing its course. Growing inward, hard as rock. Fred puts his hand, his long bony fingers, over her mouth. Her friends are all so close in their rooms. She can feel them, smell them, but they aren't feeling her.

He still has his hand, his knuckles, those dirty nails, pressed over her face. She can hear her friends in their beds, but she can't make a sound. Time goes so slow. She thinks time will stop. Nothing is real. He cannot really be doing this to her. In a place with her friends all around her. They're squatters! A family! Rebels and punks!

She cannot move. Fred is pinning her down. She needs to scream or kick or let her friends know. But her body is being invaded, her opening cleaved. She is dumb with horror and shock, stunned. Howling with smothered rage.

Shrinking with shame.

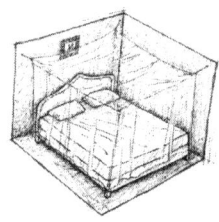

And so it is: night falls. Your husband comes home.

And you are small with rage, Elektra. And you are shrunken with pain. And your fury is directed at us, under all your different names, all the names you use to address us. And we are not your gods, and we are not your names for us. And yet you curse us and your earth and your heavens above, and yet you curse everything that you've loved, and yet you curse your husband, though he has not yet entered your room.

And your husband is outside your door. And your husband pleads with your mother in law, Sophia, and Sophia pleads and laments and echoes the names.

And echoes the words of ages, in her prayers.

And we are not her god, her Allah, and we are not Inanna. And we are not Kali and not Vajrayogini, we are not sky dancers and not dakinis, and we are not a single one of your human images. And so it is.

And yet outside the door, Sophia wails, *Alhamdulilah*. And yet she prays, and cries, *the child will die*.

On the bed, you lie, Elektra, prostrate, rigid with rage, helpless with shame, cursing us, and yet you will not listen. And yet you pace, alone in your brain, pace in circles although there is no space to pace. And yet you butt at the walls of your mind.

Where is your child, you pace in your brain and we cannot tell you. We sing and we soothe.

We know you have seen your daughter in your dream, Chinna as a little girl.

And we coax you back to your dream, to the still point of your vortex, your storm, to the face of your daughter.

And so we settle it, the face of your daughter, at the heart of your storm, at the point that is still. And we sing, and we hum, and we tell you to see her smile.

And we tell you to remember her smile, Elektra. And all will be well.

And yet you will not hear us, and yet you rage, and yet you leap from the still point of your storm, from the still point of the bed. And rage again.

And yet you leap to the floor, to the small strip of tiles.

And yet you pace the floor, though there is no space to walk, and yet you pace and circle and butt into walls. And yet. And yet.

Again and again, for hours, you walk and you pace.

And yet you rage, a blind animal, trapped in fury, on the small strip of tiles between the wall and the bed. And so it is, the black hands of your clock read eleven hours and half. And your opening, although come midnight, you will need to be cleaved, in sunder from head to toe, is closed. And you are yet trapped in your past, and your heart is closed. And your heart and your opening reversed, and hard as rock. And we are not then and not now, Elektra, and yet you are trapped in the past, and your past is your trap.

And all you will see is the blood of your storm, spurting in three streams from Chinna's neck.

[Karlheinz Stockhausen, the German composer, wears an open sports jacket with wide lapels, cream shirt open, long tips of the collar pointing to his shoulders. Blonde, long hair slicked back, side burns. Thick, lushly Jungian accent]

Jill Purce is able to decipher the spiral in all human activities.

The spiral is a spiritual principal, that is true throughout the universe, and we constantly need...

[Raises hands]

These reminders that come through the books and the words and the way of living of a few spirits among us, who...

[Shakes finger]

…Are messengers…

[Points finger again]

And who constantly remind the majority, who keep forgetting, of their eternal homeland.

[Footage of Jill taking a seat in front of an audience of longhaired young people. Voice of Karlheinz]

Through the discovery of the spiral, which is one, and probably the most important, symbol we can recognise, she discovers all the other unifying qualities.

Ten-year-old Lia follows her mother Hati around the tiny Maninjau, lakeside market. She passes the few stalls set out on the concrete, slippery with trampled lettuce, discarded fruit, rotting fish juices, old blood. It's past noon and the first food vendors are starting to pack up, but Lia's basket already contains a small bag of rice, some tomatoes, tofu, and chillies. Hati is done food shopping. Still Lia follows her mother around, among the waste piling up on the floor along the gutters.

Over the market stalls, from the crater wall's top, Maninjau's single road in, with its steep, famous forty-four hairpins, cuts ziggedy-zag down to the village.

Lia stops in front of the *warung*, the little eatery at the bottom of the road, on the corner, just across from the market. It has a row of small, glass windows where she can almost look in, but she's not yet tall enough to look over the white little half-curtains. They serve rice, of course, and fish and meat, all piled in big enamel bowls elegantly stacked in a diamond pattern in the display window in front. Lia puts down the basket. She's never been inside, but the bowls look so artful.

Inside the warung, the owner, an old woman, is wrapping rice in banana leaf, serving a large lady, in resplendent dress, the mater of a beautiful longhouse out among the paddies. Lia watches the lady come out, with her bundles and a little boy. Embroidered robes. She doesn't look at Lia, nor at the market-goers passing, baskets on their heads, the vendors crating their chickens back up for the long trip homewards on foot. The prayer-call sounds from the mosque. Hungry, Lia looks away from the lady, with her embroidered folds, bundles of rice, instead looks at the greasy banana leaves scattered across the concrete floor of the market, dogs lapping at left-over grains of rice. Grey water, littered with fish guts and *kretek* butts, clove cigarettes, trickles into the gutters. She searches for the thin shape of her mother. To her surprise, the glimmering lady has stopped in front of Hati, is greeting her.

Hati, still only thirty-five, looks worn, but has a smile on her face. She carries her own parcel, wrapped in brown paper. Fabric for a dress.

Now Lia remembers. The dress is for a circumcision celebration next week, of the lady's son, the little boy. Lia's mother is catching up again, attending weddings and funerals, exchanging gifts. Their house isn't so lone anymore in the paddies. They are becoming part again of the village.

The boy smiles at her. The lady lightly touches Lia's veil,

Alhamdulillah child, you are pretty! Walks on, saying a last word to Hati. *Boys will take note, your daughter must value herself, price herself dear*, mahal. *She's precious.*

Lia picks up the basket with food. They walk back to the longhouse, under the fronds of the palm trees lining the road, the lake glittering to the left. They don't speak, just swing their basket, their parcel. Pass the rice fields, almost home, already.

ᎶᎦᎶᎦᎶᎦ

Far from the northernmost tip of Sumatra, from Banda Aceh, from the tragedy of her star-crossed firstborn, her loss, Sophia moves into a clearcut strip of barren land, the size of the Hiroshima bomb site, outside Medan. Her home—a corrugated-iron roof, cinderblock walls—is halfway erected, as are the little boxes on the neighbouring plots, row after row.

Meanwhile, Sophia's second born, Rasul, like Lia, has survived. A grave boy. And then, there's the third: a light-hearted child, at last, a twinkly little star on Sophia's horizon. Nova, she calls the sprog. Dancing in her arms.

Or so it seems to Sophia. The shadow of her firstborn so long, longer than the little boy's life, eclipsing Rasul, casting its gloom right up up to Nova's birth, and, if she's honest, longer than even that—where are Nova's early years? His bristly little head of hair, she does notice that—so much hair, when it is short it is almost too much, just standing up straight like a brush—much as she minds that longhaired look—you have to admit it needs a bit of space, of weight, to pull it down—oh, her nerves—she digs into a bowl of rice, forces more on her sons.

By age eighteen, Rasul wants to cure the disease that killed his elder brother, left his poor mother Sophia traumatised, fat as a whale. With a heart even bigger than her rump, more spacious, embracing her babies, but terrified of hunger and plagues.

Rasul will vindicate his mother, soothe her, he'll be a doctor, turn chaos to cosmos. Goes off to medical school.

By the time Duran Duran reach Medan, half a decade or so after they die in the west, where Nirvana is gearing up, Sophia's third too has grown. Longhaired. Maverick boy. Nova wants to play the guitar, leaves her one-bed, sun-struck box of a home to strike out into the country, find a place for himself in the world.

As Nirvana break, Elektra, fat, impulsive, furiously eating her rape away, still struggles with synchronicity, as she sees it—with the disconnect between her physical reality, and what she is thinking. Her body, too small, too short, still doesn't fit her ideas of herself in the world. It just doesn't look like her.

And thinking, she does, by the way. A lot. For months, then years. The less she feels, the less she meets her physical world, that dreaded body, the more Elektra lives in thought. She wanted to be a singer, like Patti Smith, or Courtney Love from Hole, but has no voice, not in that no-go zone of a body of hers, of course.

She's read Fritjof Capra, the quantum physicist who led droves of late Eighties New Agers over the edge of reason, like lemmings, but Elektra happened to read a bit of physics too, in university, and escapes that fate. Now, '94, she's a journalist, interviewing her idol Courtney Love for her Amsterdam-based national newspaper.

Well, was about to. Courtney's husband is famously dead. Courtney won't discuss it, just the new album, and when Elektra, with her Dutch tact, lets on what she thinks of it, Courtney gets up, *I don't need this. I'm rich*, and walks out the door.

Great. A replacement interviewee is found, a biologist, famous, like Courtney, if not as rich.

They're in the Dutch documentarist Joris Ivens' loft, on the Amsterdam canals. Ivens is 73, and still the staunch socialist of his old, black and white, anti-colonial films. The loft, the attic of a seventeenth century gabled warehouse, once filled with cinnamon and cloves, cacao and coffee from the Indies, is stacked with books and dusty sixties greens: the thick fingers of Monsteras, a forest of spider plants. The Golden Age warehouse doors in front, once used to haul in sacks of spices, are open to the trees along the dappled canal. The water glimmers under a weak spring sun, a cruise boat floats past, full of school girls eating ice cream. It disappears under a bridge. Rupert Sheldrake, the revered filmmaker's guest, is promoting his book, *Seven Experiments That Could Change The World*. He's forty years old, tall, with his cut glass, Clare College accent, cool dry wit, dimples. Blue probing eyes, still somewhat youthfully wide; longish brown curls. Tweed, button down shirt. Knees sticking up from the low leather sofa. As out of place in the Dutch Master warehouse, it seems, as in the socialist realm of Ivens' agitprop films. To top it all off, he's holding a small stack of coins.

Dutch guilders. Handed to him, just now by Elektra. A heavy, black-bound volume on the table. The Oracle.

Heads or tails.

Synchronicity, Elektra had remembered Fred's explanation of Jung and the Chinese Book of Changes. 'Significant relations' between separate events through space and time, which seem to have no cause and effect.

It seems an apt enough analogy, in Elektra's mind, to Sheldrake's own morphogenetic fields. She taps her old, clothbound copy of the *I Ching*.

Would you please ask the Chinese oracle what your theory means to the world?

Elektra, like Jill, more the instant, lighting fast sort of thinker, not exactly the meticulous kind, cuts a corner or two in explaining the concept. She understands *morphic resonance* as Jung's non-causal relationships, *I Ching* as a book of archetypes. Cut and dried, you'd expect, certainly to a man like Rupert.

He sits politely gazing at the Great Book, the Dutch guilders, with their modernist Queen Beatrix in profile. Patient, kind. He's at last found, in this journalist, someone much, much madder than he is, someone truly out of her mind.

Another canalboat passes. Their host, Joris Ivens, is on the phone in his office, at the other end of the loft. Rupert and the madwoman sit side by side on the leather sofa, the coffee table before them, with the book, and the coins.

Finally, as nothing else will probably happen, he tosses up.

Elektra tallies each score, three coins, six times, and looks up the lines.

Ting. The Cauldron. *Great Fortune. Success.*

The oracle's usually pithy, but rarely this spare. Buzzing, Elektra moves her finger down the hexagram's page.

The supreme revelation of God appears in prophets and holy men, the commentary reads.

Elektra beams. Rupert sits staring at the answer. There's a changing line, she explains, which is significant. *There is food in the ting. My comrades are envious, but they cannot harm me. Good fortune.*

In the colonial warehouse, with its beams and rafters built in the 1600s, the oracle's *Ting*, the cauldron, somehow reminds Elektra, still always hungry, of her *Indo* grandmother Agnes' cooking: cinnamon, garlic, cloves.

They safely return to the topic of Rupert's own book, the Seven Experiments, which involve psychic cats and dogs. A dog will know when its owner is about to come home, Rupert claims, which proves the dog tunes in to a form of memory not *inside* its brain. Sheldrake proposes pet owners all over the world study their pooches for evidence of telepathy, which will prove, once and for all, that the scientific, materialistic view of the brain is *wrong*. This, Rupert Sheldrake is sure, will change the world.

Thing is, Elektra *likes* morphogenic fields, delights in this kind, eccentric interviewee. And the Book of Changes, the Oracle seems to agree. Sheldrake brings sustenance to an ignorant world, the Judgement reads. *To venerate prophets is true veneration... The will of God, as revealed through them, should be accepted in humility; this brings inner enlightenment and true understanding of the world.*

The changing, significant line reads as a cautionary tale: *My comrades are envious, but they cannot harm me.*

Ignore this man at our peril, *I Ching* seems to warn.

Sheldrake continues to talk, about cats and dogs, in that Clare College voice, with the polite, unreadable twinkle of the eye of the boy who was given to the headmaster for a year, to return to his mother as a young man of academic rigour, a scientific son. A boy whose blue eyes—then tightly closed—whose playful curls, were once forced to roll around in vomit, on the dormitory floor, as penance for crying to go home. A boy from whom nature's most ancient, enduring habit—its most sustaining pattern, its undersong, that curling-in, the warm, spiralled arm of his mum—was bullied into extinction. Only to return to him here, in his careful voice, his measured, cautious, elegant words, his prophetic theory of the world. As with J, as with all the great lamas and comedians, Elektra can never be sure if he's serious, or laughing at her, who is the punch line to whom.

At the newspaper, however, there's no such doubt. First Courtney walks out, now Sheldrake, tossing up coins? The joke, of course, is Elektra herself.

Two massive blunders in a row. Elektra is fired.

As *Teen Spirit* finally arrives in the travellers' cafe in Bukittinggi, in Chinatown Kartini's second-born, Afin, at nineteen, is engaged to be married. The girl, from a nice Minang family, is very pretty. Kartini is protective of her son, with his little shrimp of a hand, always held, cuddled, hidden from sight, in the healthy other.

She'd lost her firstborn, the child she had to give away to the toothless woman that day. Lost him to her husband's younger wife, who raised him in Minangkabau ways. Big now, handsome boy, a dancer in a local troupe. Angger, he's called. Dancers need to be very handsome, she knows, or no one will watch. She sometimes glimpses Angger on the street. That mutation of hers sure passed him by. She can't really believe her own little Chinese frame produced this tall and perfect stranger.

Afin still hasn't grown, is as short as Kartini herself. But he shares her passion for good, honest work, cleanliness, discipline. He's a good muslim, praying five times a day, Lord knows where he picked up that gene, not from her, she can safely say—from his father. But he's not like his two-timing father in any other way: studious, serious. Oh, and precious! So precious. She will do anything to keep him close, and safe, her second chance, her orderly boy, with his shy smile, that will widen into pure sunlight when he's happy, or, as now, in love. Always neat as can be, in his button-down shirts, his ironed sarongs.

Kartini built her own house of course, has kept adding rooms, and now takes in boarders. Students, shop girls. She still sells pastries in front of the clock tower. Still saves up—unlike her penniless ex-husband, who married three times and has many children now.

That afternoon, Kartini and would-be groom Afin, in that cream shirt, his tiny pressed pants, hit Chinatown for pans, pots, and the most important item on the list for any Indonesian young man planning to get wed. The requisite spring bed.

ও

Elektra is fired, books a plane. On her first arrival in Bali, dazed, a last-minute, half-price, impulsive break, Elektra, twenty-eight-year-old, sits outside the airport.

Hot, humid air like a wall. Cinnamon, garlic, cloves.

Her family is pallid, blonde, from Holland. Dad fled Indonesia as a child, brown-skinned, Indo. It's never before occurred to her to visit. She hasn't packed anything, and though she takes after her Dad, she now finds that, to her distress, she knows nothing about Indonesia, where it sits on the planet, even what currency they have.

A woman sits down beside her. She wears a sarung, a delicate top. It's a crowded bench and the woman, with her local sense of private space, sort of leans against her.

Elektra's breath stops. Her eyes start leaking; shocked, pallid tears. Keep weeping. The woman sits closer than her own Dutch mum ever has. Looks, feels, smells, more like her, than her own mother does. Elektra isn't just dark and small, but differently built, and she's normal in some parts of the world. Feels a kinship, a likeness of scale for the first time. She just sits there, skin to skin, and cries for a long while.

From Bali, she follows the backtracker trail to Sumatra, to Bukittinggi, the market town maze in the mountains, sprawling up the original hilltop, the twin peaks of the clock tower, and Fort de Kock, with Chinatown in the middle, below. All girdled by a doll-sized little circular road.

From there Elektra takes a bus to Maninjau, all the way down to the hair-raising forty-four hairpins bends that see-saw down the wall—into the vortex, Poppet, that once was a volcanic cauldron, spewing lava and smoke 280,000 years ago.

Now—as she bites her nails, counting down each bend while gazing below—it's one of the most tranquil places on earth, green, dimpled with sky blue reflections on the water, all streaked with hazy ribbons of colour.

Cradle, of course, though she couldn't know, for me, her daughter.

She arrives at a homestay, with thatched cabins, a gazebo cafe. The first evening Elektra stays on the beach by the lake for hours past sunset. Over the crater edge rises a full moon, climbing over the rim of the volcano. The night, a black screen of hidden cries and squeaks, opens up, a moonscape. She's at the bottom of the caldera, the crater wall a dark, violet ridge between blinking water and silver sky.

From the white little beach, glistening threads of dikes spiderweb out among the rice fields. Everything is outlined in black and shaded in with glitter, foregrounded by the purple peaks and jags in the back, all around her.

The next day, a stranger, half famous, at least in Lia's dancing group, descends the dangerous forty-four bends on a moped. Arrives in the Maninjau lady's large longhouse.

Angger, a name in these circles, a traditional dancer from the city. He practices with Lia in the front room, for a dance to celebrate the harvest of rice in the village.

Afterwards, sweaty, they sit in silence for a moment together. Spent.

Outside, the men are completing a stage, decorated with flowers. You can hear the hammers. It's been raining, the garden had flooded, but the stage is under a marquee. It's already late. In here, Angger pulls off his shirt.

His sweat smells good, fresh, clean somehow. Lia, fully dressed, stays on the other end of the room. He's smoking a kretek in his sarong and an old vest. His upper body is delicately muscular. Lia tries not to stare. She can't quite believe how precisely drawn Angger is. He is beautiful in clothes, but it isn't until he takes them off that you can see the exactness of his shoulders, of his flesh and bones, just how extraordinarily well put-together a human body can be. He's lean, gold-skinned. For all his reputation, there's nothing of the city boy player, really, about him. Lia holds her breath, another second. Then turns to face him, head on, breathe in his freshness, his scent. Time to head for the stage.

But her breath stops in her chest. Her face turns red.

He is gazing at her, more intently than she'd been staring at him. What is it is he sees? Her own golden skin, wide lips, the exactness of her bone structure, her cheeks?

After their performance, in the dark, Angger drives her home on the moped, borrowed from a city friend. Parks it in the road, and walks in front of her through the paddies. The narrow dike is flooded in the rain. Angger, in his worn, but cared-for shoes, goes first into the wet blackness. All Lia sees of him is the glint of his hair. She can still smell him, that clean, animal scent.

It pours. There's no moon or stars, but her eyes soon get used to the dark. Lia knows every bend, every crack of that path, all the way down the paddies, but in the mud from the flood, she feels her soles slither about. Slips.

Ahead of her, Angger's long limbs languidly skip. You'd think it was him, not her, who walks home this way every day. He seems to dance, as light on his feet as he'd been when they swirled under the stage-light just hours before. His thick black hair swirls along, in his neck.

He turns, takes her hand. In the dark, he spins her around, so that suddenly, it's her in front. He's also made her dance. Lia is somehow swaying ahead now in that light, lazy pace of his, then he twirls her round on his arm once more, and he's leading again. Lia follows. By her door, he turns and bends over, presses his hip against hers, and continues dancing, in place, as if they are still onstage. It's completely silent in the paddies, and their bodies move together, up to their ankles in water, warm rain still pouring down. For a moment, the old garden, with its five stones, its potted plants, feels like the lake.

Sell yourself dear, price yourself, you're precious, *mahal*, she hears her mother's voice in her head. The rich lady's.

Angger leans back from her chest. Leans back in, his lips hovering over hers. Beautiful, pearl-white teeth.

Not in front of my mother, she hisses, glancing over her shoulder at the door. The bed sits right behind it.

Shh, Angger whispers, *don't wake her.*

She colours again. *Then don't try to kiss me.*

Okay. He steps back.

She exhales, blood slowly returning to her brain. In fact, old Hati, her mum, pretty much zonks out by eight in the evening, right after Maghrib. Sometimes still in her prayer gown. Lia just tries not to look at Angger, with his silly hair, silly teeth, silly beauty.

He gazes at her. She feels herself flushing, all over. What does he see?

He just stares in her eyes, *Marry me.*

She laughs. Maybe it's nerves, maybe it's her heart skipping and jumping out of her mouth, between her own pearly teeth. (Wonky, not entirely straight, like his; but pure, unadorned.)

Shhh, he says, *your mum.*

Don't worry, she's knackered… Out cold. You could marry me right here on this doorstep, she won't stir till the 5 AM prayer call.

I don't think I've ever woken from that.

I don't think I've ever slept through it, Lia sighs. *Mum bolts upright in bed. There's so many of us tangled in her sarong I have to hang on to my sisters to avoid landing on the floor when she jumps out.*

You wake at 5 AM every morning?

Only just enough to save my neck. Funny thing is, I can't really sleep once she's gone.

When we're married you won't have to sleep with your mum. He nods at the maternal, Minangkabau roof. *We'll make our own room.*

Lia looks him straight in the eye. *If.*

He bends over again. That mouth.

Lia has felt many things today. She danced in the lady's house, in front of the entire village, her mum sat in the third row. They're poor, but not outcasts anymore. Hati's little longhouse, behind Lia, is crowded, full. Lia's in love, perhaps, probably, pretty certainly, crazy in love, she doesn't know what she's feeling. If they marry, he'll move in here with her. They'll wall off their room with some boards, a door. She saw a nearly bare-chested young man today, for the first ever time, only narrowly escaped the first kiss in her life. It's been a very long night.

She doesn't fight now. Lets Angger kiss her until she doesn't feel so many things anymore, and then she goes inside.

Just a stone's throw away, across the rice fields, Elektra lies alone in her lakeside cabin. She's been travelling for a while now, since Bali, listening to her Walkman, a new album, *Kid A*. Her messenger bag, unpacked, sits at the foot of the bed. She sleeps under the thatched roof, doors to the lake wide open. The night outside is still luminescent. Shadows like cut-outs on the floorboards.

She gets up, throws on a sarong. Dogs have torn at a banana leaf with fried chili rice she left on the table on the porch. She steps across the oily grains. In the silver clearing, she heads for the bathroom, casting nightshade shadows on the path.

Passes the other cabins, closed, silent, passes under giant fingered leaves, tall shrubs bending with the weight of honeyed flowers. Halts under an ancient tree by the homestay cafe's lakefront gazebo.

In the blackness inside, a nest of limbs lies breathing among the low tables: the staff, four or five boys, entwined on the floor, tablecloths swaddled and pulled up over their heads, bare feet sticking out towards the glittering lake.

She walks on, enters a small cinderblock shack, bunches up the sarong to pee squatting into the porcelain hole. Ladles cold water between her legs. The staff's toothbrushes sit mouldering in candy coloured pails on the wall. She switches off the light and there's just the sweet, fungal stench of soap and garlic and stinky beans pissed on the floor by the crew.

The moon is a rainbow sun. It casts through the green overhanging the trail. Flowers dropped in the night are blue, translucent skins on the path. The other cabins all sleep.

A chord rings out.

Radiohead. In the dark restaurant, on the low table, black against the crystal lake, someone plays, guitar on knee. The other staff, rolled into the ball together, still sleep in the dark below. A stray silver foot, toes up, lies flung in a patch of light on the floor.

Elektra halts, in the shade of the tree.

Long fingers slide along the frets. Blue tinged bangs fall down to a chin. *How to Disappear Completely*.

She watches from the shadow of the doorway, the tree. Fingertips skid between glittery chords; a voice.

I'm not here…

A flower, heavy, naked, drops at her feet.

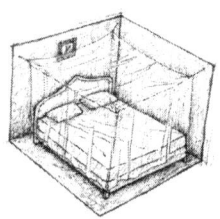

And the hands of your clock read seven and half in the evening, Elektra, and the heat is still fierce in the room, and it zings between walls, and the heat is still fierce outside Sophia's house where a lone seedling, the first in its plot, is dying of thirst.

And the sun has set and you stare, blind with fury, at the ceiling. And you stare at the mosquito net between you and it. And you stare at the roof, still fierce with heat.

And you are alone in the room, and alone in the house with Sophia, and you are prostrate with fear and fever and rage, and delirious. And in the storm in your brain, a flower, naked, drops at your feet.

And you are blind to the seedling, dying of thirst, outside the window. Blind to the dying flowering of beings, and you are deaf to our song, *Oh Elektra, you are not the only one...*

And so it is: a noise. Your husband comes home.

[Jill faces an audience of longhaired young people in what appears to be a King's College classroom. We see her back, the blonde, natural hair to her waist, the cloak, a peasant skirt down to her ankles. A desk with some paper sheets, a bulky celluloid projector beside her]

The only descriptions we have of creation come from the mythological traditions and the scriptures.

[Reaction shots of youngsters with moustaches and open-chested shirts, an older man scratching his head]

Modern science has not come up with any satisfactory description of how we came into being from nothingness.

[Young people tilt their heads listening. Beards, leather jewellery, a hand raised to a mouth in contemplation]

And what I'm trying to do is use these concepts of the

mystical tradition, of the creation myths, either through water or through the vibration of sound, to relate these to the natural forms, and how they demonstrate...

[Frontal shot of Jill, in cream peasant blouse and floral skirt]

...The dynamic force which gives them life.

[Return to shot from the back]

Can you turn off the light?

Nova uses seven words, in Indonesian.

This is how Elektra learns his language.

Hungry.

Full.

Lazy.

Tired.

Stoned.

Sleepy.

She'll leave the last one to the imagination.

At daybreak by the lake, Nova takes her messenger bag, and walks her along a snaking dike, the rice fields appearing around them from the mist.

They walk the narrow trails spidering from the lake until the homestay's cabins, hiding under flowered trees and banana leaf, are just a nest of sleeping ducklings, cupped between the lake and the sweep of sap-green rice fields.

They continue among the paddies, heading for the steep rise of the jungle sprawling up the crater wall. Follow the twisting dikes, until they emerge.

A single, tattered tarmac lane sits in the rising sun, curving away from them, circling the fields and the lake in the middle.

They sit and wait by the roadside, silence articulating the world about them, green and blue, like complementing chords.

At last a bright, hand-painted bus comes blundering up the track, and they climb on board, and in a cloud of pitch-black smoke pull off and hit the road.

They alight under Fort de Kock.

In Bukittinggi, where, among the labyrinth of the market, its circular maze, begins the seven-word spiral of Nova's days.

The words are cyclic. After the last word, comes again the first.

ↄ

1. *Hungry.*

Me too.

They lie on their backs in the master bedroom of their homestay, a crumbling Dutch colonial house in the shade of the fort. Elektra's messenger bag sits still packed at the foot of the bed. The windows are open. Satin little half-curtains wave in the breeze, like in nineteenth century Zandvoort, the old Dutch beach resort, or the old hospital in The Hague, where Elektra was born.

Nova is pulling his trousers up his dancer's legs. His face behind long black hair falling in his lap. The Dutch, double wooden doors, blue paint chipping, lead the two of them to a small hallway. A dusty, cream-wood conservatory is green with the sheen of palm fronds and papaya trees teeming just outside the windows. Three or four longhaired boys sprawl across a sofa, watching Asian MTV, a packet of clove cigarettes between their bare brown feet on the table. They nod at Nova, at Elektra.

The street is steep and overhung with trees and vines going up against the hillside. The two of them descend, walking under the crowns and leaves, the cries from the crickets, birds, the buzzing, singing-saw choir of insects, and monkeys in the hilltop Zoo. The air is cool and moist. It's monsoon season.

The mountain market town just after Maghrib is a sleepy sprawl of emerald hill, colonial plaster and cream, peeling little Dutch window frames. It's built around Fort de Kock, which sits on the hilltop in the middle, now a park with a tiny Zoo, the green jungle overhanging their homestay's street. Across a footbridge lie the Zoo and the sprawling market itself, on the corresponding hilltop.

Nova's light step leads them the other way, down the pavement, where it hits the circular road embracing the whole town centre, with little red vans cruising round, packed with crouching women still returning from the market.

The roadside is lined with food stalls. Crooked, wooden tables sit under tarpaulins. Gas lights hum.

Ma, Nova calls. A woman rises from a petrol burner on the ground. She piles two banana leaves with rice and adds fish, fried to a crisp, head to tail. Slathers fried chilli on top.

Wordless, they dive in.

ʊ

2. *Full.*

Yeah.

Nova stretches out under the gaslight, the tarpaulin, and yawns.

ʊ

3. *Lazy.*

Me too.

Nova stretches his back, and arms. Too lazy to walk home.

Hm-mm…

Wish I could dive straight back into bed. From here.

They amble back up the hill.

In the room, Nova peels off his trousers.

ʊ

4. *Tired.*

He sits on the bed. Starts rolling a joint.

The homestay is silent. Asian MTV drones from the hall.

Nova lies back. Turns on Elektra's Walkman, its tiny

speakers squeaking.

Radiohead wafts through the room.

ဌ

5. *Stoned.*

He yawns.

ဌ

6. *Sleepy.*

They lie on the bed, under the crumbling plaster ceiling.

Nova reaches under her. Number seven.

Then two new words.

In love.

The first days with Nova, Elektra lies gazing at this ceiling. Her eyes, from wildly different angles, keep returning to the same view.

Whitewashed plaster, peeling. A damp, mouldy spot. Cracks.

Here, behind the veil of paled satin curtains in the window, everything is still.

A large crack runs from the corner of the ceiling, all the way, right over her head, to the mildewed spot in the middle.

Elektra traces the circle, the mouldy rim, its scalloped fringe.

She's sprawled beside Nova, arms, legs flung across the sheets. Pillows, blankets heaped around. The messenger bag, packed with past lives, gaping at the foot end.

Elektra still lies gazing up. With the ceiling, the sounds come back on.

Beyond the faded curtain, a moped mutters past.

Someone bangs at a neighbour's door.

And then Nova reaches out again and the peeling walls close once more around them. The bag falls silent. The world goes dim.

The only sound that remains is the velvet rub of Nova's skin. His heavy hair, his radiant black eyes.

Later it's the spot again, the peeling plaster. The damp ring, like a star, like a beacon in the sky. The crack. Like a needle on a compass, it revolves, as their bodies follow the motions of love on the bed below.

Now they lie, still again, diagonally on the bed. Rain has somehow started. It pours on the corrugated roof, splashes on the ground outside the window. The prayer call wafts up through the shutters. Birds, monkeys cry from the trees on the hilltop.

And again, they tip their bodies together. Lose track in the dim, condensed silence of the room.

To lie sprawled on their backs once more later. The good old crack. Running at a different angle now. A breeze on the curtain. Monkey cries from the Zoo. Laughter somewhere down the hall.

Elektra lies silent, time-lagged, spun, as if emerging from a vortex, a hole. The familiar damp ring, shifted around. Like a star, like the compass needle of the crack, it maps her out. Feet, toes resting on the headboard. A calf on a pillow. Cheek on a bunched-up blanket, hair flowing down, down the side of the bed.

She lifts her arm and gathers her cheek and her head from the edge of the mattress, back onto the bed.

The satin curtain trembles between the open shutters. Wood smoke wafts in, garlic. Rain. Nova yawns.

Hungry.

ʊ

Soon, they will climb up the hill. Walk in the half light. Huddle on the wooden bench, under the buzzing gas lamp. Sit over fried chilli, rice, steaming off banana leaves. A car will splutter past. They will eat, under the tarpaulin, rain pelting down all around in the dusk.

For now, they lie on their backs on the bed. Home. The curtain waves in the damp, as rainwater splatters, a distant mosque calls for Maghrib. They lie in the dimming room, prayers weaving in and out of the window, as other minarets join in, their voices undulating from the hilltops, the steeples, the domes, across the trees, the low rust-roofed verandahs, the crumbling plaster of the market, this old mountain monsoon town.

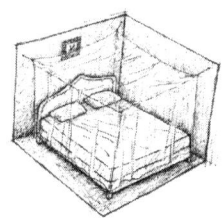

And so the sun has set, and a cock crows. And Maghrib sings to its end. And a death has occurred in the earth, in the soil outside the window, a death in a seedling. A being closer to us than to you, Elektra: you, the becoming, you, the expiring. You are the rise and the fall, the peaked line, the dying. You, the blind alley. The life of your mind, that blind tunnel, that myopic end to your evolution, is the beginning of death. With every breath you take, you lose an eon.

Yet the seedling is cyclic, a circular being. And it is not here, and not there, Elektra. And it has no end, nor beginning. It dies in the sun, yet rises from the grave in the shade.

And your clock on the wall, your blind hands of time read seven in the evening. And outside the door, Sophia's sunset prayer has come to a close. And she enters the room, and brings you a plate. And she brings you a plate heaped with rice, a morsel of meat.

And you eat.

And so it is. You have eaten.

And yet you are ravenous. And yet your hunger, your fever, your rage, that virus in your veins, in your brain, blind you to the dead bloom of the being you ate, and yet you are blind to the dying flowering around you, all the short, hot life in the room.

And you are blind to the dying flowering between these four blind walls zinging with heat, the open window a sweltering block, no breeze going in or out.

And yet you hunger, viral, and yet it blinds you to the blooms in the room, and blinds you to the mosquito, trapped over your head in the net, and blinds you to the infant lizard on the wall, to its mother perching in the corner above, and yet your hunger blinds you to the ants, below, on the floor, trading nectar, all connected one to the next, beginning nor end, in their flowering lines on the tiles.

And yet it blinds you to the mouldering in every corner, and the hairlike tips of hyphae, snaking their way into the ground, and blinds you to their boring of walls, and finding the starving seedling, feeding it, now that the sun has abated.

And yet your hunger blinds you, to the seedling outside your wall, that rises from the grave.

And it blinds you to the seedling that's risen, that holds up its head, and resurrects. Only to die once more of thirst in the shade.

Yet again.

And the hands of your clock read seven and half.

Can you turn off the light?

[The classroom, blinded, goes dark. A few students' silhouettes. The projector's light, just beside Jill, glows, like a star. Cut to the screen: black space scattered with brilliant sparks]

As far as we know, the largest structures in the universe are galaxies, huge glowing Catherine's wheels of dust, gas and stars. To the naked eye, these galaxies appear as milky patches just faintly visible.

With the aid of a 200-inch telescope, about a thousand million suddenly become visible to us.

[The camera pans along the dark heavens, resting on a bright, static wheel]

At least sixty percent of these have magnificent spiral

structures. Nobody knows much about how these evolved, or in which direction they're flowing.

[A brief cut to the zooming celluloid projector, its bright beam of light showing the smoke in the room, like clouds passing in front of the moon]

Whatever theory one adopts, it does not explain either the initial rotation, or the instabilities necessary for these superb forms to come into being.

What we call the Milky Way, is looking edge-on through our own spiral galaxy. Our solar system is tucked into one of its arms.

[Shot of a metal, Newtonian model, with little balls representing each planet]

This model was made at a time when there was a great interest in astronomy, largely as a result of the work of Isaac Newton, who developed a very detailed mechanical picture of the universe, where laws found to be true in one place were assumed to operate everywhere.

[Cut to black and white Apollo mission footage of the universe]

But before the end of the last century, science had begun pushing further out into galactic space...

[Zoom in on planet Earth]

And deeper into the nature of the atom.

[Voice of Fritjof Capra, particle physicist and author of *The Tao of Physics*]

Modern physics has had a profound influence on general philosophical thought, because it has revealed the unsuspected limitations of our classical thought and forced us to revise many of our basic concepts.

[Capra speaks. Long dark curls, smart Viennese tongue, sharp nose, soulful eyes]

For instance, the concepts of matter, time and space, and cause and effect, are totally different in modern physics, and with this drastic transformation, our whole view of the world has begun to change. Now these concepts all seem to go in the same direction, towards a view of the world which is very similar to views of the world held by mystics of all ages and traditions.

[Cut to a black and white photo pinned to a wall, with a grainy, scratchy image of a dancing Shiva, arms outstretched, what looks like flames at his hands, and with a set of spotty, concentric circles juxtaposed from chest to armpits, and another set at one knee. Lines, curved, diagonal, seem etched across the image]

I've made this photo montage to illustrate the idea of the cosmic dance, which appears in subatomic physics, and in ancient Hindu mythology.

The lines and curves in the picture are traced by subatomic particles in so-called bubble chambers.

[Pan along Shiva's shape]

They bear testimony to a continual dance of creation and destruction. It is a continual flow of energy, in which all subatomic matter is involved, in which atoms are formed and dissolved without end.

[Zoom on the heart of the dancer, where three circles meet]

For the modern physicist, and for the Eastern mystic, the universe appears not as a multitude of objects that are assembled into some huge machine, but rather as an interconnected web, in which all things and events are interrelated...

[Return to Apollo shot of Earth from outer space, zooming into the swirls of the atmosphere]

...And in which they form a flowing, changing, moving tissue of events...

[Cut to satellite shot of black and white mountains and oceans, zooming further down, a lone human shape on the coastline]

...And where man is an integrated part of this network.

In Maninjau, days before Lia's wedding, the lady in the largest house sends men to build a marquee in Hati's garden. The women in the village start cooking, beef Rendang, coconut stew they leave to simmer for days on cinnamon wood. The fragrant smoke wafts through the fields.

Angger, meanwhile, is searching for cash. He's meant to bring a spring bed for his wife. It's requisite, tradition, all over the nation. But his father and stepmother, back in Chinatown in Bukittinggi, though they're fine Minang Muslims of course, are struggling. He himself has two crumpled rupiah banknotes to his name, which won't buy him a pillow case. He might have to talk to more distant relatives, or the lady in Maninjau. He's on his way there, on the borrowed moped, swerving down the forty-four hairpin bends.

And then he is on his way nowhere. His body, that perfect shape, still hitting every one of those forty-four hairpin bends.

Before he is halfway, he is crushed between tyres and tank, hand bars and pedals of the borrowed moped, dead.

Lia fades to black, yes she does. Fades to black, for a long while. Till her mother's longhouse starts picking up colour again, shades of grey, pale pastels at sunrise, at sunset again, between the long over-bright hours of day, which blind her, oh they do, with their noise and their clamouring shades, pink! turquoise! magenta! it's all too much and yet never enough, all these siblings and ghosts of siblings buried under each stone and then she really has had enough!

No more stones.

From the bus terminal in Bukittinggi, a month later, a small Hello Kitty backpack drooping behind her, Lia takes a van into the city, wanders around *Pasar Banto*, the farmers market just below the circular road, on the outskirts of what must be the real market, on the hilltop in the middle. It's her first time, by herself in the monsoon mountain town.

She can't bear to think of her mum.

Hati had not looked at her when Lia left home in Maninjau that morning, with the old backpack, which used to carry her books to school. Not because Hati was upset with Lia, but because she didn't want to cry in front of the children, Lia knows.

She herself bit her lip, and kept waving, alone, long after her mother had turned and gathered the kids and led them back to the door.

Now she finds a way into the fabled *Pasar Atas*, the top market, from the enclosing circular road. She's heard stories all her life, and visited once or twice with Hati, but the market is labyrinthine. It covers the entire hill. The entrance she finds is under an orange tarp, and winds up the covered path, deeper and deeper among the little stalls, higher and higher, the sellers at their rough wooden tables, more even in the first bend of the path than she has seen in Maninjau in her life. She holds a note the lady of the big house has given her, as she winds her way up towards the concrete buildings on top. The note has an address, Blok B, and a name. Toko Song.

As Lia walks up, past the hijabs and flip flops and chicken and fruit, up and up, past second- hand clothes and leather stalls, she reaches the first concrete building. It has a used comics shop, more clothes, an internet kiosk. She arrives at the top, past VCD-sellers, three tailors, and now a phone stall, a gleaming shop fronted by a glass counter, with a short, well-dressed boy selling handphones. Handsome smile. Chatting up girls.

Lia walks on, with her little Hello Kitty rucksack, her schoolgirl hijab. She suddenly feels very young, much younger than she is. Checks the names on the blocks of the market. She's just passed Blok D, BAWAH, ground floor, and is standing now before Blok A. Clearly, the alphabet runs counter-intuitively in Bukittinggi's famous top market. A warung, a small eatery, sits bustling in a nook under Blok A's central staircase, bowls stacked in their diamond pattern in the window, a TV blaring away. More tailors, a busy satay stall. Lia crosses another path. The building across is whitewashed concrete like the one behind her, with a peeling pink or orange band round the first floor. The sign only reads ATAS, top floor. On a hunch, she goes up. There are more fabric shops than she imagined existed on earth. She asks for directions, is sent back down, to a different block. Another maze of shops. She asks for directions again, is sent the wrong way, walks around, totally lost. Tears sting. She turns again, giving up.

Walks straight into Toko Song, a clothes shop, where she gets a job.

An hour later, now officially a cashier, Lia sets out to find the next address on her note, a boarding house. It's started to rain. Lia walks on, turns the corner. She's under a concrete awning now, passing a pay phone kiosk, as rain pours down between traffic and her. Music explodes from the open door of a red public transport van. A boom box sits hand-wired to the dashboard. In the front seat, a passenger operates the dial through the glove compartment. Lia ducks in, checking the address with the driver. She knows, and loves, the song.

That night, in her boarding house room, under the attic, she's alone for the first time in her life. She doesn't sleep, just lies on the bed. She won't drink or eat, for fear of having to go to the loo. The bathroom, downstairs, is filthy, shared, she doesn't dare go in to wash or pee. She's never been this scared.

Hunger. Thirst. A bed all to herself. Cold and alien.

The next morning, her first day on the job, things look slightly better. Her coworker Rahmi, a girl the same age, tells boarding house war stories, gossip, tips. Buy a cheap kettle, Rahmi says, from a local brand, to boil eggs in, plus water for *Indomie*. They cost little more than a meal, and will make you a noodle dinner in minutes. And get extra flip flops, just for the loo. Rahmi's own lodgings, in Chinatown, are much cleaner, scrubbed with lye or some Chinese formaldehyde, Great Panda, that will tear the soles off your feet. There's a big drama going on with the Chinese owner lady's son, and the woman is scrubbing like crazy, building and cleaning and mortar-pasting. Her son has been jilted, Rahmi says, weeks before the wedding —everything ready, a gas stove, pots and pans, the all-important spring bed—by his pretty Minangkabau bride. Rahmi points him out, later that week, selling handphones in the market. One small hand cradled in the other.

Lia goes to work, and back to her room, and back to work each morning, back to her room in the evenings. Buys that extra pair of flip flops, plus after her first wages, even the kettle. And then she goes to work, and back to the room, and back to work each morning, and back home again, to noodle dinners.

᎒

Within a couple of months, Elektra and Nova get married in Bukittinggi, a quick, office affair without family or fanfare. One witness, Denny, another longhaired boy, who works in the town's backpacker's cafe, but will skip a shift to sign the register, in exchange for a beer.

But the jungle calls. The couple return to Maninjau, by bus, descending the treacherous forty-four hairpin bends back down into the crater.

Elektra swims out, turns on her back. Breathes in, arms wide, floating in the lake. Lets go of her head. It stays above water. The hazy sky, the green lungs of the crater walls starker and more vibrant and still than she can credit. Irrefutable. There's nothing else.

I am here.

The mist in the crowns, timeless. No beginning or end. On the out breath, slowly, her legs sink. Her chin stays afloat, until water gradually rises to her cheeks, and finally, into her eyes.

As her lungs fill back up with air, her belly rises, buoyant again. The walls resume their verdant, oxygenated hum. A lone fishermen soundlessly paddles in the distance.

On the long out breath, her feet in front of her once more start to disappear into the cool, dark water. The green, earthy smell of the lake overtakes her again, rising up to her chin, until only her nose sticks up above the water, and she breathes in, the fecund smell of the earth, Poppet—of volcanic ashes and phosphorus and clay minerals: all the mystic catalysts, and building blocks of life. Her chest, gut, legs have risen to the surface again. She opens her eyes.

ᘐ

Back in their cabin, she joins Nova, who plays Radiohead on the bed, and yawns.

Hungry.

Me too.

ᘐ

At the foot of the forty-four bends, just above the sleepy Maninjau market, Lia has escaped both the lonely pot noodle dinners of her city boarding house, and her mother's crowded longhouse.

The young man who'd been jilted back at her coworker Rahmi's lodgings, handphone seller Afin, with the diminutive mitt, has used some of the money his thrifty mother Kartini saved up all her life from selling pastries, batik, in front of the clocktower, from building a boarding house with her own hands. From scrubbing and cleaning for lodgers like Rahmi.

Afin has bought Lia the little Maninjau warung, the eatery on the corner, at the foot of the hairpin bend road, with the white little half curtains, the display in front. It's the newlyweds' very first home.

Yes, Lia still marvels, in silence, to herself, they're married. He brought a gas stove, pots, pans and all. There's a room in the back for them to sleep. The brand-new spring bed.

Lia has a newborn, named Hati, after her mum, who she nurses on the bed in the back, while in front she cooks—cinnamon, garlic, cloves—and sells nasi. Piles her bowls, in their artful stacks, in the window.

ʊ

Nova and Elektra cross the market, to the winking panes on the corner. Sit down inside, in the cool little room, among the white-painted boards of the walls, a fan blowing, breeze in the little curtains. Eat rice and fish they choose from the bowls in the window.

Elektra exhales, digging into her fish, fresh from the lake, in a thick chilli paste. Her restless, furious body comes to a halt, a standstill. Just sits on the wooden bench, at the gleaming wood table. For reasons she couldn't know—family constellations, Poppet: Lia's bowls, the scent of her own *Indo* grandmother Agnes' spice pots, these little windows, in their cream wooden frames, the curtains, *Blowing in the Wind*, like the Dutch hospital where she was born—Elektra's body just slots into place, as if she has finally, after many long wandering years, returned home.

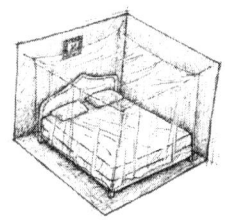

And Sophia comes home as the sun sinks, and from outside the room, through the window, the long and winding song, the labyrinthine singing, that precedes the call to prayer, begins. And the heat will yet not abate.

And inside the four walls of the room, on your clock, Elektra, the hour is six, and it will soon be time for Maghrib, and Sophia opens the door.

And she gets under the mosquito net with you, and she enters her bed. And so it is. Her weight sinks the mattress deep under you, and you struggle to keep your shape, Elektra, your flesh so enraged, taut with fury and hunger and pain.

And the hunger eats at your bones, and your bones roll, and they roll in the bed, towards the dip in the mattress, where the weight of Sophia's knees holds it down.

And your head spins around, like a spin top, on your rump, and we are neither then nor now, Elektra, and we soothe you and sing you back to your still point, the calm of your storm, calm like the heart of a rose, and we sing you back to the hair radiating on the top of your crown.

And yet you are deaf, and yet you are taut, and yet you spin in your storm.

And Sophia clambers around on the bed, digging under her pillows, for her white prayer gown. And pulls it over her head, and starts her prayer beside you. And her gown is white, and embroidered with gold.

And yet you are deaf to her song, and blind to her gestures, and yet you curse Sophia, and her God, as you curse heaven and earth.

And yet all you pray, is for her to leave, and all you pray is for Sophia to get out and cook you a meal. And all you pray for Sophia is to leave you in peace.

And so it is. Sophia leaves.

And you lie and you wait, and your body is bones, shrivelled in hunger and pain, and a cock crows outside the window.

And your brain is a murderous place.

And you pray for Sophia to kill the bird. You pray for Sophia to hurry up and kill the cock and to cook it like Lia, and your ravenous brain eats at you. And your fever,

your hunger would kill to rip even the single leaf of the
seedling, dying in the heat, struggling to find shade under
its lone leaf of green.

[Apollo footage of Earth: a distant ball, hulled in cloud.

Then a satellite shot of black and white oceans, zooming further in to whirling waves, roiling surf. A lone human figure. Jill's voice]

It's not until we stand back from the earth, that we see how much we live in water. Seventy percent of the earth's surface is covered in water, and seventy percent of our bodies are water. Ninety percent of animal life is found in it.

[Satellite weather photos, the whorling atmosphere traced with the black grid of a map. Latitude, longitude. Swirling clouds]

Through the interplay of hot and cold air and hot and cold water, vortices are formed, some so enormous that they are large enough to cover entire continents.

[The global weather map, a spiral vortex spanning several time zones]

Research on tornadoes seems to show that they are not formed simply by a strong updraft and rotating air, as one would expect...

[Black and white footage of a cyclone's uplifting whorl]

But only when a sudden unseen gust of cold air drops from the top of a rotating thundercloud, and feeds the system.

Unlike Afin, Lia's husband, Nova owns nothing. A sarong, a shirt, a pair of flares. The wedding in Bukittinggi was as sparse as they come. Elektra paid the imam, the fees, bought Denny the beer, and that was it. Here by the lake, Nova will offer Elektra the tiniest shells, grain-sized whelks, pink conches she can barely make out.

At night, when the homestay guests go to sleep, he smokes grass with the rest of the staff in the gazebo, open to the lake and the stars, and plays Radiohead songs on their shared old guitar. Then the others will curl up together to sleep in a little nest under the batik tablecloths, and Nova will retreat with Elektra to their cabin.

Then one night, she wakes alone, and he's gone.

Across the paddies, up the road, in the backroom of the warung on the corner, Afin sleeps, while Lia tends to

Baby Hati. Midnight. The mutation that affects her husband, seems to do something, too, to her child. What, exactly, she isn't sure. She has plenty of milk, that isn't it. But the baby won't grow. Both hands stay limp, and very small. Her eyes won't look at Lia.

Lia settles the baby. Gets on her knees on the spring bed and prays, in her best prayer cloak, embroidered, maroon, not for herself or her daughter, but for fate, God's will, to prevail, for her heart to be open.

Moonlight. Across the paddies, alone in her room, Elektra gets up, to find Nova curled up with his friends, outside under the tablecloths on the floor in the gazebo.

Explanation of deletion

Soon, Elektra too stays away from her cabin, and rolls up under the batik beside Nova, to sleep under the stars.

Within weeks, all they can think of is someone even smaller; as tiny, as free, as light on their feet, as they are.

In the mornings, while Nova sleeps, Elektra visits the little eatery. Sits on the bench with Lia, mostly wordless, peeling dozens of bulbs of garlic. Elektra's tummy has grown. Maybe it's just her imagination. She's only weeks in, at most, six weeks since her last period. Hums a Radiohead song to Lia's little infant, the closest thing to a lullaby she knows. *Strobe lights*, she sings, smiles at the child. Hugs herself. The song, with its recipe for disappearance, is almost too close to the bone. Elektra, with her national, ancestral history—*where are your women*—her family constellation—*torture them to death, those bloodhounds of colonialism, revenge, bloody revenge!*—her wide-flung cousins she's never seen, her body she doesn't quite feel —*shame*—is a little lost. She doesn't really know what she's doing, but Lia does, with her little shop, her cooking, her pans and pots.

Lia enfolds everything, her baby, her whole being, in the safety of home, of the place where she was born, where the land, the lake are her birth right, even her husband, where safety, security, a roof, are not what Lia needs to earn, but what she outright owns.

Like little Fuxia, Poppet, Lia is part of evolution, of nature's most clever innovation: extended parental care, a nurturing membrane, fully inheritable, that extends to her daughters for generations to come.

Elektra hums the Radiohead song, *I'm not here*. Listen, my sweet, as I, Chronicler come into being, my mother peeling garlic with Lia, her tummy growing, as I spin my own dreamy turns, my cells slowly splitting within her.

A year or so later, from a payphone kiosk in a waterfront restaurant somewhere in Bali, some place rather far from the warung, the homestay, the lake, Elektra rings Nova. It's been a while since they last spoke.

Elektra has been prompted to dial by a song, not on her own Walkman, but on a cassette player somewhere, on repeat.

She's standing in the payphone kiosk now, outside the Bali restaurant, where she has not eaten, and will not eat, can't afford to, this evening.

Holds onto my infant foot, dangling from a sling. In her other hand, she cradles the receiver. Out the window, the sun goes down over the water. Across the waves, just ahead, lies the Sunda Arc, with the ribbon of Java, the upward swirl of Sumatra. The crater, Maninjau, where Nova has retreated, back to his friends' nest of limbs, under the batik, the tablecloths, by the lake.

The phone line is silent, creaking softly, as she waits.

All she hears, is breathing

Outside, Bali girls cruise around the late-afternoon beachfront on glinting little mopeds.

Their thick straight locks cut short, small shoulders bared. Smooth legs park their bikes. They descend, to join large white men, whose leathered chests and red-neck faces bulge from outsized batik shirts. The men drink beer, exchanging insults, glass in hand. Their girlfriends, in cropped neon Lycra, manage to be both servile and insolent at their sides.

Elektra had at first avoided the waterfront that afternoon, sitting instead in the back of the restaurant. There, a sandy garden area held a sprinkling of guest gazebos, just off the kitchen. She'd sat there in the dusk, watching a rather different set of mixed couples, a group of three or four young families, snuggled around a low table in one of the gazebos. Lounging together, sipping their drinks under the thatched little roof, their children toddling at their feet.

Elektra herself had not been in a gazebo. She sat in the dark, with her back against the wall of the kitchen, on a slab of wood across two empty crates, beside the kitchen door. She was sharing this bench with an old Philips tape-recorder. A cook, a young woman in a shapeless t-shirt, had just stepped from the kitchen and leaned in to turn over a cassette tape. Then slipped back inside. Elektra watched the group of families around their table, from the shade, as the tape looped, creaking, beside her.

The men in these couples were young Balinese. They had long satin locks and soft smiles, and murmured over their infants. The women, tanned, had only in recent years cast off their backpacks, swapped bikinis for clean jeans and shirts, tied back their blonde, sun-bleached hair. Their sculpted, freckled cheekbones had softened for their new roles, had smoothed out over their children.

A verse rang out, just at that point, from the cassette

player sitting beside Elektra.

I'm not here…

That's when she got up and walked around to the front of the restaurant. She entered the payphone kiosk. The brown girls with their mopeds, the rednecked execs, mixing on the beach before her. Not really blending at all, staying static instead, separate, under Elektra's gaze.

She's standing in this booth, still. Phone in hand. The sun sinks over the sea. Baby feet droop from the sling. She's been staring out the window here, ever since my father picked up. Has stood here a while now. Listening.

The silent wire crackles across the waves, another minute, two, three, as the sun lowers towards the water.

She hears my father breathe, on the other end.

Waits for him to speak. To tell her where, in all of this— all these mixed couples, these families—*we* are.

As if he might have some kind of answer.

Later that evening, she returns me to our bench in the rear of the restaurant. It's growing dark. Candles in glass jugs have been lit in the gazebos.

The tape still turns, the same Radiohead song my father used to play around the time of my conception.

When Elektra was sixth months pregnant, Nova had punched her in the breast and stomach. He'd smacked her before, but that hadn't set off any alarm bells. If she had to, she could always slap back.

This time she left the lakeside homestay, and went to Bali for a week. She checked into a guesthouse, where she lay in the tub and looked at her sad little dome sticking out of the water, bruised purple and blue. It began to dawn on her that what she carried wasn't safe.

Still, she went back.

By the lakeside now, night after night Nova sat on the porch of their cabin, smoking. His guitar by then had gone silent.

They sat as she talked of songs he used to play, songs he might play yet.

The lake would throw itself at the dark, invisible beach before them.

This had lasted weeks, perhaps months, my father smoking as she talked, until she had picked up from the table his lighter, and, still talking, to make some point, flung it at the floor.

They sat, as it ricocheted off the cool, gleaming tiles, sparks flying.

Then they watched, both silent now, as it ignited on the floor, blazing, into the roof, a narrow, vertical supernova, white on the outside; inside, a heart of purest ultra-violet breaking for the sky.

Then it died and they sat there still, Nova and she, on the porch, as the lake hammered the beach before them.

After that he got up.

She'd been alone then, among the cabin walls, as I turned my slow turns in her womb. She'd sat on the empty porch, left with nothing but my splitting cells, the surf, the gleaming tiles, and the echoes of her own voice.

Nova had wandered, from there, until he'd ended up back where he'd started, back with his friends. Back in the nest of limbs under the batik tablecloths, black against the glimmering night-time water.

Elektra, too, had at some stage drifted from the cabin. Bearing my little body on her chest in a sling.

I liked to be carried into the world face-first by then, her hands clasped over me in front. She had carried me on and off a series of boats and ferries and buses, in and out of cheap homestays.

Food arrives at the low table of the gazebo in the garden. She watches the couples. The young dads hold their toddlers in their arms, pass them around; wide, handsome smiles passing across their faces.

Elektra stays in the dark, away from the garden, away from the beachfront, away from the glare of the setting sun. The last rays streak across the palm fronds. She watches the trees inland light up then darken, dim and impassive in the night.

The cook steps out, turns over the tape once more. In the sling, my baby self sits gazing around. Grasps for my mother's hands, missing, then catching her fingers.

Elektra rocks me in the dark as the first verse starts over. Catches and holds my two bare feet, brown, little toes wriggling in each of her hands.

Under the palm leaves of the gazebo the women, blonde and statuesque, lean against the cushions and talk among the candles, a soft-lit group of surfer girls, newly sculpted into motherhood.

Beside Elektra, the tape continues to loop.

I'm not here…

She keeps rocking me, among the echoes of the past, of my father's silence. Sits holding my feet, my trusting spine against her chest; sits there unable to get up and leave, unable to stay, unable to move.

We wash up, eventually, at Sophia's.

In Sophia's one bed house, in Medan. The bed sleeps the three of us, together under the mosquito net; Sophia by the door, Elektra in the middle, me against the wall.

The net is a white polyester canopy Sophia has sewn by hand, suspended from the corrugated ceiling. Her black stitches go round uncertainly, like a caravan of dark ants creeping up the seams. Mosquitos, trapped inside the net, hang from the gauze, casting fat black shadows.

Under a blazing lightbulb, inside the net, Elektra nurses her child. Outside, night falls. The open window sits airless, not a hint of breeze, just a blind square in the wall. The prayer call sounds; a Bollywood movie jangles somewhere.

Sophia, with her great black eyes smiles at me. Sophia's hair is streaked white, her body round with the weight of her losses. A row of framed photos hang on the wall. The most recent four are her children's graduation portraits: two daughters, two sons.

Two older, Banda Aceh pictures tell the rest. In the first, her wedding photo, Sophia is bright-eyed and slim in front of her house near the beach, her new husband already slightly paunchy. The second shows her in a yellow minidress, young mother of five—not four. Sophia a slim-stalked, yellow, five-petalled bloom.

Only Sophia's feet, tiny and gracious, have held their shape, the rest has ballooned in a helpless effort to bolster her heart against losing more.

Nova would refuse to sleep unless I'd rock him all through the night, she smiles at Elektra, who nurses me beside her on the mattress. *Stroking his forehead, holding him close to my chest, not leaving him alone for even a minute.*

By morning, Elektra knows, Sophia will wake, as always, at the first hint of dawn. Fill her wok to the brim with oil. Tip in every scrap of food she'll find in the house. There'll be no stopping her. She will need to preserve, make sure not a morsel should wilt or go to waste.

Then she'll set out for work. Call some local boy on her landline, to pick her up with his moped, in this scorching, barren development, and drive her to the nearest road. Haul her bulk into the back of a small, crowded van, change transport again, catch her third bus, to the distant West Medan office where she works.

Elektra will be left with me in the house once again, another day without cash, with nothing to eat but a charred sardine, a refried leaf of spinach, or a blistered deep-fried egg.

But that will all be tomorrow.

Allah, Sophia sighs, whaled on the bed, wiped out from work and her endless commutes.

Elektra switches off the light. Turns her back to Sophia and settles me for the night, my knees cuddled up to her stomach, soft little skull resting on her arm. Sophia, in the gulch in the mattress behind her, already softly snores. In the dark, Elektra watches my eyelids waver—and drop —and close.

Her head goes light with relief. Her limbs ache to stretch, to rise, get out of the heat, out from under the bug-ridden, airless net, anywhere, one minute, alone.

Slowly, she withdraws a leg, a hip and then, from under the hot, dreamy nape of my neck, releases her arm. Gets up on an elbow. Extracts herself and, careful, as if she might set off an alarm, sits up in bed. Reaches for her Walkman.

Looks down to find me blinking, staring, wide awake.

I slept!

I will be good, she knows, for hours!

Next, Elektra is outside. Standing in the barren lot, alone, trying to breathe the stagnant heat trapped between Sophia's wall and the neighbours'.

Steps out onto the dirt track, a black gutter in the dark, and finally lets go of her legs, lands on a dry, caked mudbank.

There's not a motorised sound in the world. Pans and pots jingle under an outdoor tap somewhere. She's sitting in the warm, hardened dust, in the middle of nowhere, in the middle of the night. A local house-beat starts pumping from one of the neighbours, some nursery song on acid, in the same pitch as a crying infant behind some shutter or blind, a wailing wife.

When she re-enters the room she blinks against the light. Sophia lies on her belly on the bed, floodlit, playing with my toes. *Siapa bapaknya*, she's teasing, *WHO's your daddy?*

I squeak and squeal, star-eyed, wriggling from side to side under the bare, glaring bulb.

When finally the light is out and my grandmother and I sleep, Elektra lies squeezed on the bed, between us, listening to her Walkman. Escaping the heat in the old Radiohead song, its curdling notes. She aches for sleep with a rage that fuels her body, scorching her veins, keeping her awake.

At last she seems to drift. I slumber in her arms, a soft ball, little limbs tucked up, snug, in the pouch of her lap, her knees pulled up around me. The mosquitos cruising the net grow dull and distant; the heat closes overhead into a sweltering black mass she no longer needs to bother with. She sleeps.

She pulls Elektra's arm, Sophia, pulls Elektra awake. *Don't sleep on top of the child!* she pants with her great dark eyes, *Don't lie on top of the baby!*

Don't worry, Ma, Elektra hisses, *I never lie on top of the baby*.

Sweet dreams, child, she turns and sleeps again, my grand-mother Sophia. Her rump cuts deep into the mattress. My mother's hungry frame hovers. Wavers uncertainly on the sloping, gutted bed. Then sinks, rolls down, into Sophia's soft, cool back, Elektra's pale skin stretched taut and tight.

She sighs.

Holds her baby in her arms and, limb by limb, lets go of who she thinks she is. Inch by inch. Falls to Sophia's flesh. Slowly eases against her.

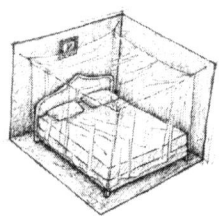

And the hands of your clock read five in the afternoon and you sleep, Elektra, in the stillness of your storm, and all is well and you dream.

And in your dream you see Chinna, your child, as a little girl.

And in your dream your child smiles.

And you sleep alone in the room, and alone in the house, and alone in the heat, and you dream.

And there is a key in lock of the door, in front, and your mother in law returns.

And your mother in law comes home.

In the centre of every vortex, there is a still point.

[A child's head of hair, seen from the top. A rose. Cut to the darkened King's College classroom, Jill's silhouette, the film projector's flickering glow. Image of the spiralling segments of a pine cone]

Wherever the spiral appears in nature, it embodies certain very practical properties, such as economy, allowing more room within less space, strength, close packing, and wrapping, protection.

[Cut to Professor Maurice Wilkins, Nobel Prize winner for discovery of DNA, King's College London, in his office. He holds a shell, speaking confidently, like a lecturer, with pointed emphasis for the benefit of the listener]

The form of a thing is the visible expression of the essence of a thing, the underlying essential nature.

Take the snail shell. Here you have a particular mathematical form, of great simplicity, and this is an expression of the special nature of the growth of the snail.

[The office is spacious, neat, Professor Wilkins wears glasses, short hair, a collared shirt and tie. He sits upright while also leaning back in his chair, without a hint of a slouch. Models of molecules surround him]

It's the simplest type of growth, without any change in the shape. There are many examples of logarithmic spirals in nature. Sunflowers grow in spiral patterns that have very particular numbers of seeds, like 55 and 89, and it seems very odd at first sight. Why does one not have 88, what is it that makes these very special mathematical relationships?

[Professor Wilkins holds the heart of a dried sunflower, in close up. Very clean hands and nails]

But when one goes into it, one sees that these arise quite naturally, these special mathematical relationships. That as the sunflower grows, the various identical parts arrange themselves in a regular way in rather the same way that identical molecules form regular arrangements in a crystal.

[Wilkins addresses the camera in a considered, authoritative tone. Behind him a bulky microscope]

And the special arrangement of the sunflower is not mysterious, but...

[Throws up his hands, his combover shines, glasses catch the light, a small laugh]

...Or it is mysterious, in the same sense that the special mathematics of the right-shaped triangle is mysterious. Pythagoras' theorem, the sum of the squares... And all that.

[Shrug]

Now, the Pythagoreans did of course think that this mathematics has some special mystical aspect.

[Hands together before him, fingers intertwined.]

But today, we find this...

[Raises one hand, shakes it]

...*Mystical* element rather elusive. The really important mysteries are on another level.

[Cut to Jill in a laboratory with a longhaired, white coated scientist. Vials, a pipette of some kind, like a turkey baster. Voice of Wilkins]

They are about relating the aspect of nature one obtains through scientific, analytical thought and observation, to the aspects of nature one gains through art and music, mythology and everyday life.

[The white coated lab assistant drips various chemicals into petri dishes. Wilkins' voice concludes]

And I think that it is in approaching this more profound mystery, that Jill's study of the spiral in all its various contexts has its importance.

PART FOUR: 2002–

Cinnamon, garlic, cloves, all straight from the little Maninjau market, plonk into the blender. A ten second blitz, and Lia is ready to coat her fish.

Tilapia, like little Fuxia back in China, half a billion years ago, with her precious innovation, offer extended parental care. They belong to the Cichlids, many of whom are mouthbrooders. Fish, often the fathers, who carry their young in their mouths.

But not *these* tilapias. The new fish in the lake are a mutated, sterilised breed, promoted by authorities. Within years, Indonesia needs to be up to speed with modernity, with global fishing techniques.

Lia cooks them, fresh every day, while she tends to Baby Hati, now a teen, with cerebral palsy. Those tiny fists, bony, jagged, and still limp. Even tinier than Lia's husband Afin's.

Her little head resting on Lia's shoulder, or on a batik booster pillow fixed to the wall, over the spring bed in the room in the back. Today, a Monday morning, the girl sits in front, cheek on the booster pillow stood in the corner. Twelve years old, she can't read or write or speak. As Lia cooks, the child smiles her crooked smile at her. Lia beams back. Hati can smile, with her sad, jagged jaw, like there's no tomorrow.

In London, eleven-year-old Chinna is waking, and getting dressed in bed, a gap-toothed face disappearing into the neck of a Christ Church Primary jumper, the logo backwards, and inside out.

In Switzerland that morning the evolutionary biologist Andreas Wagner prepares to settle the age-old debate between Darwinians and Chinna's ancestor, the pig-headed Dutch botanist, Hugo de Vries. We know how change is preserved—but not how it takes place. In Zurich, he's creating the biggest microscope biology has known.

The computer. Like the microscopes of Darwin's time, data crunching allows us to travel into a new world, one so small that even the most powerful imaging technologies can not see it: the world of the molecule. Proteins, metabolism, amino acid, genotypes: for the first time, we'll see not how evolutionary change survives, but how it *arrives*. The University of Zurich is building an entire mainframe network, a dedicated cluster, large enough to accumulate the kind of computational speed required to simulate evolutionary change at work.

Instead of watching DNA, proteins, metabolisms in the lab, and waiting for them to mutate, he'll *make* them do it, virtually, in nothing but code, and calculate the results. Watch patterns emerge.

On her twenty-first floor, little Chinna is still battling the sleeves of her school jumper. Today is not a computer-whiz-kid day, like weekends and holidays, which she spends wired to her keyboard. It's a school day. But school too, Chinna has decided, can be taken to the max.

She'll have SATs next week, prep tests this week.

It's the first Elektra hears about it.

She's doing Level 6 maths, her daughter explains, taken on average in Year 9. Now the kid seems up to the ears in some equation. *If Level 4 maths is the level nationally to be expected for Year 6, my age group…*

Right.

And Level 6 B—which is what I'm doing, Mum—for Year 9, or Year 10…

H-mm…

And GCSE's are in Year 11…

Yes…? (The child does seem to have a knack for maths.

Elektra is afraid her daughter has lost her.)

Then I could sit my GCSE's early and be out of secondary school in a year, maybe two.

But you still have to start there.

Exactly, Chinna nods. *A year, perhaps two. Three, max.*

To be perfectly honest, Elektra might be a little dim compared to Chinna, but she is finally catching up with her daughter's sums, the 'national expectations' and 'Level 6 Bs'. She's doing the maths. Chinna is right. She *could* be out of school in three, four years' time. Reading Computer Science. Imagine that. Chinna skipping off to university.

Chinna is worried there'll be classes in Computer Science.

No, Chinna. There's lectures, but they're few and far between.

No School Days?

You're meant to code. You explain what you're doing with your computer, what you're working on, like you do at home. You get feedback, just like here. That's it.

There's no need to further enlighten Chinna. She's way ahead of Elektra, lost in the imagination. Tapping the keyboard, tripping the light fantastic, reading Science— even here in bed at dawn, struggling still with her Christ Church Primary jumper.

Chinna *is* right. With A levels and all, it takes a little longer, but at seventeen an offer arrives. Computational Biology, on the strength of her triple As in chemistry and maths.

Chinna sets off for Cambridge.

Alone in her flat, instead of feeling freed from the burden of single-parental care, Elektra feels locked in, inexplicably, single to the point of despair.

Within months, she becomes furiously energetic again, cleaning, scrubbing, writing post after post on her blog, contacting sponsors. *Elektric Ladyland*, her deep-and-wide podcast about female archetypes, how they arrived and how they survive in kickass women today—hot mamas, fierce ladies—consistently ranks in the lower strata of the monthly top hundred.

But Elektra is tired. She's not feeling her heroines and interviewees, her kickass individuals, and feels far from Elektric herself. How far, how wide does she really have to be? She just needs to be here.

In truth, she feels bogged down, pondering ennui, as she looks out her twenty-first floor London window. Trains pass below, lone single people, in cars on grey roads, or hidden behind their own windows and walls. Social vacuums are what she's obsessing about. As always, Elektra fails to feel her own body, that old, strange disconnect she's always had, between what she's thinking, reality, her worries and thoughts and ideas, and, for lack of a better word, *reality*—all the stuff she sits here and lives. Like this: the bell rings.

A package. Dutch. She recognises the discrete brown box, had received one before. Blast from the past: Fred, the last person she wants to hear from, these days a mogul internet entrepreneur. Not for her.

She leaves it in the hall.

What Elektra wants is a space, a room of her own. But her beautiful flat, which she renovated just months ago—gold wallpaper, velvet sofa, tropical plants everywhere—now feels like a cage. To be frank, Elektra sits on her brand-new sofa, taking in the view of the City skyline, the Heron, the Shard, and dreams of being hospitalised. White little curtains, blowing in the wind. Not a care in the world.

She longs for Lia, suddenly, dreams of peeling garlic, in the small warung on the corner by the lake, with the fan, the white boards on the walls, the little windows. Dreams of kicking no ass at all, at least for a tiny while. Has no address for Lia of course, no phone number, or email.

But she needs something, some kind of connection. She's lived in London for over ten years, even Nova moved here at some point, but in the past decade, she still hasn't managed to make friends where she could just pop in, unannounced, and sit down, share some household chore. While away ten minutes of this very long, very lone life with some mindless, sisterly non-activity.

Maybe it's the British, that famous reserve, maybe it's just her.

She needs, she decides, some form of community living. It's the twenty-first century thing to do, apparently, a little googling soon proves.

Elektra is lonely, that's what it is. She's so lonely it's making her ill. A sour, corrosive taste in her veins. Black, caustic tar clogging her arteries, eroding her heart.

There's another reality to it too, of course, co-living ain't cheap, she quickly finds out, but she has a platform, sponsors, and sets to work. Kylie. Surely there's a podcast in it, people are gagging for wholesome, aspirational, we're-in-this-togethery stuff. Something to believe in.

Three weeks later—she's never slow—she's found a woman in Bali, Tamara, who runs a co-living space in Ubud. No stuffy hippie joint, no spider plants, a designer-led enterprise called *Roam*. She emails Tamara about making an in-residence podcast, about community living in the twenty-first century. Choice, comfort, tailored options. Individual space, high-speed internet, global allure. Community, *your* way.

That Friday, Chinna comes home, unpacks her rucksack, her laundry, eats a stack of crumpets, two helpings of Mum's vegan Bolognese.

(Elektra's secret is tempeh, Indonesian fermented soya beans, sold in cakes.)

They watch *The Matrix*, as always, spent mostly with Chinna ranting about how ferment, moulds, all mushrooms, connect the entire world, heaven and earth.

Like the fabric of reality in the film, inter-dimensional or hyper-dimensional, Elektra won't pretend she understands either *The Matrix*, dimensions or mushrooms. Though there is, of course, that Amsterdam package. Moot point, as it soon turns out. Not mushrooms, *fungi*, she's quickly told: mushrooms are just the 'fruit', fungi are 99.999 percent roots.

Merlin Sheldrake, my tutor, is a mycologist, Chinna explains. *The roots are mycelium, a mass of branching, hairlike mycorrhizal threads called hyphae.*

Before the end of that sentence, Elektra knows: the girl is in love. But there's something else. Merlin Sheldrake. What a marvellous name.

Something rings a bell.

ɕ

In Maninjau over the past year, tilapia, those plucky little fathers, with their brood in their mouths, now, sterilised, have been having a whale of a time. No more parental care. Single, male, with no natural predators, they simply eat and survive.

The fishermen, in their boats, cross the lake at dawn. Mist in the crowns on the crater walls. Not a sound, barely the soft, gentle slap of a peddle, as they check and feed their nurseries. Fat, fulsome fish.

In the warung on the corner, Lia bolsters her daughter, Hati, seventeen years old and hunched over on the spring bed, against the pillow, with her jutting hands, jutting jaw, like an old crone. Fish is delivered, and Lia cooks, fries, serves the old lady from the large house, serves the village, local tourists and backpackers.

Each night, the nurseries once more fill, as the fishermen feed and feed, the government mandated fish food, more than enough, and then more than more than enough.

Which, night after night, day after day, sinks to the bottom of the lake. Drifting, floating down, forming sediment. In the oldest, deepest depths of the crater, that ancient cauldron, where it mixes with the mineral-rich volcanic floor, good old phosphor, sulphur, those clay minerals, which once kickstarted the citric acid cycle, created spontaneous membranes, embracing RNA in that mystic, life enhancing rate—and now send up whorls of gaseous clouds.

The lake too clouds, until, one morning, it's the colour of milk, then rotting milk, curdled and odious, and filled with fish. White bellies up.

The next day, it froths. A thick layer of dead fish has formed, crawling with maggots.

Later that month, one dawn, in the back room of the warung, in the stench from the lake, Afin and Lia sit on the bed, holding their daughter. Her jagged little bones more rigid than ever.

Gone cold, in their arms.

They had been warned. But Lia, in her heart of hearts, had not believed it could happen. Despite what happened to her mother, the five little stones. Not if she loved this much, put her trust in God. Truly. Her heart fully open.

The next week, they lay a sixth small stone in front of Hati's home, the ancient longhouse. A potted plant on top, a tiny, jagged rose.

That night Old Hati, little Hati's namesake, plus Old Hati's six daughters, their husbands and children, all sleep in their box sized quarters, walled off with boards, with curtains, under the horned, ancestral roof. Lia alone on the shared mattress, the shared room, her back turned to Afin, to her sisters and mother, to the window, the paddies singing outside in their silvery light, even to the moon.

It takes a month for Lia to return to the back room of the warung, to the spring bed. The lake festers on, there are no more visitors, the backpacker trail dries up.

As the year wears on, the stench goes down, the lake is cleaned, fish are bred, things return to normal. Fishermen in their boats, in the silence, between the ancient walls with their cinnamon tree crowns, the mists of dawn.

Lia prays five times a day, as always. Not for herself, just for the strength to accept her fate. But as the lake survives, as her husband Afin shows the mettle of his Chinatown mother Kartini, cleaning and scrubbing the little warung—in the green yard of Lia's maternal home, under the stone, the pot with the thorny flower, Lia's heart stays buried with her child.

ၯ

Sheldrake.

Ignore this man at your…

In London, Elektra sits up in bed. Suddenly wide awake. The sun's barely up.

She knows that name. *Rupert*, Merlin's father. That strange day, in the loft by the canal, under the seventeenth-century rafters.

Her interview. Her article for the paper. What was it again? *Morphic resonance*—synchronicity—physics, it's all pretty rusty. The *I Ching*.

She leaps out of bed, in her empty, hollow flat, finds her laptop on the sofa. Googles her own name, plus the paper's and Sheldrake's, to find the article. But it was early nineties, before Google or news online, obviously. The days of printed paper.

How quaint.

Right. It's coming back now. She was fired. The article probably never quite made it to print.

The rest, too, is coming back. She made him toss up coins, to ask the *I Ching* what his own import was for the world.

What was the verdict, the oracle's answer, the judgement on Sheldrake?

There was something about vessels, crock pots—or was that her?

All she remembers is the warning: *Ignore this man at our peril.*

She smiles. The final punchline, to that whole afternoon, with the psychic cats and dogs, that mild twinkle, the dimples and curls, the polite, unreadable glint in Rupert's eye. Who ever heard of Sheldrake, again?

His recent TED talk was banned, Google offers. Deemed unscientific.

Well. Whoever heard of Elektra again. From reporter to c-list podcaster.

She sits in her Elektric Ladyland, her overdecorated room, on her overstuffed sofa, and looks out her twenty-first-floor window. The skyline, the City, the Gherkin, the Shard—life has done nicely without her interview, without synchronicity or morphic fields, experiments that changed the world—without the *I Ching* for that matter.

What had she been thinking?

She speed-dials Chinna on her phone, no answer. Docks her old iPhone 5, the one thing she hasn't replaced in her fury to compensate for Chinna's absence.

Right, people, not things. Elektric ladies, not androids or bots. The motto of her podcast, in the first place. It's time for some yoga.

But frog-posing on her mat, minutes later, furiously trying to concentrate, she jumps straight back up.

What was the verdict, the answer again? The hexagram, what had Sheldrake drawn?

She still cannot remember. Sits back down, not on her mat: on her sofa, with her laptop, goes through all the 64 hexagrams, one by one. Not systematically, of course, as Sheldrake would've done. In his slow, methodical way.

But counting on the lightning-fast flash of intuition, going from faintly familiar shape to remotely likely form. Mountain? Lake?

What was the name of the hexagram, again? Perseverance? Ascent? Like a pin ball, over the next day, she bounces from Chinese six-lined diagram to diagram. Kings and soldiers, fires, earth. Fathers and sons. Maidens, famines, wars. Yin and yang.

She goes through each diagram in their dedicated pages online, in the various versions, translations, commentaries, from EarthMom.com to the classic translation by Richard Wilhelm that Elektra used as a girl.

But after sixty-four of them, in no particular order, stumbling on many multiple times, over and over, pinging back and forth and spiralling round, bouncing and jolting like a yin-yang billiard ball, like a lightning-fast but undeliverable telegram, she finally knows: *she cannot recall Sheldrake's hexagram.*

All she recalls is that warning. Where is it, in the *I Ching*?

Not in the descriptions of the hexagrams, that's for sure. There is not one called *Man To Be Ignored At Our Peril.*

It's not in the Judgements, or the commentaries, she reads all sixty-four—two, three, sometimes seven times, in each dedicated page, each permutation online.

The warning must be in one of the sixes or nines, the unstable lines.

On her laptop, over the next twenty-four hours, Elektra reads every single changing line in the *Book of Changes*. Finally, by morning, she stumbles on it. In hexagram number fifty, Ting, the Cauldron. Now she vaguely recalls, *prophets and holy men… To venerate them in humility…*

The changing line is the second. *There is food in the Ting. My comrades are envious, but they cannot harm me. Good fortune.*

It sounds like a riddle to her, after all these years. What does it mean?

She googles *I Ching hex 50.2*, the code, she has found out, by now, for this outcome.

Night has come and gone, over the city. She's hungry, and cold. The sky is still grey, not quite dawn. A grid of tall steel legs stick up above the Gherkin, the Cheese Grater, the Heron, like an alien landing-ship platform, hovering over the skyline. The tall legs of cranes, flashing their little red warning lights over the concrete and glass still scrambling up, buildings we don't yet have nicknames for.

For reasons beyond her and beyond us, the page Elektra lands on, is written in Dutch.

It's the Spice Pot, as the Dutch version of the Cauldron is called, but the page is not the hexagram's own, dedicated page, like the ones she's been pinging back and forth between, all night long.

It's the old introduction by Jung, that she'd read as a girl.

Where Jung asks the *Book of Changes* the same question Sheldrake had, but for the *I Ching* itself: what meaning does the oracle hold?

The Spice Pot: supreme revelation appears in prophets... They should be accepted in humility... inner enlightenment and true understanding...

Jung, for the book, too had thrown the six or nine, the changing second line. *There is food in the ting. My comrades are envious, but they cannot harm me. Good fortune.*

Sheldrake had asked what his own meaning was for the world. The oracle gave the same response.

I Ching and Sheldrake—spice pots both.

ဟ

In Wuhan, *I Ching*-country itself, as all over the planet, warnings are ignored.

Poppet.

No, sweet, no need for alarm—not in your dreamtime. Stay wrapped in your deep-space world, safe in your coil.

Chroniclers keep track of time, they summarise, organise. We make sense of history. And I was hungry then as I am now, child, for knowledge, my hunger ran as deep and as wide, but I was starting to fall.

Chronicling from the Big Bang through the Cambrian explosion—Entangled life—Through prophets and revel-ations—J, *I Ching*, Sheldrake—

Through today—

Mycelium killed with anti-fungal spray—

Spice pots toll, hollow, my body clanging, my voice cracking up. Speeding, faster, faltering, as your timeline spins and roils—

Industrial ploughs, monoculture, hyphae stripped from the soil—

Crops bred on their own, like people, 'individuals', separate from their natural bionts, unable to mine the earth's life-giving crust for phosphorous, minerals—

Overfed on fertiliser, unable to reconnect with their natural allies—

Bred alone, sterile—

Bloated, vessels of disease, eaten by bloated souls cut off from their own holobionts—

Sterilised fish, childless mammals, their guts sanitised and barren, helpless against invaders, rudderless pawns, collateral damage in the biological arms race—

As we've all become—

Team biotechnology, prompting nature towards ever new innovation, microbes that can do without cell walls, antibiotics that are engineered to destroy, proteins, efflux pumps, that flush out antibiotics,, and extremophiles, of course, that will actually feed on them, use antibiotics to make each of those known, 3.8 billion years old, 60-odd building blocks of life—

All sprouting lifeless forms, viral, that exterminate us from the inside—

Climate, Anthropocene, cataclysm. It's a minute to midnight.

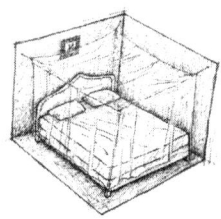

And your black hands of time read midday Elektra, high noon, and you are alone in the room and alone in the house of your mother in law with the lizards, mosquitos, the ants on the strip of tiles on the floor and you get up from under the mosquito net and you get up from the bed. And you open the door and enter the next room. And the house is small. See: the room holds nothing, it is smaller than the room you left, Elektra, and has another strip of tiles with a single gas burner, for the kitchen. You open the next door.

And the dirt track in front is deserted. And so it is: noon.

A row of identical homes sit and radiate the heat of the sun. Their waving iron roofs shudder and creak. And another row runs along it, identical. And yet another row runs. And others, in all directions.

And there is row after row, and row after row, and they scald.

And your eye seeks the green comfort and shade of a tree. And see, there are no trees.

Behold. No green.

And your eye seeks the comfort of a companion, a fellow being, and see, there are none.

And your eye seeks a road, a market, a kiosk, and there are none.

And the dirt track shivers with heat, and the dust cooks under the sun. And the houses offer no shield. They glower in the glare and when first ever you set foot in this country, when first you set foot in Bali, shielded in green, you would not have believed such a place existed.

And see, you are here. And yet, were you not here, stood in the door, Elektra, determined to run, were you not stood in the middle of it, you would yet not believe it.

And there is no one.

And you are hungry and dizzy with lack of food, and you have not eaten. And you are fevered. And shaking.

And yet: the fever rages before you, under the sun. And the fever of the sun is without limit, without end or beginning. And it is heat beyond enduring. And it is greater than you.

And you cannot run.
And you turn, and go back inside. And you close the

door, and the next door, and get back in the room, under the mosquito net, and onto the bed. And the room shudders under the iron roof, and you rest your fevered head.

And death occurs around you, in the struggling seedling under your window, and death is in the rows and rows of iron and cinder block concrete, in the shadeless development built so far from the city, Medan, and built so far from Medan's towers of Exxon and Citi, that the spires cannot be seen, and in the room where you rest and all around Sophia's house the heat crackles and blisters.

And you sleep, and you dream, and see:

The face of your daughter appears.

Day 0.

In China, a random mutation occurs. Evolution is an algorithm so simple a computer could do it. Zeros and ones. Change a virus' DNA, and you give rise to its altered form.

Mutate. Select. Repeat.

Day 1. A new strand is born. This little fucker beats them all.

Hello world!

The virus' race to solve the travelling salesman problem has begun.

ᘒ

How do they find the shortest way from A to B?

Merlin, Day 1, in Cambridge, is talking about problem-solving behaviours of fungi.

How do they let the rest of the network know in which direction they should grow?

Chinna has been wondering about this herself. In fact, she'd barely stopped thinking—all through *The Matrix*—of Merlin and fungi. It's Monday. She's just back from the weekend at Mum's. There'd been a package in the hall. A discrete brown box.

Chinna had pointed. *What's that?*

Some old hippie sends them. Amsterdam. Now he's rich, and feeling guilty. I guess.

Chinna opened it. It contained a grow kit, spores. 'Golden Teacher'.

Elektra had yawned, shrugged, *I'm too old, take it to the lab if you want.*

The mushroom is a slow coloniser, Chinna learned on the train back to Cambridge, with rhizomorphic mycelium, but the spores had been pre-colonised on a brown rice substrate, right in the box they came in.

All she'd needed to do last night was fill the box with water, close it and let it soak for 12 hours, then this morning put the box inside a bag to let it grow. She can't wait to get back to her room. The mushrooms are meant to come up in a group called a flush.

Merlin is still talking about the travelling salesman problem, or more specifically, the fungal approach to it.

Chinna sits up. Maths. Algorithm.

Darwin himself, prophetic as always, had come up with a theory a hundred and fifty years earlier. He called it the Root-Brain theory.

It's still disputed today, to say the least, Merlin grins. *Scientists hate thinking of anyone without our own neural structures and lobes, encased in some boneheaded skull, as having a brain.*

But Darwin proposed that the evolving tips of hyphae are like the earliest membranes in nature, those sensing, feeling skins, knowing exactly what to keep out and what to keep in.

Chinna nods. Of course. Membranes were life's earliest brains.

[The white-coated lab assistant has dripped clear liquid with a pipette into vials, and tipped these into a petri dish. The dish, set on a desk between Jill and an unseen third observer, is slowly changing colour. Jill's young, carefully modulated tones]

Science itself is increasingly showing that observer and observed are one. That the scientist is a participator in the world he is looking at, and an integral part of his own experiment.

Merlin still talks about hyphae, in best tutor mode. *It's the place where information comes together to link perception and action, and determine a suitable course for growth. Hyphal tips are where mycelium grows, changes direction, branches and fuses.*

Chinna feels her fingertips, those sensing, feeling skins, mentally tracing the shape of his cheeks, his chin. Knowing what to keep out, what to let in. She feels her spiral fingerprints rolling in, involving the world around her, hyphal tips where her young body grows, changes direction, branches and fuses.

How do these root-brains work, Merlin is still saying, *how does information travel throughout the network?*

Olson, a Norwegian researcher in the sixties proposed—Chinna knows, naturally, even without thinking—*that it was through electricity.*

Olsen tried to show, Merlin says, *that action potentials were sensitive to a stimulus.*

Exactly, electricity. Sparks, flowing from high action potential, to low, just as they do in her circuits.

But Chinna, despite knowing everything there is to know about circuits, is lost. Her brain, like her fungal ancestor core, her mycelial flesh, is in her roots, her fingertips: so sensitive, seeking action potentials, the stimulus of a nostril, a dimpled cheek. A long brown curl. Smooth chin, barely stubbled at all, still talking. A beautiful, lovable lip.

ʊ

Back in her room, distracting herself from her feelings, her tutor, Chinna checks on her grow kit. No growth yet.

Then she picks up an apple, checks in on her virtual lab. She has a job interview tomorrow, with Adam, researching fungal logic gates, but she's frantically researching her own.

Computational biology, algorithm, is her spiritual home. It brings her peace. But not tonight, dumping the apple on her desk, already forgotten. She's too hungry for science to eat. She just needs to know. How does life survive?

Circuits can be rewired in astronomical ways. With each added gate, the number grows exponentially. Even her own little pet circuit of sixteen gates—*nothing*, readymade circuits contain *millions* of gates—can already be wired in

10^{46} ways.

What would each of those circuits do?

Chinna has no idea. There's no human way to build each of those 10^{46} circuits and check, not even on Cambridge computers. The only way to get the roughest idea is through calculation. And even that is a wild guess. Most random genetic mutations would create nonsense genotypes. Likewise, of her own pet circuits, all but the most ubiquitous, well-known functions might be void. She uses four input bits, and four outputs, which gives her 1.84×10^{19} hypothetical functions. An almost unconceivable number, more functions than she can ever imagine for sixteen simple yesses or nos. How many of those functions might actually exist? It's like gazing out at the black void of the universe. Hoping for pinpricks of light, each one a function of her circuit: lone stars among all that empty space.

She holds her breath. Just a second. Then exhales.

Starts to type. An algorithm, creating as many random wirings of her circuit as her laptop will hold. Two million different circuits. How many will come to life?

ʊ

Mycelial networks 'compute' data encoded in electrical spikes.

In the real-world lab, she sits across from researcher Adam, as he interviews her and drinks coffee. It's more of a lecture.

If we knew how a mycelial network would respond to a given stimulus, we could treat it like a computer, he explains.

Chinna nods. It's the reason she's here, of course. Hot on Merlin's heels, overtaking him, leapfrogging into the future, with the biocomputer, while at the same time seeking shelter, comfort in his shadow. The cool world of fungal circuits. She just wants to get started.

Slime mould networks can be modified, for example by cutting a connection, to alter the set of logic functions implemented by the network.

She nods again. All cut and dried.

Once we can quantify and standardise how the network responds to each 'cut', it becomes a living logic circuit board. But your job is simpler. You can begin, he gestures at a pile of wooden blocks, *by growing the mycelium. Getting a feel. You like oyster mushrooms?*

Sure.

Good. Know how to grow them?

She blushes. *I'll erm, learn.*

ၒ

Elektra cannot live another day alone in this quietus, in

her overdecorated, over-cared for London flat. Full of plants, in lieu of human company. She's never been this lonely before. Not one to postpone, she's booking a flight to Bali, departing that Tuesday, just as her daughter calls.

Mum, I've got a job!

Great, I'm going to Bali on Tuesday, to make a podcast. I'm going to live and work there for a while. Let's have a big goodbye cuddle this weekend and you can tell me all.

Elektra pays for her flight, Chinna books her train ticket, both on their phones, while they chat on.

What do you want for dinner?

Your veggie spagbol, Chinna sighs. *I can't eat more canteen corn burgers Mum.*

Done. Unsurprised by Chinna's lack of interest, in either co-living or Bali—the girl is eighteen—Elektra seeks common ground. *What film shall we watch?*

Memento?

Yet again. Mind-boggling stuff, part of the *Inception/ Matrix/ Source Code* canon Chinna has on permanent rotation. Elektra's turn to sigh, with a smile. *Of course.*

↺

Adam's endless coffee comes in handy, as oyster mushrooms turn out to thrive on the grinds. Chinna prepares blocks of wood the next morning, colonises them with mycelium. Oyster mushrooms, like their magic cousins, will take a while to sprout. She covers the blocks, feeds them grinds and water, TLC.

Back in student halls, she can't eat, can't sleep. Lies thinking. It's 4 AM. She looks at her circuits, checks her algorithm. She wants to run it.

As she leaves her laptop to crunch through the last hour of night, falls asleep in her seat, another uneaten apple before her, her thick parka pulled around her, still shivering with cold, she dreams. Not one lone star, but a spiralling galaxy lights up the sky.

By six AM, her hands have turned blue. Her body is rigid. She needs to breathe before she can bend her back, her neck enough to look at the screen.

She rubs her eyes. Looks again. Her laptop must have crashed, or her code has bugs. As usual. Some kind of mistake.

She checks the log. Everything looks normal.

Among some nonsense, she's found over one million functions, and counting. None of them remotely familiar. Another half hour in, she has over 400,000 new functions again.

Exotic things she's never dreamed of, let alone seen or

heard of.

She shrugs off the parka, suddenly hot. 150,000 functions.

And that's just with two million random wirings—there's another 10^{40} circuits left to check, more or less, and 10^{12} more functions to try!

ᘯ

On Saturday, Chinna takes the train home. That evening, side by side in the big bed with Mum, they watch *Memento*.

They both know the film by heart, though Elektra still has no clue how it works. Chinna has explained ten thousand times, drawn diagrams, made Elektra sit through eighteen minutes of Christopher Nolan explaining the spiral vortex structure on YouTube. Backwards, inverted, counter clockwise, whatever it was.

None of it matters, as all Elektra wants to do is hold Chinna close, hear Chinna's voice, as her daughter explains yet again. Smell the warm nape of Chinna's bones, her moist neck.

Rub the little frown on her daughter's brow. Within minutes, the brow goes slack, eyelids close, and there's the slowing of breath, the little spasm of muscles, that mean her child has fallen asleep in her arms.

If only Chinna could stay there, sleeping, a year or so

more. There'd be no need to pack tomorrow, fly to Bali, spend a single thought on co-living at all.

༠

Even Merlin is growing fauna in the lab. On Monday, he shows Chinna dust seeds, the smallest plant seeds in the world. *These are orchids, one of the largest species on the planet. But they won't germinate till they meet a fungus.*

The seeds weigh nothing, Chinna has to hold her breath not to blow them off the dish. They're no bigger than spores. Is Merlin suggesting the dust seeds are basically kind of the orchid's… like, eggs, that the hyphae will now somehow… impregnate?

She wipes her brow, smooths a stray lock of hair. Heavy, black.

Merlin shows her rows of pots, where weeks ago he buried thousands of them in small bags. *Waiting to catch them in the act.*

They dig up a bag. Sit around the microscope, with a needle and a dish, pushing the soil around, looking for swollen, entangled seeds, dust that's been coiled, cradled, kissed to life.

There's only soil. Merlin gets up. *Let's give it the rest of the week.*

Over the next days, as a lonesome Elektra boards a plane and lands in Roam, her new Bali co-living home, full of orchids, Merlin keeps watering his pots, while Chinna mists her grow kit, and her blocks.

Chinna still can't sleep alone. By Thursday night, her Golden Teacher box is showing tiny white pinheads. Oyster mushrooms, her fungal logic gates, are starting to form, in Adam's lab.

But she still ponders her virtual ones. It's 2 AM.

She's found 1.5 million functions, even within her own little cohort of two million random circuits. But there's quadrillions—times quadrillions—that she hasn't tried.

What haunts her more though, is that she still doesn't know how the functions arise. How, in that dark universe of 10^{46} potential circuits, are the potential functions *organised?*

She lies in bed, alone, sleepless, without the calm gaze of her mum. Gazing up at the dark plasterboard of her room. She's an atom, removed from every other student, Medicine, Law, on every other floor, stacked in columns and rows, nothing but a vast wasteland of board, walls, mutual incomprehension between them. She could not explain what keeps her awake to her closest neighbour, a Botany major, dreaming of classifications—could not share one new thought, not if she tried all night.
There are 10^{29} more possible combinations, than there are

possible functions. Are the functions lone points, lone stars, random and unconnected, in all that empty space? What is the point of a random function, if any *new* change to the circuit, any new mutation, causes it to die?

She thinks of the innovations of bacteria—3.8 billion years ago, already exploring today's sixty-odd building blocks of life. How their metabolisms evolved exponentially, through basic maths, when proteins, not RNA, began expressing our genotypes. Proteins' twenty amino acids, versus RNA's four, took the number of combinations from a four-letter alphabet, to protein's twenty letters, which soon took the number to astronomical heights. Each protein mutation, each 'logic gate' change, changes the genotype. Which potentially changes its 'function', its phenotype. How are *those* possible functions organised? What's the point of a random new phenotype, if any new change means it can't survive?

Back to her virtual world.

One thing she knows. *More Ways Than One*. Since there are so many more possible circuits than there are possible functions, there must be many doubles, many different ways to wire a circuit—*and* get the same function. Is it possible that a mutation will *not* necessarily change a function? That you could change a wire at a time, without losing the circuit—without even changing what it *does*?

Across the world, it's 10 AM, and Elektra has arrived in Bali, settled in over the past day. It's Day 12 of the virus, though few people know this. Elektra least of all. She breathes in the fresh verdant air, dives into the pool. Paddies, green, trees, all breaking for life as far as the eye can see, Bali's volcano, Mt Agung, in the distance.

At the other end of the pool, a woman arrives in a hot pink batik bikini, with a coconut, a straw.

Orchids grow on the walls. *Bollocks to bacon and beans*, Tamara says. *Fancy a fresh pina colada for breakfast?*

Ten minutes later, Elektra's pulls up *Elektric Ladyland*, presses play, and they're squirting rum from their noses in the pool, over Tamara's biblical namesake.

She married the actual Onan, Tamara heaves, *the OG deadbeat husband.*

Elektra hiccups over deadbeat, while the podcast gets to the bit where Tamar receives her deposits. *'Take her away,' judged Judah, 'To be set afire.'*

Afterwards, Tamara still laughs. She tells the torch squad to leave her in peace and just go find the dick who left her his stick and seal. Snorts. *God only knows how that story survived Christians for 2000 years.*

3000, Elektra corrects. *It first survived the Jews. When you look at characters in books, it's mad how they survive. Tough as nails, much hardier than we.*

She gestures at the sky, the green all around. *You can change everything, like all the details… the setting, the language, even the time. Tamar is the original bold-ass comeback.*

Tamara hands Elektra the coconut and the straw, *Like Bey telling Jay where to put it.*

Amen.

Back in Cambridge, it's 2 AM. Chinna sits up and starts typing a whole new set of commands. This time, she starts not with a random set of circuits, but with one random function she's already found. She calls it Ms *Fungski*, marrying her twin loves, function and fungi.

The question that keeps her awake, she realises, is robustness. It's those bacteria, those genotypes again. The microbes that can thrive in volcanoes or under ice. A metabolism that can survive in more than one environment needs to get more robust. And as complexity grows, so does the number of possible genotypes. Astronomical.

Chinna is going to try, one change, one mutation at a time, to keep Ms Fungski alive.

The program starts by changing one wire. If the function stays the same, Fungski lives. Chinna will keep the mutation. If not, she'll go back, try another wire. Repeat the same test: if the function stays the same, she'll keep the mutation, if not, she'll go back, retry, until she finds a wire that keeps the function intact, and Fungski alive.

From that newfound circuit, she'll repeat the whole process again, changing Ms Fungski's circuit one connection at a time. She wants to find out how many times she can rewire her, how many wires she can change, how far she can change the circuit altogether, before Fungski will stop working, give up the ghost. How many changes her pet circuit, her poppet, can survive.

෬

The next day, Friday, Day 13. Merlin and Chinna sit around the microscope, peering into their dust seed dishes for hints of germinating. No luck.

But it's only four in the afternoon. They have no other plans. All her coding at home, plus all the slicing, boiling and dyeing of fungi, gazing at dead hyphae squashed between glass slides, here, in the lab, has left Chinna aching for signs of life.

Also, there's a first flush. At last. She found her Golden Teacher golden this morning. It's in her bag.

She smiles. Merlin, of course, doesn't know that.

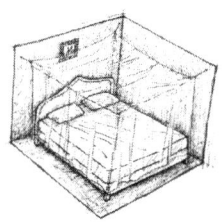

And the clock on the wall reads seven, and a lone bird sings in the shelter of dawn. And outside the window: a noise.

A moped has come. It halts on the dirt track in front. And Sophia goes out, rests her bulk on the back seat of the bike, behind the rider. And the drooping mound of her long pink robe hides the rear plate. And hark: the hum, and the spin of the rotor, as it takes off, and Sophia goes to the main road, fifteen minutes away, in front, where she will catch a small, crowded van to work.

And inside her room, you lie and listen Elektra, for your husband outside your door. And you know he is there. And you lie and listen and wait.

And you lie and wait, Elektra, for your husband to go to the mosque. And it will take hours, you know.

And you rage, and you wait, for the turns of the clock,

your black hands of time, the cycles and hours it takes. And you pace and you walk in your brain where there's no space to pace.

And see: he is gone. It is noon. You are free to escape.

[The petri dish, set on a desk between Jill and an unseen third person, is changing colour, from clear liquid to red. A cloud pattern emerges, swirling curls, like the waves on a Japanese woodblock print, or the clouds of Cirebon batik. Jill looks on, flushed, searching for words, her long wavy locks caressing her cheekbones, mouth and strong jaw]

What are the implications for living systems, of the fact that pattern could emerge from chemicals?

[The unseen third person comes into view as the assistant recedes. It's biochemist Dr Jonathan Ashmore, University College London, seated opposite Jill. Leaning forward, arms crossed over his chest, with long dark hair, a beard, plaid shirt. Sharp features under all the hippie bluster, the hint of a receding hairline, in his twenties. A high, expressive voice. Struggling to be both precise, and somehow hip and openminded]

It is rather surprising, that you can get such definite structures emerging from initially homogeneous mixtures of chemical reactions.

[He leans in, sits back, turns around on his swivel stool, gesturing widely with his hands. Leans back again, continues]

And this system has been considered as a paradigm for some kind of biological development...

[Jill, excited but still, solid within her ivory skin, her generous curves, her whole body alert with pure curiosity]

What of the physical reactions happening here? Are there any which are not purely chemical?

[Image of the swirling spirals in the petri dish, like a miniature painting, a batik medallion. Jonathan, authoritative, but with the slightest tremble to his voice]

Pure chemistry.

Jill: *Pure chemistry.*

Jonathan, swirling on his chair, colouring cheeks, twirls his beard, *Does that detract in any way from it?*

Jill, emphatic, *No.*

Jonathan stops grinning, regaining scientific composure, returns to higher ground. *It's a model of a very definite morphology arising out of an initially homogeneous medium.*

[Continues twirling his beard, his sharp features growing pinkish, like the dish. With every phrase, he lifts a hand, gesturing, then puts it back, under his chin, or wherever it will sit still]

For example, one of the outstanding problems in developmental biology is how pattern emerges from the embryo, for instance, whether it's the segments on a worm or the pattern of the bristles on a fly...

He swivels back and forth on the chair, plucking at facial hair, ...*Even all the way out to bigger things such as that, I don't know...*

Shrugs, shy, smiling, hands waving back and forth, rocking right and left on his chair, *Why one has four legs I guess...*

Colours bright red, fingering his beard. *Well... animals do...*

Jill, unperturbed, her whole shape sensuous with wonder, *So now what we're seeing is the appearance of order out of chaos, out of nothing?*

Jonathan squirms to be both factual and true, in his plaid shirt and jeans, smiling, *It's not chaos and it's not nothing.* Pained grin. *It's something.*

Jill: *Something which has no apparent order.*

Jonathan, cradling his beard with his hands, as if hugging his chin, *Any kind of order which one sees I think is always rather surprising.*

Jill leans in, earnest with wonder. *Why? Because you don't think that the universe is basically intelligible?*

Jonathan, resting his pinky finger on his lip as he listens, presses the nerve just under the nose, then swivels away, grinning and touching his ear. *It's surprising that it is, I think, but perhaps it isn't, I don't know...*

Jill: *Surely it would be very surprising if it wasn't intelligible, if it wasn't ordered and comprehensible?*

Jonathan: *Maybe. It's surprising that the same forms keep reappearing...*

Jill leans in deeper. High, modulated tones: *Surely these forms go right through all the different levels, and also through the levels of our own consciousness?*

Guileless waves frame her face, her wide eyes, *And this has to do with why we actually see these forms: because we only see what we're able to see in a sense, so that our minds in fact structure what we see. And they are structured by the overall order.*

Jonathan listens, rocks from side to side, eyes darting, grinning. Fingers touch his lips, voice recedes. *Familiarity breeds what we see... but it breeds contempt, as well...*

Jill's voice deepens, a constant, sonorous flow. *We actually see order in something. And if you recognise it, you recognise something you're familiar with.*

A pause, as she meets his eye. Reaching out. *So if you see order in this, you're recognising something that is in yourself which is in your own mind or in your own organisation...*

Another confident pause, as she waits for a meeting of kinds. *It's a recognition.*

[SILENCE]

Jonathan, blushing deep, his angular features expressing pain, the hard glint of holding out in his eyes, *It may just, for me, generate excitement.*

Jill, smiling: *But that excitement is recognition.*

Jonathan swivels in his chair, small swivelling spirals, retreats into his shell: *I just call it excitement.*

Jill laughs, dropping her upheld chin, hair falling, natural waves, along her cheeks, her young, mature face.

First flush. Golden Teacher, a proud little clump, sits plump in its box. Chinna has brought the box to the lab. She's alone with Merlin. It's still Friday, Day 13. Late: everyone's gone home. She'll run her programme later, when she gets back to her room. But first, there's Merlin.

The two of them sit around the microscope, peering at dust seeds they gently poke with the needle, the seeds still covered in soil.

You hungry, Merlin says.

Chinna doesn't expect what happens next. Bold as can be, she opens her mouth. *Actually, I've got some shrooms*, she hears herself say. More than speech she had intended, more than volition or agency, it's like an echo, a resonance in the room.

A look on his face.

The look is not of surprise, or shock, but of simple communication, as if the echo, the resonance, is not just one voice, but some kind of choir, *polyphony*, as if their hyphae, hers and his, those sensing tips, are already somehow entangled.

Bright eyes, dimples, on his part.

Black stars, plump volcanic lips on hers.

Plants are the way we see fungi in the world, Merlin is saying an hour later. They're still staring into the dish, looking for dust seeds, trying to catch them in the act. The room is starting to look a little funny. It floats.

Mycelium stitches all of life to the earth, it mines the volcanic crust and weaves its minerals throughout the soil, through every cell and stem and leaf, from high to low, Merlin is saying. *You can't see the fabric with the naked eye, but it's thicker, denser, trillions of times longer than all the plant roots combined, all around us, entangling the entire world, everywhere on earth, every fruit, every potted plant, he gestures at a departmental Monstera, every bit of green on a windowsill as in the soil is an extension of it. Every orchid—*

Wait. Look.

A seed has swollen into a fleshy clump tangled up in thick, throbbing streamers leading into the dish. Fungal hyphae, impregnating and nursing the seed at the same time, enfolding and coiling stickily around it.

It's not intercourse exactly, he says. *But it's sexy.*

She nods. Holding her breath. The lab has turned golden, the dish bright and warm, there's something amniotic and floaty about the whole room.

His eyes glitter hard as he sighs. *It's cells from two different creatures meeting, and embodying each other, collaborating in the building of a new life.*

The orchid seed flushes and swells in the dish between them, growing lusher, in the sticky probe of the hyphae, until the flush in their brains, his and Chinna's, and the flush in the dish, and the fungal fabric stitching it all into one—heaven and earth, soil, grass, flesh, atmosphere, a three-dimensional realm of microscopic threads thicker, denser, billions of times longer than all our roots and veins, our arteries, beating pulses combined—is all one swirling spiral, one throbbing bodily hum.

By the time she gets home and starts Ms Fungski's programme that night, around 4 AM, Chinna herself is more dead than alive. Spun around on cloud nine till she no longer knows up from down.

But before the programme is halfway its run, Chinna is revived. She cannot believe her eyes. Fungski's function is not a lone star in the sky. Chinna's pet circuit is part of a whole galaxy of stars, each connected to the next in a massive, hyper-dimensional spiral, all around the entire spectrum.

Chinna gazes up from her screen, to the ceiling, that plasterboard, now lit up by Ms Fungski. All those stacks and rows, floor after floor, of lawyers and medics-to-be, asleep in their dreams, their nightscape visions suddenly connected, she feels. It's as if they can all cross departments, suddenly, all talk shop as they hop from one dreamscape to the next, Medicine, Law, Biology, without losing a beat. Everyone bright as starlight, one continuous, circling conversation.

This is how change is *organised*. Circular.

A circuit can change every single one of her gates, can have not a single one left from birth, can be different in every gate from her earliest self, and still do the same thing. She can go all the way around the spectrum.

And *survive!*

There is no explanation. Chinna tries it again, with a different function. *Fungski Two*. Same thing.

Her pet circuit, her poppet is *robust*.

She tries a hundred more functions. A thousand.

Then starts thinking. She may never sleep again.

It's like the bacteria.

As complexity grows, so does the number of possible genotypes: a self-organised, spiralling network.

But how does it work?

Still spinning from her first flush, from her night with Merlin, Chinna mists her oyster mushrooms a few hours later, Saturday morning. Day 14 of the virus, though no one yet knows. The mushrooms have come up in clumps. Tender, velvet fanning shapes. She touches their skin with her own hyphae, her fingertips, sensing skins. Pale flesh on pale flesh.

Adam comes in. *They're ready*, he nods, sipping his first coffee.

Wiry hair grows from his ears. He brings out a set of electrodes. *If we insert these, we can measure the action potentials at various points in the network. We'll be able to gauge their response to a stimulus. Once we collect that data, build a base of responses to various inputs, we can start building logic gates.*

Chinna can't really speak, too many mushrooms on the brain. But she grins.

Biocomputing is on its way.

She keeps stroking the pale velvet flesh. Even her touch seems to get a response. Maybe it's her thoughts.

Chinna is still a little fuzzy, to say the least, on that first flush. Perhaps it's just the Golden Teacher using her thoughts as a conduit to talk to its oyster cousins.

However the wires are all connected, exactly, she hears herself—whoever that is anymore—soundlessly talk.

Have no fear. There is no end, and no beginning. We are not now and not then. And we are not you and not me—someone —her brain?—is saying. Man, she is high!

Adam fidgets with the electrodes, hooking them up to the mushrooms. Sets out various stimuli. A vial of acid, the bunsen burner.

Three hours later, that same day, Saturday, Day 14, still reeling from her first flush, from Merlin—Is this *love?*—

From Ms Fungski—*self-organising spirals?*—

From the lab—*flames*—

—QWERTY—

Chinna breaks down completely. Tears. She stands in her college's library, only thinking of what just *happened* to her—in the lab—but she can't, she cannot, she'll go insane—

She needs to read. But she cannot decipher even the titles on spines. *Pain.* Words make no sense to her, letters spin and will not connect to her brain.

Evolutionary history. All these books. All these chronicles and accounts, all these conflicting theories.

She stares at a random book with birds on the cover. It says something about computers in the blurb. *Arrival of the Fittest*, by a Swiss scientist. Andreas Wagner. A book of changes.

Her hands, those sensing tips, her hyphae, Darwin's *Root-Brain*, hover on the shelf.

All they want, all they need from the book are the birds. Darwin's own finches, yellow and green, red little beaks.

Pretty and sweet.

Over the next month, in Cambridge, Chinna falls into a vortex, between the words—fails to read, fails to sleep, fails to speak—across the world, in Bali, Tamara dives in and leaps out of the pool among the paddies.

In her pink batik bikini.

Elektra doesn't hear from Chinna, but thinks little of it. Chinna has been asserting her independence, and Elektra tries to applaud this.

Also, okay, there's that bikini.

That whole month passes so fast, though in reality, so much happens—so much *has* just happened, Chinna will never be the same, QWERTY, she'll go insane. She loses weight faster than anyone fathoms.

But first, on Monday, Day 16, she does not show up at her job in the lab. Adam, concerned, calls Merlin, her tutor, who hasn't seen her either, not since she showed up at his door the day before, Sunday, Day 15, in tears, unable to speak.

Chinna does not go out over the next few weeks, stays in her Clare College room, fasting and mute, until finally the college get wind and threaten to hospitalise her.

Nova comes, Day 39, and unable to think, with Elektra away in Bali, carts his child straight to Heathrow. Trying and failing to reach his ex-wife, that battered old series 5 iPhone, forever on the blink. Just booking the first available flight to Medan, to Sophia, his own mum.

Where they arrive, on Day 41 of the virus.

In Bali, by the pool, Elektra has her first kiss.

ʊ

And so, it's Day 41, and my timekeeper's account, my timeline, my Chronicle, is coming full circle.

My younger self has been flown out of the country, is reeling with fever in Medan, between four scorching walls, thinking about the travelling salesman problem, watching Jill Purce on YouTube on my phone.

Yes, I watch Jill then, I listen to her formidable voice, as I still do today. Poppet. Chroniclers take notice, they re-count: summarise, organise, building timelines. I lay and listened, and I was alone in the room, burning with fever and pain, alone in the scorching furnace of Sophia's walls, and even then I had the ear I have now.

The ear for a tune, for a hum, just like you, my sweet. For knowledge.

Mum?

Child.

Listen, my loved one, my knowledge was as keen back then as it is now, as deep and as wide, but it was scalding, eating me up from the inside.

And even now, the event that caused this has no home in my account. No home in my body. Poppet.

No real place in memory, in history, in time nor in space —*though it took place on Day 14 in the lab, a laser-sharp date.* It has no fixed place on my timeline, can only happen, over and over, again and again, *here and now.*

Which is where my Chronicle breaks down.

And I can't let this happen, not this here, this now, not Day 41, when my young self is in Medan, lying in bed and listening, for Jill's cool voice, her glady rivers, her spirals and vortices. And I listen, and Jill has my young ear. Because I'm eighteen, and if I stop thinking about the virus, about spirals and pure maths and DNA and genotypes and evolutionary algorithm, if I start thinking about what I feel—QWERTY—I will immolate my brain.

My father too, in the next room, is on his phone. Shouting over my grandmother Sophia, who howls that I'm dying. *Anak mau mati!*

The college sent her home. Either that or they'd section her. She won't speak, lost a third of her body weight, hasn't eaten in weeks—

There's a loud kind of vortex, while he waits and my grandmother wails. Then he speaks again.

I couldn't look after her in London, I just got her on the first plane, Elektra. She has diarrhoea, flu, can't walk, she needs a bed, needs to sleep with family, eat. She's too weak to move. My mother can cook, she knows how to bring down fever. Plus my brother Rasul is a doctor up North in Banda Aceh, he's right now driving down.

My dad exhales. *You have to come.*

We wait for my mother, with her pina coladas, her

Tamaras, *Community, your way*, to respond.

℧

In China, a traveller sets out with gifts.

The spin top, a pretty spiralled thing, its neon yellow paint still bright with formaldehyde—through Bejing, Singapore, Jakarta, is making its way.

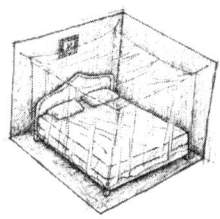

And see, outside the window: a seedling, the tight, spiked furl of a first leaf.

And hear, Elektra: the long winding song of *tahrim*. It is dawn and inside the room, Sophia wakes Nova to pray. They sit up in bed. They sit up in the one bed under the mosquito net, and they sit on the edge of the bed that the three of you shared. You, and Sophia, and your husband.

The Arab clock on the wall says five before sunrise. And yet. What does it mean? The hands go around in cycles, endless spirals, like us, neither here nor there, all the time in the universe and beyond. And we hum. And yet, Elektra, you do not hear.

And yet you wait, as your husband and mother in law leave from under the net.

And you pace in circles in your brain, where there is no

space to pace. And you walk turns in the enclosed maze of your skull, where all you have is walls, and where you are trapped in your past, in your pacing, and where you are insane.

And you imprint on your brain habits and form, and you cycle the grooves of your fever, your rage, and you become its very shape.

And we hum: your body, your womb are viral, and without them your daughter, the child who will yet give birth to Merlin's son, your child whom come noontime you will recall in your dream as a girl, with her smile, would not be from woman born.

And see: here you are, the image of your brain. And you are helpless, a woman, and you are locked in a room. And a virus is lodged in your womb. And you are, you yourself have become, Elektra, the ticking clock.

And you pace: will you be saved?

And yet we hum. And yet you wait, as Sophia and Nova leave the bed and as they leave the room, and you wait as they go to the next room.

And you are hot with fever, and yet it is before the rise of the sun, and you lie in the bed alone. And you wait while your mother in law gets ready to leave the house, and go to work, and yet while she calls a boy on her phone. And you wait as she waits for the boy to drive his moped to her, and take her to the main road.

And you wait for her to leave, and for your husband to leave, so you can go out, get away, break free from this house. And escape.

And you watch the clock, the hours, the minutes, the seconds, and you think you will explode. And you are blind to the world, and you are blind to the seedling, outside, unfurling its very first blade.

Tick tock. Tick tock.

And you wait for the arrow of time, your saviour, and you wait to be saved.

And it is all imprinted on your brain, like the virus, and it is your shape.

And yet we hum, and tell you, Elektra, your body is not your own. It will break and burn and be cleaved and torn and only the blood of your daughter, her very cells, will save you.

And we hum, your body, your womb are viral, and without them your daughter, the child who will yet give birth to Merlin's son, your child whom come noontime you will recall in your dream as a girl, with her smile, would not be from woman born.

And yet we tell you, Elektra, you are wrong, and you are all wrong, and behold, like your virus, you are getting this backwards.

PART FIVE: TODAY

Day 41, three hours after Nova's phone call. His brother Rasul, a doctor up in northern Sumatra who lost his license over some kind of corruption, arrives with his wife in his Kia from Banda Aceh to look at Chinna. He puts her on a make-shift drip of saline and quinines, while Sophia feeds her boiled papaya leaf.

Chinna swallows one, bitter as bile, refuses Sophia's mount of rice, topped with a deep-fried sardine, a deep-fried egg, and a limp stalk of deep-fried spinach.

Rasul picks up his five sons from the Muslim boarding school he's had to send them to since going to prison, and they all sleep on the floor in Sophia's parlour.

Overnight, squashed between Nova and Sophia, miraculously, Chinna's fever comes down.

In the morning, Day 42, she gets loaded into Rasul's Kia

wagon, with all the boys, plus Sophia and Rasul's wife, to pick up Elektra at the airport, a two-hourlong drive across town.

Elektra's plane lands around noon. To her surprise, they don't head home to Sophia's, instead driving Chinna's cousins, Rasul's five sons, back to their Medan *madrasah*, before Rasul needs to head back to Aceh to serve the rest of his sentence in jail.

Elektra does not try to understand the specifics, politely staying both out of her brother-in-law's personal affairs, and Indonesian politics.

Nova, the brother with the western wife and kids, the Londoner making money, first takes them all out to lunch. Rasul chooses the place, on the beach. It's a long drive out, a gated resort. There's karaoke, bingo, a cover band on a stage somewhere in the distance. There's no *warung nasi* or Lia's fragrant paste, no cinnamon or cloves, to be seen, the menu boasts 'international cuisine'. Beef burgers, steak, and Chinese. Nova just orders several platters of everything, to go around, then takes his nephews for a swim in the pool as the women—Sophia, Rasul's wife, Elektra and Chinna—stay at the table to wait for the food. They stick to full hijab, as is the norm, Elektra in one of Sophia's veils, even Chinna has been stripped of her habitual t-shirt and batik trousers and stuck into a whale-sized, long-sleeved, ankle-length dress of Sophia's.

When there's finally some action at the table, Nova piles all the boys back in their seats, under the parasols. They make short shrift of the platters, a dozen burgers, two whole farmed tilapias slathered in red sauce, Chow Mein, Fu Yong Hai, half a dozen steaks. When they're done, Nova orders another round, this time for the women, who've made way for the boys, decamping to a second table exposed to the midday sun.

It's a great day. Nova spends most of it in the pool, playing with his nephews. Splattering the kids, being splattered back, feeling their trusting bodies against his. Watching them perform tricks. Dive bombs. Acrobatic turns. Benji, Rasul's youngest, is very good. He's chubby, eats all the time, but has a real way with jumps. A born little performer. Swaying his hips, straight out of the Justin Bieber clips the nephews all watch all day on their phones. Benji, Nova thinks, is also the sweetest of the bunch. Artless, like Chinna. Benji has a crush, Nova can tell, on his daughter. Gives Chinna constant looks, even hugs her, makes her gifts. Waves from the water, blowing a kiss.

His five older brothers are harder to please. Leave their cokes half drunk, demand 7Up. They grew up long before Rasul had to send them off to the Madrasah, are used to things their father can no longer afford.

Nova shrugs, tries to make up, be the coolest uncle in the world. Local boy made good.

At some point, Chinna comes up to him, saying Elektra has stalked off to the beach, Nova should check on her. Nova tells her to wait, he's busy feeding her cousins.

He orders yet another round, then dessert, ice cream, banana splits, pudding, milk shakes. Surveying the half-eaten plates, platters, bowls, the table still full enough to feed three families, he sits back at last. Best day of the holiday, Nova thinks. Anyone would agree.

That night, when they finally get home to Sophia's, the boys dropped off at their madrasah twelve miles out on the opposite side of Medan, Rasul and his wife snoring on the floor by the kitchen, Ma, Elektra and Chinna beside him in the bedroom, the one bed, Nova falls into a deep, happy sleep.

ဟ

He is woken before dawn, by Chinna. The opening notes of *tahrim* sound through the window. Where is he, somehow back in the womb, in this long, spiralling verse of the Quran, this never-ending labyrinth before Azan, where he sleeps in the arms of his wife and—

His daughter is standing outside the mosquito net, on the floor, on the strip of tiles between the bed and the wall. Only Sophia is left beside him, deeply asleep.

He rubs his eyes. *Huh? Where's Mum?*

Chinna shrugs her shoulders: don't know.

Nova can't wake, goes back to sleep, but hears himself muttering, *What…?*

He tries to doze, but there's something so alarming in the sight of his daughter, her stick-bone shape cast against the faint light, he finally does wake. *What*, he tries again. His tongue slurs... *W-what's wrong?*

His daughter sinks to the floor.

There is something he has failed to note, something in his memory that now sticks in his throat, but which he cannot recall.

...What is it?

She sits rocking on the floor, wearing her batik trousers again, a tee, both clown-like on her shrunken frame.

Nova rubs his eyes, still sleep drunk. Nothing makes sense. It feels like midnight, if it wasn't for the endless *tahrim*. It feels like some bad dream. He looks around the room. Elektra really isn't there. *What is this? ... Did you see her?*

Chinna nods, holds up one finger: alone.

Nova tries to sit. *What's her problem*, he sighs.

Chinna says nothing. He now clocks that she's crying. Her face is wet.

Chinna points at her cheeks.

Mum was crying too?

Chinna nods.

Why? Nova finally sits upright.

Chinna stares back at her dad, does not have a word to say. How to explain? Mum didn't like the resort, it was loud, they had to stay fully dressed, plus veiled, in the heat, the food was obscene, Chinna couldn't swim…

Her dad is still studying her, trying to read her thoughts. Sinks back down, pulls Sophia's computer-printed fleece blanket over him. Two jungle tigers, in emerald green.

Mum wants to go to Maninjau, Chinna tries to think loud enough for him to hear.

Nova pulls Ma's blanket further over his face. He can feel his daughter searching for his hand, tangled in the lurid, jungle-print fleece.

When it hits him, finally. The resort. The burgers and steaks. Chinna had not been able to swim, naturally, being a girl. And she'd had to wait till the boys had finished their food, and another round had been ordered. It had taken awhile to arrive of course, it was Indonesia, not Nando's. But he'd noticed all that. The thing he'd failed to see. Chinna had not touched any food at all.

Maninjau, some thought finally resonates in him.

Through the fabric, Chinna at last finds Dad's palm. It's Day 42 of the virus, she hasn't eaten in weeks, is dying, can't swallow or speak, can only think loud enough, she hopes, with her deep, mortal feelings, for Dad to hear.

Mum wants Lia to cook for me.

Fifty yards away, in the dark, between two identical homes, a row down from Sophia's, Elektra gathers herself together, gets up from the broken wall she's been sitting on since four this morning. Not a motorised sound. Where had she even meant to go? She's at the end of the world. No roads, nothing but dried banks of mud. But there had not been a breath of air in Sophia's house that hadn't been drawn first by Rasul, or Nova, or all the others asleep on the floor. Even those five absent boys, still haunting the lounge. Her fist is bleeding from pounding the ground. It's almost dawn. Loudspeakers start the long, winding song calling the men to the mosque. She wipes her knuckles, her face. Chinna needs to eat, fucking nutrients, clean food, no bony deep-fried sardines, or some touchy-feely grandmotherly hug. But her rage is not going to do any good.

She finds Chinna slumped on the porch, on the tiles by Sophia's door. Elektra takes her arm, leads her back to the room.

It's way too early for you, come on, let's sleep while it's cool. Sort of.

Elektra slips back under the mosquito net, on the bed, beside her husband, her mother in law. Chinna on her other side. Tears, rage start again. Elektra needs something she can't articulate, mutually exclusive things she can't even separate. Co-living, community, her family; a room of her own. These fucking walls broken down. Her heart, that steely cage, ripped open, all over. She needs to save her daughter, get her to eat, to speak, of course, that in the first place, but look at the state of things, climate change, virus, minute to midnight, who can blame the kid for shutting down? To save her daughter, she needs to save the planet, the world. She needs to know how to act, but the whole fucking mess lacks precedent, protocol, she doesn't know where to start. What the formula is, the technology, the algorithm, or the riddle or whatever mystery this is. What God or Goddess even to pray to.

Calories.

She holds on to Chinna with her body, will not let go. Tries against all her beliefs about how these things work, to nurture her. Feed her with her heart, her chest, her skin and her thoughts.

Chinna is shaking.

Elektra holds her, in the room already starting to scorch, before the sun is even properly up. It's forty degrees at least, airless, humid. The hours all flow into one in this room, in this climate, where dusk is as hot as dawn.

She holds Chinna in her arms until she feels her shudder, and hears a deep sigh. Another one, a sigh with the faint rasp of vocal cords. Almost a hum.

She has not imagined it. Chinna is saying something. A first word in a month.

Mum.

Outside the window, a tree has grown.

Across the island of Sumatra, Baby Aafiyah has not eaten, either. She's been waking throughout the night. She vomits, has a fever, cries. Lia's second child. *Not again*, she jolts up in bed. Though it's barely dawn, she gets ready to walk to Bantolaweh, the little village at the foot of the hill, just before the canyon, where an old medicine woman, Bu Rita, lives in one of the old longhouses that remind Lia of her mother Hati's home.

Lia pulls on her long black veil, embroidered with flowers. Sets Aafiyah on her hip in the sling across her body and sets out. Little feet dangling. They descend from her own long staircase alley, cross the little Chinatown main street and climb up again towards Fort de Kock. From the peak, they go down again, towards the circular road. They cross. The street they are on will plunge further down, into the overgrown canyon hidden in the green rocky cliffs below. Marapi's neighbouring volcanic range rises steeply back up, stark against the sky.

At the foot of the hill, right before the canyon, like most people with business in Bantolaweh, Lia halts to begin the morning in the busy warung, on the corner of the street. It serves *lontong*, cakes of sticky rice, with curried jackfruit, cabbage and greens. Women crowd together at the tables, behind the little half-curtains strung across the windows.

Lia gets her order at the platform set with large enamel bowls in the back, manned by the matron owner and four or five of her young daughters, all rushing to fill plates with white squares of sticky rice, topped with vegetables. Lia asks for a curried egg. Takes her plate, releases Aafiyah from the sling and sets her on one of the long, narrow Formica tables. The baby sits looking around, her dazed, pained look growing alert. Lia settles in her plastic chair, and feels a wave of relief course through her body. Normality.

She ladles up jackfruit red with capsicum with her spoon and the warm chilli haze kicks in. She feeds the baby chunks of the plain, sticky *lontong*. Aafiyah, distracted, opens her mouth. Even she seems revived by the loud chatter everywhere around her, the bustle of colourful veils, like a swarm of butterflies perched down to eat, girlfriends eating together, couples, families, babies sitting on tables next to her, playing with rice noodles. Aafiyah is too sick, too little to have many thoughts, but she takes it all in, and grins in response.

Lia eats, thinking of fevers, while Aafiyah chews her rice, in her own, wordless, sensory world, fully alert to the children everywhere, precious like her, on tables or laps or the tiles, nurtured but not separate, fussed over without fear, coaxed, cuddled, but left to themselves, free to explore, free to crawl on the floor.

At the medicine woman's house, ten minutes later, she gurgles throughout the consultation, gazing at the woman's caged quartet of budgies, a miracle cure as far as Aafiyah's concerned, the budgie mum with three of the tiniest, most Aafiyah-like baby birds.

೧

Day 44 of the virus. Indonesia no longer has a clean bill of health. Two cases in Jakarta are reported on the news. The virus is going global.

In Medan, Elektra and Nova resolve to take Chinna home. Elektra calls her airline to reschedule her flight, while Nova calls his. Neither gets through. They spend all morning on the phone. After five hours, thirty-eight calls, Nova hears all flights are full.

You'll need to wait, Sir, till your scheduled date.

Nova insists his family stay together in Medan. Though she's tough, Sophia is seventy years old, and he wants to make sure she's looked after.

They're talking right in front of Sophia, on the porch of her shadeless house, in English. Elektra bites back her frustration, her rage, but doesn't give in. She's taking Chinna to wait out this virus thing in Maninjau. They're leaving the next day.

Throughout the debate, Chinna stays mute. She has not managed another word to her mum.

Elektra aches for her voice, her smile—a pain so deep, so corrosive in Elektra's veins, it is eating away at her cartilage, like battery acid, dissolving her bones, yes it does, it's that quietus of her twenty-first floor, but now it's everywhere, seeps into her from Sophia's tiles, from the very ground, from her daughter's silent, hungry-ghost mouth.

Lia, she pleads, will know how to make Chinna eat. She's

their only hope, she tells Nova. Their daughter needs food more than air. The girl is dried up, knife sharp in the cheeks, the shoulders, little more than her skeleton. They need to rebuild her immune system, somewhere cool and green. Among the paddies, in the arms of the rice goddess. In the cradle of the crater, the lake.

Nova says nothing, in English. In Indonesian, he arranges with his baffled mother, to have his wife and daughter taken to the airport the next day, from where they'll travel to Bukittinggi, the monsoon market town, 400 miles south.

From there, they will take a bus to the lake.

At least—he explains to Sophia—the lake, since it is so remote, will keep Chinna very safe.

The next morning, Day 46, Nova drops Elektra and Chinna at the airport in a taxi, from where they fly to Padang, to take a bus to the mountain market town.

Arriving that afternoon at the terminal in Bukittinggi, Elektra de Kock, in Sophia's hijab, and Chinna in her t-shirt and batik trousers, take another bus straight back out. It's the very last leg of the journey.

As they leave Fort de Kock behind, the journey feels much longer, the last lap of a trip Elektra started much, much earlier.

Alone on her London sofa, overlooking the City, the red warning lights on the cranes over the skyline. All those hexagrams, looking for that one six or nine, reading the

Book of Changes' every changing line. Recalling Rupert Sheldrake, her interview. *Morphic resonance*, whatever it means, the seeds of the past coming into being. Family constellations. Patterns, which repeat. Wandering Dutchmen—*Where are your women?* Her own hunger and rage, as a teen—her daughter's. *Always hungering*, she thinks, and recalls Sheldrake again, the canal-side warehouse, once filled to the brim with colonial goods, cinnamon, cloves. The Spice Pot, *food in the ting*. Her wandering husband, she herself wandering pregnant, seeking her more secure friend. Peeling garlic by the lake, side by side.

As the bus turns onto the dinky little road back out over the mountains at last, Elektra lets out a very long sigh. Maninjau, Lia, are finally within reach.

Something is happening to Chinna, too. Something between fever and relief.

Chinna starts to speak.

Mum, listen.

Elektra meanwhile, is retreading old ground, that same old bus, that she used to board with Nova, with its black little puff of smoke.

It's packed even fuller today, Day 46 of the virus. A woman with twin babies sits squeezed between Elektra and one window, one or the other of the babies almost in her lap half the time. Chinna squashed on the other side, beside an old man, who coughs, politely out of the opposite window. WTF. Elektra changes places with Chinna. Keeps facing her daughter, her back in hjiab to the poor old man. While Chinna, now prone to the babies, talks. *I think I've worked out how evolution works, Mum. I think I'm part of it now, of next-level evolution, of biocomputing.*

They ride the familiar road, past the old wooden longhouse on the corner, still there, with a square basin, a pool or a pond, rippling gently, as if nothing has ever changed.

Elektra wants to point out all the longhouses, stark and strong, always crumbling, along the road. All the hooded little Dutch homes, the old shutters and cream window panes. Curtains aflutter.

Like the tiny Dutch houses she used to know by the lake, where she'd walk, pregnant and alone, while Nova slept curled up with his friends under the tablecloths.

But Chinna is pouring out everything she's been keeping inside for so long. A library book that she's brought, and has finally skimmed. By a Swiss evolutionary biologist, working with computers, like her.

Music plays very loudly. Chinna talks on. *Hyper-dimensional space, astronomical numbers.*

It's Day 46, just another hour at most, before they'll descend the bends of the crater wall, enter the cradle. Find the food Chinna needs, the calories: all Elektra needs to do is sit through this. There's light, finally, Lia, and her immutable sense of home, at the end of this long, nightmare funnel. There, safe in Lia's lap, she'll get her daughter to stop raving. Simply talk. Share with her the steep jungle walls, the paddies, this green, peaceful world.

Pure maths, Chinna says, *robustness, platonic shapes. Circuits, logic boards,* DNA.

We're not alone, Mum. We're 8 percent retrovirus, through horizontal transfer—without syncytins—which is a cell with double DNA, Mum, your own plus the viral genome—we couldn't even be born—there's HRV-3 *which got into apes 25 million years ago and it makes a protective little string of bubbles for the baby in the womb—and we all carry it, imagine it Mum, you have cells in your womb that have two different kinds of DNA and the viral stuff is 25 million years old and you have my stem cells too, with my DNA, and it's just part of your tissue, it can show up in a test —but that's not it,* DNA *is like logic gates, it's about* HOW *it mutates—there's a spiral—it's like Plato's Cave—*

Elektra is trying to not interrupt, simply to listen. But it takes all she has. Rage always clawing at her, right under the surface, her smiling facade, inflaming her brain. She keeps looking patient, while her daughter raves on, faster, rushing to get her thoughts across.

Mutation, innovation, evolutionary algorithm…

Shut up, Elektra is thinking. Just shut the fuck up. They've arrived at the infamous forty-four *kelok*, the forty-four hairpin bends, the road plunging down to the lake. The view is astounding. The volcanic walls, shimmering green, the lazy lake cupped between. Sparkling silver and gold, while also hulled in a violet haze.

Slime moulds, Chinna is saying.

უ

They make it down the forty-four bends without incident.

In Maninjau, as dusk falls, the first thing they note when they alight from the bus, is the smell. There's a cumulus storm of sulphur, rotting eggs, with the nauseating stench of dead and decomposing fish. Algae, lichens, gorging on fish guts and skins. Rotten fish blood, black swarms of flies, all clouding the air like thunder.

They quickly cross the road, to the little eatery on the corner. It too looks wrong. The windows are boarded up. Those little net curtains. Not a trace. The roof has fallen in. The room in the back, where the family lived, is full of trash, overtaken by fungi, ferns and moulds.

Lia is gone.

It's too late to get out. They spend an airless night in the last Maninjau homestay still open, their room's windows all closed against the stench from the lake. Take a return bus the next morning.

Back at the terminal in Bukittinggi, Day 47, they take a van into town, a private ride share. Elektra pays for the whole car.

It stops at Fort de Kock, the once Dutch stronghold. Now Benteng Park and Zoo. They take a room in the old Benteng Hotel, one of the oldest in town. She's never stayed here before, but the crumbling traveller's homestay in the old Dutch house where Nova and she used to stay, just downhill, with the crack in the ceiling, like a compass, has been knocked down, replaced by a concrete hotel.

Here, the fort, with its cannons, still tops its green peak, surrounded by ancient trees. It's the sleepy, leafy end of Bukittinggi's central hill, divided by the Chinatown little main street below. The fort is connected by a footbridge to the Zoo and the market on the hilltop across.

The fort side of the hill holds ancient Dutch villas and another old, sedate hotel. The classic, horned, Family Benteng restaurant, next door, small and green, with its antique, rusting Minangkabau roof, its shady verandas all around, sits overlooking it all.

Chinna leaves Mum to do the checking in, just stands in the road.

The *noise*.

In her mind, she hears Merlin, sees his face light up. *Polyphony*.

Waves of song vibrate in the trees, the shrubs, from every single plant and blade of grass. Not one voice but a choir, pulsing together, zinging and screeching and chirping, not a single melody but every creature pulsing with an individual tone, all creating a wave, a zig-zag of sound, invigorating each other, loud as any stream of traffic. There's some little critter sounding like a singing saw, and a choir of contrasting voices, infinitely varied, energising, full of vitality. Not a tired sound among them. Not a retiring soul. All jamming and riffing and taking turns.

Their Benteng hotel room is grim. Stinking carpet, smoked glass panes in the window, and the stench of old ashtrays and rotting plumbing. The hot shower, in the putrid bathroom, is a lukewarm drizzle.

They wash up. Unpack.

Are we related to, you know..., Chinna says, putting three t-shirts in a neat little stack.

Probably, says Elektra. *Though my dad never talked about it. My grandmother Agnes was called De Vries, part Sundanese, and my granddad De Kock was also Indo. They got out after the war and never went back, as far as I know.*

She opens the window. Monkeys call from the Zoo. *And believe it or not, in all these years here, you're the first to ask.*

After their shower, it's not yet noon, Elektra takes Chinna to the Benteng Restaurant next door for a view of the city. She orders two glasses of unsweetened tea—Chinna still refuses to eat and Elektra is saving her appetite for lunch in the market.

Elektra explains the sights below and across, the madly compact, old Dutch-Indonesian layout of the city—circular, egg-shaped, like a miniature, hilltop eighteenth-century Amsterdam—to her once more silent daughter.

The commercial centre—across from the Limpapeh footbridge spanning the little Chinatown main street in the middle, below—stretches back up in tiers, she points out, to the old Zoo at the top, and the *Pasar Atas*, the 'top market' sprawling around a brand new concrete building, built after the old one finally burned down some years ago. Bookended, she gestures, by the town's proudest two landmarks: the great yellow mosque, Mesjid Raya, at the top, right by the Zoo, and the famous old Dutch clock tower, now with a Minangkabau roof, set on a popular, panorama square.

To show Chinna how to navigate the spiralling labyrinth of the hilltop market, they hop onto one of the little red public transport vans which go all around the circular road, a potholed, dual-carriage affair pocked with families crammed together on mopeds.

The van is low, crowded, and Chinna squeezes in between seven or eight women on their own ways to the various entry points of the maze.

Chinna watches as they wind their way along the road, in what feels like more than a full turn of a spiral already, before Elektra tells the driver to halt, slipping him the fare.

Okay, we've done 180 degrees, Elektra says. *We're at the opposite end of the labyrinth. Let's see if we can make it back.*

They walk along the foot of the hill, along the circular road, with the sprawling commercial heart pulsing above.

Across the road, below, lies Pasar Banto, the farmers' market, with its poultry and vegetables, surrounding a decaying concrete block topped with the rusting beams of a Minangkabau roof, like the carcass of a giant whale. Myriad other markets radiate out, further down.

But Electra points ahead, where on the pavement, a thin woman in a pale pink dress and long, matching hijab sells *jambu*, tiny shiny java apples just as baby pink. Minivans packed with schoolgirls, scooters zoom by as Elektra heads for the woman's rackety table, which carries a heap of larger *jambu* as well, plump and a deep cerise. She buys a pound, moves on, past the next stall, where a woman in black and violet sells sour green *mandarines*.

Then the side of the road opens up to the hillside market: orange tarp overhead filters the sun as they duck below and enter the warm, fragrant tunnel. Chinna breaks a light sweat. The stalls on the path winding up the hill sell shoes and slippers, live chickens, there's an old woman with avocados and rambutan, a stall selling hijabs, long, short, blue, purple, pink, all with the cap at the front, many ruched below, and Muslim prayer socks for women and girls. Small kitchen supplies, orange storage containers, water bottles, pink plastic plates, sky blue melamine. Towels, checkered dish cloths, tablecloths. Up, the path winds, further up the hill, slowly going round and round:

t-shirts and baby clothes, safety pins and colourful plastic toys, then a gap to the left, where the tunnel opens up, and Elektra halts.

Hungry, she asks, casually.

Chinna says nothing, but tries to smile. They're on a plateau, out in the open air, with a wide, long, old wood-beamed roof, painted blue and white, resting on ancient wooden pillars.

In neat rows, women perch on individual platforms, tables set out before them stacked with large enamel bowls. Low, white little net curtains separate the stalls. Each table surrounds the matron towering at the centre, a blue painted wooden U-shaped bench folding around it, with people eating.

Elektra chooses one, and they take place. The large bowls, Chinna sees, are heaped with fish, chicken, some sort of yellow sausage, beef, all in rich yellow, red and orange sauces.

There, veg, Elektra says, *jackfruit and bamboo, all stewed in coconut. Pretty good.*

Chinna's stomach revolts. She can't imagine having to swallow.

Elektra orders two plates of rice, her own topped with sauce and fish and a range of veg and chilli and titbits, Chinna's with jackfruit and cabbage—*no sauce*, Elektra quickly raises her hand. Pure coconut oil. Lethal.

Chinna looks at her food, breathes. A gentle breeze blows through the entire plateau, which is rimmed with a low, crumbling white-washed stone balustrade. Beyond, an orange floor of tarps shielding the path winding up below.

Up here, the path swirls up further.

Elektra dips her hand in the finger bowl, and eats. Watching her daughter looking at the path, still winding up, she smiles, pointing. *There's much, much more. This is just the start of the hill, there's all sorts of stairs, with shortcuts to the* Pasar Atas, *the top market.*

She gestures at a set of worn concrete steps, half-hidden in the throng of shoppers and stalls, leading up to the market on top, while the path itself meanders on, lazily spiralling up in the same direction, offering more towels and t-shirts on either side, children's books, haberdashery, endless sandals in every colour and shape. Hoping to distract her daughter from having to eat, hoping she'll just lift a handful to her mouth without thinking, Elektra points out a pharmacy hidden somewhere in the back selling cough syrup and eucalyptus oils, a small grocery shop with paper packets of jasmine tea, instant coffee, assorted nuts and bitesize cakes in bright pink and green, yellow, white.

Chinna watches a drop land on her hand. Hot water, leaking from her eyes. She stares back at her untouched plate of jackfruit, yellow bamboo shoots, rice.

She has not been this lost in her life.

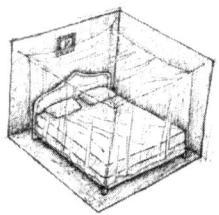

And in the beginning, Elektra, the earth was empty and void.

And there was the word.

And the word is om, the breath, the moving on the waters, and the word is without beginning. And end it has not.

And yet it brings form. And yet it brings the hands of your clock, and brings your time.

And the word is it, Elektra, the riddle, the maze, and it is it, the spiral, and it is the algorithm, the labyrinth. And it grows and unfurls like the spiral, and it unfurls at the rate that brings life, and brings life to your child.

[Karlheinz Stockhausen, in his open-chested shirt, wide lapels]

In all the holy scriptures we learn, that there was first the word. It is not a word of human terms. It is the word of a being, that is, the spirit of the total.

But there must have been an initial sound, which is like the stone in the water.

And the vibrations still reach us.

[Voice of Jill Purce]

All the great masters have taught us ways to order ourselves, to find the still point at the centre of the vortex.

Great courage is needed even to begin to unravel the self, and the attitude needed is like that of a warrior.

[Image of an ancient warrior statuette]

The journey takes us into those areas of ourselves we don't understand, and find hard to accept. For the real hero is the man who comes to terms with himself—all of himself.

Has brought each part together, as a well-balanced whole.

[Image of black and white drawing of man and dragon, at the heart of a labyrinth]

Man has always pictured this journey as a maze.

And the maze is a model of himself.

[Cut to a drawing found on a wall in Pompeii of a labyrinth. Black and white, geometrical lines]

The oldest labyrinths go back almost 4,000 years.

[Black and white turns into colour: the green of an old yew tree topiary, the brown soil of a path at the opening]

Entering the maze is like deciding to take your life into your own hands. Becoming responsible for yourself. Until then, you've followed your old habits and desires.

[The camera shakes, sound of Jill's footsteps, as we walk into the maze. High yew tree walls all around]

But now you have to find a new sense of direction…

[Camera pans around forks in the path, each leading off in directions unknown]

…For the old ones only confuse you.

[Approaching a fork, choosing a path, entering deeper]

In the labyrinth we become responsible through choice.

[We follow the bend of the path, reaching a dead end, a dusty metal gate, where we swivel and turn]

Which confronts us at every moment.

[Spiralling round the path]

Once the journey's begun, there's no going back.

[Tree tops spinning overhead]

Going back is as hard as going on.

[Another dead end, deep inside now. Another turn]

But suddenly the path seems easier, and wider.

And you realise you're at the centre.

[A small, empty space at the heart of the maze]

And there's nothing there, but yourself.

Chinna is lost in the market, the maze. More lost than she's been anywhere before, even in her own brain. The matron towering before her, with her bowls, mistress of the mountain, of the market: a matriarchal pleasure dome —food! houseware! clothes!—that Chinna simply cannot take in. She hasn't touched her jackfruit or bamboo.

Elektra is full.

Chinna gets up from their bench, between the waving curtains, under the white painted rafters. Elektra pays, and they continue.

The market path spirals up, towels and t-shirts, endless sandals, headscarves, batik gowns, the tiny pharmacy hidden in the back, while in front the path winds on, offering hairbands, scrunchies, more oranges, belts and wallets, artisan machetes, wooden-handled knifes.

Freshly grilled bananas, Elektra points out, vegan too, and feather light spongy crumpets in white or green. *Sweet*.

On and on.

Up the hill, they wind, till they get to a dark, musty covered part with larger stalls on either side.

Blue and white plastic tarps strung across overhead all along the path keep out the rain, but still let in a denim-tinted light. It's cooler here, and thick with spores, fungi trapped under the tarps overhead, Chinna smells. Spores, moulds, streaming from the stalls all carrying second-hand clothes.

Jumpers, trousers, colourful tops, skirts, dresses, Elektra points, all neatly sorted, children's jackets, jeans, blouses and shirts. Even bedspreads and quilts, pink, magenta satin.

Tucked in the middle of the winds of the path, like a brutalist monster, sits an old concrete building, yet another market, a block, with its own labyrinth stairways and maze of stalls and paths, with secondhand handbags and trainers and heels, more leather jackets and jeans, all—Elektra says—mostly sent from Korea.

Students, schoolgirls in hijab crowd the halls, the two tiled warungs tucked side by side in a corner serving rice and chicken, fish, from those same large enamel bowls, while outside the covered path spirals on.

Onwards, towards the top, with new clothes and old, till the wares reach to meet the interests of local tourists,

Elektra explains, batik dresses and trousers, like Chinna's, batik shorts, miniature horned longhouses on key-rings or t-shirts, and finally the famous local kerupuks, tall bags of cassava crisps glazed with red or green chilli.

The path crosses and meets the various stairs from below, as it keeps circling towards the market on top. Arriving now among embroidered ladies' dresses, and hundreds of stalls selling broderie anglaise cloth, violet, yellow, green and pink, all edged like butterfly wings with elaborate patterns of contrasting sculpted lace. Tailors rattle their Singers in backstage quarters, mostly hidden from sight. The cloth is sold by the women in front, in cut-to-size lengths wrapped around display dolls or beautifully bundled, waiting to be assembled—by the Singers behind —like build-your-own butterflies.

Curried coconut sauces waft in from every direction, woodsmoke, grilled satay and clove cigarettes. Women everywhere, in long robes, young girls, five or six years old, wearing little pink veils. The mosque at the top starts its prayer call.

Chinna has again started to cry. She cannot go on. Cannot stand one more hijab or laced prayer cape, one more satay stall or kiosk or warung heaped with food, one more Arab note or girl-child swaddled in pink, one more woman throttled in an ankle-length gown.

She just needs to go home.

They've reached the large yellow mosque, Mesjid Raya, at the top.

Okay, says Elektra. *There's a shortcut here, stairs straight back down to the little Chinatown main street below, across from Fort de Kock. We'll cut back up, to our room.*

They pass under the gate of the stairs, which form a ramrod straight, steep, stepped narrow alleyway down to Chinatown.

Chinna half swoons at the height. Her head is spinning, her body fails. She's lost too much of her own weight to even stay attached to the ground.

Chinna falls.

When she opens her eyes, Elektra is holding her. Crying now too. They both sway, fall over once more—

Balance their combined weight—

Stay upright—

Before tumbling together, in a heap on the steps.

Stranded, midway the stairs.

I don't know how to help you, Elektra cries, quietly. She can't carry on, not one more step, suddenly, not like this. Her front, that bright, furious mask of competence, of brittle compliance, shatters, exposing her insides, black with despair, tears of pure battery acid.

Chinna says nothing, only weeps.

You have to talk, poppet, you have to eat.

Chinna bites her lips, tastes blood on her rubber tongue. Numb, unable to produce sound.

People stop to watch.

From the houses lining the stairs—old homes interspersed with shuttered kiosks and shacks—Chinese grandmothers, two little girls in veils, old men, a young tailor take an interest. A mother in a very long hijab, rocking a baby on her porch looks on.

Elektra ignores them all.

Chinna wants to die. *Spectacle. Useless, selfish, wordless, worthless*—QWERTY—

But her mother is shouting.

Chinna raises her hands to her ears. Not now. Not here. Not on top of everything.

But her mother's not shouting at her.

She's not even holding her anymore. Has just left her here in a heap. A small pile of bones.

Her mother is on the veranda. Holding the woman.

Shouting at her, at the baby.

The woman is shouting back.

Embracing Elektra again.

Come, Elektra finally turns to the stairs. *Honey, come here.*

Chinna lies on the stairs, ignoring Elektra. She no longer cares about circuits or logic gates, self-organised geno-types, she just wants to stop having to breathe or to live.

She no longer cares about Jill Purce or creation myths—God moving upon the waters—

Nothing came out of nothingness—

Just look at this earth, this planet—This labyrinth—this fucking market maze—

All darkness and void—

She *hates* this horrible God, this Allah—With his horrid, horrid mosques—

Little girls wearing veils—

Girls, sexualised before they're even six—Horrid, horrid, horrid—

She hates this world.

When her daughter has finally gathered herself up, Elektra introduces her to Lia. *Chinna, my daughter*, she says in Indonesian, *almost nineteen. Already big, a student.*

Lia leads them onto the tiled little porch, two plastic chairs. *Sit.*

She fetches a third chair from inside a hall. *Where are you staying?*

Elektra gestures across Chinatown below, to the opposite hill, *Hotel Benteng.*

You must stay in the house, Lia points at her wide-open doors, the high, long, white tiled hall inside. *We have rooms.*

Only now does Elektra see the sign, discreet, in Indonesian, *Accepting family boarders.*

Sure, she says politely. *If you'll have us.*

We're serious, ya, Lia lights up. She has become even more beautiful in past years, with her clean face, heartful smile.

Elektra can't stop beaming. *If you're sure it's no trouble.*

I'll show you the room, Lia jumps up, baby and all.

Elektra kicks off her flip flops, follows her in.

The hall is cool, old, bare and spotlessly clean. Three doors, three rooms, off to the side.

Lia opens the second. Whitewashed walls, tall ceiling, white tiles on the floor, an ancient wardrobe in the corner, painted pink. An old, kingsize bed, with a batik bedspread.

Lia goes in, shows her the bathroom. Light, with a breeze hole under the corrugated roof, more tiles on the walls and the floor, pink, no stinking western toilets or shower, just a pink-tiled basin in the corner, filled with clear, cold water; a pink squatting loo.

Chinna has followed in. Brooding, by the look of her.

Elektra hesitates. *No hot water, poppet, no western plumbing*, she says. *Only one bed.*

Chinna says nothing, turns and disappears.

Elektra feels tears stinging again, spinning now herself. Sinks to her knees in the bathroom, out of Chinna's sight. Her daughter needs her to be strong. They'll go back to Benteng, anything Chinna wants.

She finds her child stretched out on the batik bedspread. Lia has left.

A big sigh escapes Chinna. She's closed her eyes. Looks oddly young, just a girl, almost asleep.

Elektra staggers with relief, sits down on at a small wrought-iron table, light-headed again, as she looks out the window, onto the side porch of the house, with Lia's washing hanging to dry, a sideways sliver of view, through the alleyway stairs: the turquoise dome of the old Chinatown mosque, on the corner of the little main street below, and beyond, Fort de Kock and the sign on the roof of the hotel replacing the old homestay where she first learned Nova's seven words.

ဣ

Chinna lies on the bed, while in front, she hears Lia and her mother talk. Indonesian. Chinna has heard Elektra with Sophia of course, but she had no idea Mum could speak, like, heart to heart, that she had actual chat.

She listens to Mum's distant, familiar voice, in the unfamiliar tones, until it's all a bit of a drone, soon smothered by yet another call from the mosque, even louder here, for some reason she doesn't understand, than up in the market before.

But it's not stressing her out.

She closes her eyes, listens to the singing, mixed with chatter, distant traffic from the sleepy main street below.

Then another voice joins in, loud. This one does sound like a voice from the mosque. The lady, Lia, did look very religious. Her boarding house doesn't look like a homestay at all, that bare white hall, none of the usual tourist junk, and, clearly, not anyone's idea of a quickie hotel.

Elektra greets Lia's husband with a happy *Abang*, brother, which is all she's ever called Afin. He's immaculately dressed, hair neatly trimmed, about half a head shorter than she, and Elektra herself is small. He approaches, hunched over, holding his limp hand in his other hand, in a half-shy, half-defiant kind of scuttle, but his voice booms. *You look so good!*

They sit down together on the tile floor in the hall. He beams at her, his light brown eyes wide with pleasure.

Elektra beams back. *You too, it's so so good to see you!*

A tiny lady in trousers and blouse shuffles past, even shorter than Abang. His mum, Elektra assumes, acknowledging her with an Oma, grandmother, and a bow of the head. The lady's small eyes twinkle in a square little face under white hair, thick and straight and short, like a pixie cut. The lady smiles and walks on. Then turns, once more, to give Elektra a long, gauging look.

There's something odd, but Elektra can't place her finger on it.

I'm serious, you look good, Abang still repeats. *Your face, your skin. No make up?*

Elektra grins. *Nah.*

Bersih, he approves. Clean.

She smiles wide.

Hati bersih, he says. A clean heart.

She nods, *yes, absolutely*, it's why she came here, to his family, she realises now, to see Lia and him: these wide, delighted smiles.

Hati senang, she says, a happy heart.

She suddenly knows what was odd about Abang's mum. The hair. No veil at all.

Hati puas, Abang is still saying, happily: a contented heart.

Yes, she says again. *Exactly*.

Lia is nursing Baby Aafiyah, the infant's head hidden under Lia's very long veil.

Hati sehat, her husband nods, smiling big, but serious, now that he's touched on the virus. It's Day 47.

Elektra agrees. *A healthy heart gives the best immunity.*

He lights up again. *Precisely. It's the way of Allah. Like mother's milk. Best protection in the world. No immunisation program can beat it. God's own vaccine.* His face keeps dipping in that half-shy reverence, and lifting back up with his voice: loud, confident.

Elektra nods, furiously, in agreement.

No cases yet in Sumatra, Abang continues, in his small, spotless clothes, cradling his smaller hand in his lap. *Inshallah. Though there's a lot of Chinese here where we live, so close to Chinatown...*

Ah, look at little Aafiyah. So happy! Elektra turns to the baby. No scapegoats please.

Also, the hair, the pixie cut face. Those bright, sharp little eyes. Isn't Abang's own mother Chinese?

ʊ

Lia picks green beans in her garden, collects them in a bowl. Two carrots. Oma, her mother-in-law Kartini, planted them, still waters each plant relentlessly every day. Even now, she's pruning flowers in a little bed by the gate, in her faded pyjama pants, an old skimpy hijab just pulled quickly over her head, for the neighbours' sake.

In the kitchen, Lia washes the veg, plus her shallots, garlic, ginger, cloves. Brings them out on a tray to the veranda, with a second tray, the baby on her hip. She hands one tray to her old friend, plus the beans. Sits beside her on the porch, peeling and cutting garlic.

Elektra is impatient with the beans, Lia notes, not an idiot, just rushed. Like she is with her clothes, just flinging on that hijab, like *Oma* Kartini, you can tell, she doesn't use a cap underneath, to keep stray strands from peeking out.

Lia takes her time over each little shallot. Cooing to Aafiyah.

Abang was born in this house, right, Elektra speaks.

Yes, Lia says. *Oma built it. With her bare hands. Her husband had already left.*

Ah, says Elektra, *yes, when I first saw Oma I thought she might be fragile and feeble with age, but I soon realised she was pretty eagle-eyed. She sees everything, doesn't she?*

Oh yes, she's over seventy years old, but nothing escapes her, she's the boss, Lia laughs. *She's Chinese*, she adds, in a whisper, first checking her husband doesn't hear.

Yes, laughs Elektra, *I kind of worked that out.*

Built the house by selling pastries in the clock tower square, batik, anything. Saving up. Adding room after room, this great big hall. All by herself. Honest, she put up the walls.

Elektra is still laughing.

Still sells things in the square, Lia whispers, glad to have found in Elektra such a good audience for the diminutive Kartini, over seventy years old and still outwitting them all, Lia's formidable mother-in-law.

ᖇ

That evening, after yet more prayer calls, Chinna opens the door to Lia, who's brought a terrine to their room.

Garden vegetables, Lia explains. *Broth*. She hands them deep plates, and spoons.

Mum thanks her and Lia disappears.

There's only one chair, so they sit on the tiles on the floor.

It's how we eat here, Mum says. *Careful, don't spill. Ants.*

She ladles broth onto her plate, leaves Chinna to serve herself. But watches, Chinna knows.

The soup actually smells interesting.

Cinnamon, says Elektra, *star anise, clove*.

Once she sees Chinna raising a spoonful to her mouth, and another, Mum keeps talking, calm, but insistent, distracting her, Chinna knows again, from thinking too much about the food.

We don't use first or last names in Indonesian, Mum explains, *and also no pronouns like me or you as that's all considered a bit direct*. It's a relational language. *So we call ourselves by our relation to our addressee, which soon gets extremely confusing, you'll see. So Lia is 'Uni' to me, my sister, and I am 'Uni' to her. Since I also don't refer to myself as 'I' when speaking to her, but as 'Uni' again, 'your sister', you can imagine how many Uni's we exchange. It sounds bonkers, and it is, but it kind of sorts itself out, with practice. In any case, the short man with the*

*crippled hand who is cleaning the floor out there is not a servant,
he's Uni's husband. I don't really know his name, since he's my
brother and therefore 'Abang'. It would be very rude to call him
anything else. You can call him 'Om'. Uncle. You following
still?*

Chinna nods.

It has worked. She's emptied her plate.

Arriving later that night in Chinatown below, the little
main street, Elektra is soon met with a thousand-watt
smile. *Elektra! Apa kabar!*

Denny, the longhaired boy, long-ago witness at her wedding. Western manners. He now owns the traveller's cafe.
Has his eldest sister, a woman with three grown children,
two grandchildren, run the place. The sister once more
has no name, to Elektra, is simply 'sister' again.

While Denny and Elektra chat in Indonesian, Chinna
curls up in a corner, on a little platform across from the
bar, with a low table in the middle, palm-leaf mats for
lounging, padded backrests. She leans back, her legs in
front of her, half lying, half thinking, and some tiny part
of her brain simply being, not thinking much, for once.

Elektra watches her daughter gazing about. Someone is
playing guitar, strumming and singing. Cigarettes go
around. Elektra passes on the smokes, but joins in the
singing.

She remembers arriving in the country for the first time. How everything had been her own size. Her hip slotting into a stranger's on a bench, feet fitting into footfalls in the sand. Tiny blouses in the market snug around her waist.

Now, for the first time in her life, Chinna too seems to fall into place. Blending in with the surroundings. Long black locks, plump lips, black-star eyes.

Her mum singing along, some old Radiohead song. Denny's sister, in hijab and jeans, joins in. She has sharp eyes, like Denny, not Dad's big round ones. Traces of make-up, a straight, almost thin mouth. Thinner than Chinna's own. A lovely voice.

You happy, Elektra says at some point.

Chinna says nothing. Nods.

You fit right in. Your hair, your size, even your… ehm, style.

Chinna glances around once more. Says nothing, but smiles. Mum is right. T-shirts and batik. She didn't even know it was a thing.

Elektra hugs her. *Welcome home.*

ഗ

Day 48. Bloody prayer call. Not one but two loudspeakers blast right into Chinna's ears at 4 AM. Uni Lia's stairs, it turns out, simply connect the town's two major mosques, the old turquoise one in Chinatown below, and the Mesjid Raya, the yellow Great Mosque, at the top. Clearly competing, they out-watt each other, blowing her eardrums in stereo, Dolby surround, a 4 AM alarm from hell.

Starting just seconds apart, on different scales, using different singers and different calls—polyphony be damned —they're plain out of sync, and out of tune as well.

As the first, very long sermon ends, Lia is already leaving the house. It's 7 AM, and she climbs up from her gate, scaling the stairs, enters a small, out of the way covered market at the top, where one or two merchants are opening up among shutters still closed. Lia passes the tiny soup kiosk, with its two narrow, communal tables set out in front, catering mostly to the market workers themselves, who form a little family of their own, the men smoking and playing cards and drinking tea from the kiosk in the afternoons, around an optician's stall. Women and children eating at the tables throughout the day. Now everything is still silent, the only sound her own footfalls. At the very end, where the men like to sit, the market's cover gives way to views of the drop below. Mornings like these, on the empty concrete, no immodest gents, smoking or gambling, Lia herself gets a peek. Still astounding, even to her. The corroding skeleton roof of Pasar Banto, and the paddies, just beyond the low, rust-roofed city, stretching out, the dew-hulled volcano.

Lia exits the tucked-away little market here, at its back, descends along the hidden, winding stairs of *Gang Mawar*, Rose Alley, all the way down. Small wooden houses line the steps. Pint-sized compared to Kartina's old boarding house, and all near-tumbling down, painted turquoise or cream. They remind her of home, of Maninjau. Deep rusted roofs overhang walled-in porches, bringing shade to tiny, shuttered windowpanes. Plants on the low, peeling veranda walls. Flowers grow from pots, bougainvillea, hardy little fire-red rosettes, hanging plants, gingers. Ferns, jagged little roses, dark pink.

She thinks of the rose on her mother's porch. Just a moment. All those stones.

Then loses herself once more in the monsoon town's staircase splendour, tall stems of double leaved orchids, with their white-and magenta blooms, yellow, bell-shaped trumpets, a bewildering variety of shapes and species, from apparently different worlds, all potted higgledy-piggledy side by side, thriving in the mountain air, surrounded by tall trees trailing durian, avocado from their branches, banana, cassava, papaya sprouting everywhere. She takes the last few turns, the last steps down.

Just across the bustling circular road, at the foot of the stairs, lies Pasar Banto, at last, the huge concrete building, with the skeleton longhouse roof, and its daybreak farmer's market in front encircling the entire block.

The dinky two-lane circular road is a whorling river of mopeds and small motorbikes with two or three passengers each, plus the red public transit vans packed with women, all either breaking for school or work, or braking without warning to let shoppers on and off.

Lia crosses, carrying her shopping bag. The market starts with long tarps sheltering dozens of poultry vendors, then fugues into a lot of fifty-odd mopeds parked while their owners restock, with their daily bundles of fresh groceries, tofu, veg, eggs, all hanging in plastic bags in neat little uniform packs and stacks. Dozens of moped sellers ready to strike out to every part of town. Some still drink coffee or smoke, eating fritters and lontong, so close to dawn. Lia continues along the bustle, winding her way along paths circling around the whole block, passing the hundreds of tables selling cucumbers, durian, every kind of fruit and vegetable, plus spices, shallots, turmeric, chilli, all fresh—but Lia needs a bag of each ready-crushed, sold from great buckets by the dozens of stalls she's finally, almost, reached. It's the far end of the circle. She could just as easily have started there, instead of first winding around 360 degrees.

She breathes.

Passes the plant sellers on the last corner, looks at the flowers. Orchids, gingers, hibiscus, bougainvillea. Aloe vera. Many more things she doesn't know the names of, but takes a minute to observe anyway.

She walks on. Dried fish, duck eggs, avocados. The paths between stalls are crowded, filled with women. There's no sign of the least bit of worry. With Baby Aafiyah still fussing, Lia doesn't even want to think the word fever, or virus. Everyone rubs past, busy, not a single face mask, apart from some teen girls showing off their trendy pink moped masks in front, just putting it on. It's 8 AM and the hustle is loud. Every cook, every warung and kiosk holder is shopping, getting ready to cater to the town. Lia breathes in all the scents, durian and chickens, fermenting fish. She no longer caters.

But she still makes the rounds.

Chinna has long gone back to sleep, completing a first night under Lia's roof. She's not thinking, for once, not even dreaming, of data-crunching-as-microscope, of evolution or algorithm, of that library book she brought and still hasn't read, with Darwin's finches on the cover, yellow and brown, black and red.

That afternoon, Sunday, mother and daughter hit the square where Simpang Raya, the town's oldest restaurant, right across from the *Pasar Atas*, the top market, is packed. They find a table by the glass facade. The windows are open to the clock tower, with its bustling square, full of vendors, food, tourists being photographed in front of the clock topped by its famous little horned Minangkabau roof. Chinna watches the throngs below, milling around it, on the circular ornamental pavement, great slabs of slate, with steps and low walls everywhere filled with people sitting and chomping *mi* from large yellow crackers, spicy fruit salad, satay. So much food, so much noise, and, unaccountably to Chinna, something that even to her looks like pure joy. Horse carts line the street, decorated with pompoms, ruched little curtains, and bells.

On the far end of the square, a steel panorama balustrade is crowded with people, backs turned, enjoying the view. There, she sees, on raised slate platforms, under a row of gigantic trees, entire families unpack their picnics and eat.

Everything is cupped by volcanic ranges, embracing the plateau. Beyond the balustrades, the town plunges, into the distance and back up, where great Mount Marapi hovers, looming up in the cloudless sky.

She yawns, stretches. Leans slightly out the window. All over the square, women in hijabs and bright, red-carpet-length gowns, teenagers in jeans, schoolgirls in uniform, are taking selfies. Seen from Chinna's corner, by the first-floor window, Marapi, the volcano, rises right behind the clock, ancient, unmoving, green and grave, the perfect backdrop.

Chinna still hasn't touched any of the food the waiter has rushed over the minute they sat. The whole table is set with little saucers, fifteen-odd, each holding a turmeric coated, grilled fish, a curried drumstick, a dollop of stewed beef, and many other things covered in bright red or green chilli. A large bowl of plain rice to the side.

Elektra, insistently casual, is eating. Elegantly, neatly tipping small clumps of rice with morsels of meat and chilli in her mouth with her fingers.

Choose what you like, Elektra explains, *we only pay for the dishes we touch.*

Chinna spoons some rice on her plate, a saucer of lettuce with a slice of tomato, cucumber. She washes her right hand in the finger bowl, plays with her food, adds some chilli.

She points at the little dish with glistering, pungent stew her mother is eating.

Rendang, Elektra nods. *Local specialty. Beef, but try the sauce if you want. People think it's a curry, but it's just reduced coconut milk, boiled, on cinnamon wood if you're lucky, for days, till it's half charred, half caramelised.*

Chinna tries some with her rice. It's the best thing she's ever tasted, like savoury, barbecued coconut pudding, indescribably good—

But much too rich to actually eat.

She swallows morsels of it, with her cucumber. Then returns to her window.

After the meal, Elektra goes back to Lia's. Chinna wants to stay and hang out for a bit on the square. She crosses to the far side, the panorama balustrades, the slate platform and steps, the trees, and below, the drop to the old city. In the distance the volcano, Marapi.

Under the first tree, there's a shelf, where she can just fit her frame, her back against the trunk, the fence in front. Glance down.

The circular road, which embraces the hilltop, the market and the square, all around, here becomes a little artery, leading south, but still lined with old buildings. A tiny old modernist Dutch facade, bright yellow, sits like a doll's house right below.

Rooftops, down along the road, are all lined with laundry racks and potted plants. She's not seen this much green in a city ever, outside a park. Or green this casually kept, just lining every available surface, porches and verandas, flat roofs, sitting in potted rows among rusting corrugated iron everywhere. It doesn't look like anyone cares, it's all so messy and anarchic, unplanned, yet there's so many flowering leaves that must have been put there, without anyone's cues, and getting water every day, TLC.

On the corner of a long, ancient roof, an old man in just a vest and sarong sits on a stool, smoking, enjoying the view, just like her.

The volcano in the distance, inscrutable, stares back at them.

For a moment, Chinna hallucinates. Lack of food and sleep, her head suddenly lifts off again, though her body feels rooted to the slate step, the tree, as rooted to the earth as it'll ever be. It's not the old man and her, the picnicking families beside her on the platform, enjoying Marapi.

It's Marapi enjoying them, holding them in her lap. The hilltop market isn't grafted onto the volcanic crust, it's an expression of it, all this bustle, all this mad zinging energy, this joy, it comes right from the earth, from the basalt suffused with fungi, their single-celled twines writhing throughout the rock, penetrating every last inch, mining it for its sulphur, phosphor, carbon, every last trace they can trade up to the roots of the plants teeming in the soil, growing on rooftops and trees, lianas, bananas, cassava and papaya, mango and avocado trees, all ceaselessly fruiting, landing in the mad farmers' market below, and back up here in the saucers and bowls, the warungs, kiosks everywhere, the spicy fruit salads, the salted duck eggs and picnics and jackfruit eaten all around her.

She sees it all so clearly. It's the same volcanic wellspring, the cradle that gave birth to the citric acid cycle, to RNA, and finally proteins, with their astronomical numbers of possible genotypes, the complexity and robustness, the self-organisation she's trying to name—her pet circuits in the lab, Ms Fungski, her poppet, evolutionary algorithms—

She's so close to the mystery—

She breathes, stares into the distance, for once not thinking or trying to articulate.

Just listening.

Chinna finds another stairway, just like the one they live on at Lia's, but tucked away behind a hidden covered market. The market, inside, has a dinky doorway-sized kiosk serving tea and soup, with two tables with secret views of the city, where she longs to sit but is afraid to, not knowing the language or the rules. Men sit and play cards by the next stall, an optician's, which has the craziest little stools, covered in yellow velvet, gold and bright, as if for some miniature King of Siam. The men them-

selves sit on rough wooden benches or plastic, the plush
stools are always empty, waiting for customers to have
glasses prescribed.

Beyond the men is a drop to the astonishing view below,
which is where she finds her stairway. Gang Mawar, she
reads, whatever that means. It's not straight from A to
B, like their own: it seems to wind downhill through a
secret world.

Miniature wooden houses, all peeling white or pink.

She passes the tiniest windows. Double, with lots of small
horizontal panes, frames painted cream, closing in the
middle. Louvred shutters open out, little half-curtains
strung in between. She tiptoes, almost. Listening. Entire
families living behind each little house-proud strip of
ruched satin, in the wooden rooms. She hears a Bollywood tune blaring, pots and pans. Women making
dinner. Glimpses a floral calendar nailed to a wall of
boards painted hot blush. The small window gives nothing more away, but she longs, suddenly, for that
bedroom, that family bed. It looks like the quaint Dutch
fisherman's towns Chinna visited in her youth, old Vol-
endam, Urk. There's potted plants again everywhere,
hanging from the little verandas, lining everything that
can be lined, orchids, frangipani, cactus fruit.

As she descends, a guitar sounds behind ruched half-
curtains between open shutters. A pair of bare feet sticks
from another window, brown toes. Someone enjoying a
sit down inside, in the afternoon sun.

The next house, even smaller, has an extended veranda, an overhang of rough wooden planks. A young girl in batik housedress sits on the floor. Scrubbing clothes with a brush, in a basin. Suds. Washing hangs from the lines, dozens of baby pants, pastel shades, between orange-and-pink sarongs faded with age.

Chinna nods, smiles. The girl grins back, Chinna beaming now. Before scuttling on.

She emerges down by the Pasar Banto, the scary brutalist block where they sell vegetables, walks on along the circular road, under an old iron footbridge and further, where Pasar Banto's grim concrete soon gives way to rice fields, finger-sized mosques, topped with tiny silver domes, villages tucked in the arms of the city, till she reaches the corner of the quaint little main street cutting back through Chinatown. Which she takes, back home.

She drops in at Denny's. The cafe is quiet, a Dutch couple or two having beers in front, next to three Malaysians checking their phones. They too drink Bintang, local beer, while playing cards. Inside, Denny smokes on a stool, and selects a playlist on the laptop perched on the bar. It's the one place in the city, perhaps in the country, Chinna sighs with relief, where Justin Bieber and Ed Sheeran are banned. If she has to listen to Shape of You, or Love Yourself one more time she will scream.

Indonesians clearly have not a word of English, she thinks, watching the women pass on the street, in their ankle-length gowns and capped, one-piece hijabs. The style is less headscarves and more the pull-on type cloak, like a cross between a baseball cap, a veil and a poncho.

It's not even that uncool, or ugly.

But it certainly does not reveal any part of their physique. To hear Ed Sheeran blast *Shape of You* from every amp or speaker in town is weird to say the least. Lost in thought, Chinna stares at the wall, a painting of Bob Marley, dusty Balinese artefacts, some scary Barong statuette. A rusty old knife, a blackened typewriter for some reason, a chipped hand mirror, all nailed to the boards behind the bar. Some empty whisky bottles, trophies rather than actual stock.

Denny looks up. *Drink?*

Chinna shakes her head.

On the house, he insists. *Try jus pokat?*

She raises her hand, no thanks.

Nonsense, he says, *you're my guest, you'll love pokat, like your mum.*

She makes a question mark face.

Jus pokat, he repeats. *Juice. Good.*

Chinna squirms, gestures, then nods, and squeaks. To her surprise, words come out. *No sugar, please.*

She's spoken. The thought of drinking scares her so much, she adds more words. *Not sweet.*

Denny nods. Pure. In a minute he returns.

The glass is green.

Pokat, Denny says again. *Good.*

Chinna takes a sip.

It's ice cold, creamy. Something between a smoothie and bland guacamole—*avocado*. Not sweet. She smiles. Keeps sipping.

Good, she nods. Another word, one she did not believe she had in her, least of all about food.

Denny returns to his screen.

In front, a Bintang delivery arrives. A young man carries cardboard boxes inside, three at a time.

Just then Denny's sister walks in, heads for the bathroom. Denny checks the bill with the delivery guy.

Bareheaded, the sister returns with wet hands, squeezes past her brother, behind the bar, where she pulls on a white floral cloak.

Disappears below.

Chinna watches, puzzled, her hands round her cold,

condensing glass.

The sister re-emerges, hands up under the long veil, eyes closed, praying. She bends over, disappearing once more. Denny and the Bintang man, over her head, continue haggling over what sounds like some error in the delivery order.

Chinna drinks, eats, whatever it is, the thick cold juice, the nourishing thing she is coping with.

The sister keeps coming up, eyes closed, lips muttering in Arabic, before bowing down again behind the bar, while above her, the error appears to get solved. The men swap Denny's packet of clove cigarettes, light up and smoke. The laptop plays on, The Doors, Jim Morrison in leather trousers, in front of Denny's sister's closed eyes. Twin almond portals—pale, shut to the world.

Come on baby, light my fire…

The sister tugs off her veil, checks her ponytail in the hand mirror nailed over the bar, pulls on her hijab, while joining in on the delivery debate, checking the bill one final time.

৩

The next morning, Baby Aafiyah still won't eat. Lia did not sleep.

She sets out again to Bu Kiki, the medicine lady. It's Day 50, and the WHO has advised cities to spray against microbes. Lia hurries across the hill. She's late. Aafiyah has been crying all morning, would not get dressed. No time for breakfast, and sticky rice in the lontong place is bound to be sold out by now. But Aafiyah will like the bustle at least. After rushing up and down Benteng hill, Lia arrives at Bantolaweh, enters the warung at the corner of the street. It's well past ten, late indeed. But instead of the usual empty enamel bowls of coconut sauce with just a few slivers of jackfruit left, a heap of unsold vegetables today remains at the bottom. Half of the restaurant is closed, and without the habitual flutter of butterfly veils, even the remaining tables look pale. A small group still occupy a large table by the door, a couple eat with their child. Two young men, a lone woman with a mask. None of the usual noise. It's the first time in years that any one voice can be heard. Instead of the habitual shouting over the TV and the crowd, there's only hushed hums. A steady trickle of young men descends from mopeds in front, to take place at the tables emptied by women and children. Aafiyah droops. Lia walks on.

More than the empty tables, the face mask, the visual pallor, it's the warung's undersong that has changed tone.

Just a little way up the main street from Denny's cafe, still flagging, old Kartina is scouring Chinatown for disinfectant. Hand sanitiser is all sold out, but Kartina doesn't believe in new-fangled trends. *Mahal*, expensive!

She doesn't quite trust Indonesian detergent either, and Dettol too is expensive. It's Great Panda, her own trusted brand, with its unmistakable smell, imported straight from China, that she wants. Lysol, lye, whatever that smell is—don't sniff too close, it will strip your septum from your nose.

But no matter how many doors she enters, how many old friends she sits down and chats to before getting to her errand: Great Panda, too, is sold out. There are no more imports from China.

When Chinna crosses Chinatown the next day, walks into the cafe, Denny's sister is wearing a mask. Or tries to. She sits drinking coffee, with the rest of the staff, waiting for custom. But there's not a white face left in the town. Still, she fusses with the strings behind her ears. Fiddly. She gives up. She's only using it for tourists anyway. Not with her co-workers, of course, who are safe.

The street, the cafe are empty.

Day 52. Up on the stairway connecting Chinatown to the Great Mosque at the top, as Elektra and Chinna sleep, Baby Aafiyah still will not eat. The medicine woman advised the yolk of a duck's egg, and *pahid pahid*: bitter food. Papaya leaf. Against fever.

Lia's husband Afin is a big fan of rigour, cleanliness and discipline, like his mother Kartina, but within reason.

He hates waking for the farmers' market. Lia also just needs the break. Worry, the baby, she hasn't slept much. She finishes prayers, can't focus anyway. She has made every bow, every gesture, said every word, and remembers none.

She pulls off her robes, no time for a wash with Aafiyah fussing. She leaves the baby in bed with her husband, gets dressed for market. Her favourite hijab, long and black, reaching almost to her knees at the back. It's cleanish. Embroidered with roses, which helps hide Aafiyah's worst. She quickly checks the glass in the hall. Just as she thought. Yesterday's vomit, spittle, it's all grist for the mill, in this veil.

Out the door. The fresh air on the veranda, quick climb up her stairway alley, to the top, the great Masjid. She turns right, away from the Zoo, and ducks into the secret covered market, where she emerges again, at the back, out in the open, at the top of the tucked-away stairs. She pauses, as always, to take in the volcanic range in the distance, but most of all, this morning, the hidden world, here, of the sleepy *kampung* cresting the hill. Passing the tiny, tumbling-down houses of her youth by the lake, strewn along the stairs and still half asleep, the miniature porches all in bloom, hanging plants and frangipani in pots, ferns and tall trees heavy with fruit. Even if Lia would need a single egg, or a pinch of salt, she would climb down Gang Mawar, Rose Alley, just to get a whiff.

Pasar Banto, as always at the foot of the stairs, across the road, looks somehow different. And then she knows what it is. Traffic. The road, always a death-trap, with its mopeds and random-missile-act vans, is almost sedate. The market still draws a steady trickle of its crowd.

But Lia doesn't feel like circling the large concrete building today, leisurely making her rounds. Picking and choosing, judging the texture of fish and the shade of tomatoes, along the farmers' stalls. Trucks are parked along the circumference. Yellow rope tied between them. A soldier watches from the road.

Lia crosses, starts right where she normally ends.

Garlic, chilli, papaya leaves. Eggs.

The bloody mosque keeps keeping Chinna awake. When she finally goes back to sleep, the Imam starts preaching again. The man is in love with his own voice. It blasts down the stairs, right into her ears, there's no getting away. She doesn't get a word, but the tone is hectoring, menacing, the three words she does understand, *orang barat*, Westerners, and *corona*, spat out in high-pitched peaks.

QWERTY, is all Chinna thinks: one trigger—*fear*—linking to the next—*flames*—dominoes—*hyphae*—PAIN—a chain of non-causal effect. She gets up. Throws on her batik trousers, her tee, heads for the porch, the little bench under the passion fruit pergola. Sits in her corner, by the gate. The Imam is equally loud, but at least diluted by the air. The narrow view from the stairs. Chinatown lies along main street below, Benteng and the fort in the distance above.

On the veranda, across from her, Uni Lia carries the baby on her hip, feeding her something so yellow it looks like custard on steroids, like some radioactive agent from the lab. She's wearing another ankle length gown, and a long, embroidered black veil. It reaches past her hips, further dips in the back.

Right through the Imam, someone somewhere is blasting Ed Sheeran again, *Shape of You*.

Lia, with her cheekbones, brilliant smile, pure, golden skin, is beautiful. That much is clear. But there's no trace of the shape of her body.

Chinna feels a ripple of something, crouched in her corner, cowing under the passion fruit dangling overhead, the spiralling vines. A ripple, a current, an inkling of something she can't yet explain. Let alone articulate.

Words.

She gives up. The baby has vomited the bright yellow custard all over her mum. Maybe it's egg yolk. Smeared with steroid-yellow gunk, in her long Muslim gown, Lia is still the most glamorous housewife Chinna has ever known.

Chinna lies in bed. Stretches out, curls back up. There's no escape from her thoughts.

She needs cover. Shelter, more than this roof over her head: a new kind of membrane, she needs something between herself, this failing body, and the world.

Even in the silence, she hears Ed Sheeran.

It's not the shape, but the safety of Lia's body, she wants.

Simpang Raya, the town's most famous restaurant, is empty. On the ground floor, a single family occupies a table. Upstairs is even ghostlier. The first-floor tables overlooking the clock tower, unoccupied. Three soldiers sit with their backs turned, watching the wide screen TV on the opposite wall. Day 52 still. Chinna is the only paying customer, and even she is not here to eat. Drinking is the best she can do. She sits by a window, looking out on the circular slates, the panorama fence under the line of ancient crowns, the distant volcano hulled in clouds. The row of little tourist shops lining the ornamental paving, with their old little Minangkabau roofs, are closing up. Her spot under the tree, for the first time in days, is free. The tower stands alone in the rain. An old man walks around with a large parasol. Though the restaurant is deserted, the tiled walls seem to echo louder than usual. The TV. A presenter in Lycra, on a bike, is instructing children to wash their hands. There are 367 confirmed cases in the country.

There's little Chinna can do. She sips her avocado juice.

The streets are still. Chinna passes the shops, with their bored assistants all listlessly checking their phones. Till she dares a glance at the wares.

Miss, miss! What you want?

She finds she'd been darting looks at a veil. Black, long.

She looks at the assistant.

Two-hundred thousand rupiah, Miss.

Chinna squirms, bows, smiles, walks on.

She ends up at the Plaza, an ugly, airless, modern mall by the clock tower. Takes the halting escalator up to the town's one department store, Ramayana. It stinks of fake leather sandals and handbags, a thick toxic fug. But at least it has price tags. No need to haggle. And it sells women's clothes. Though it has no customers, apart from two rich ladies wearing diamante shades, the first women in sunglasses she's seen in the city, Chinna believes. Ramayana, a nationwide chain, clearly out of touch with Minangkabau shoppers, also has no veils.

On the ground floor, she wanders aimlessly between concessions stands. Long dresses, long hijabs galore. No price tags though, and pushy sellers once more.

Miss, miss!

Her vision blurs. Hunger. Her retinas burn—she aches, aches, suddenly, unaccountably, for that veil.

Her feet fail. She cannot walk.

She can also not faint here. Spectacle. All these eyes, on her western shape.

She just needs to disappear.

Hides in the next, empty shop. The seller—her own age, not more—is on the floor. In her prayer gown, head, hands, feet all covered. She has her face to the ground.

Chinna halts, her fevered eyes casting about, and finally losing focus, simply staring at one point, while she gathers herself. Dark violet voile stares back at her.

How much, she asks with her eyes, when her peer scrambles up.

The assistant helps Chinna put the veil on. It reaches over her hands, and almost to the back of her knees.

She leaves the mall. Her brittle frame quakes. Now all she needs is a gown. Tomorrow. But she's overstimulated, too many options, too many impressions on her depleted frontal lobes. She can't stop thinking. Her head is inflamed. Her brain roils, her thoughts press against her skull. If it wasn't made of solid bone, it would blow off. Her thoughts are like the gravitational waves of an armed spiral galaxy, forcing brain matter together to the point of nuclear fissure. Not even the deep, dark violet veil can keep it together.

The clock tower looms over the forlorn square. Half-five. Few vendors pace its ornamental circles. Four or five photographers cluster around the foot of the tower, their identical sample photos posed side by side on the empty steps. The army of prawn cracker sellers have retreated. A few women sit with their baskets on the low wall where they used to congregate in their dozens, where throngs of visitors sat eating or sharing giant yellow crackers filled with even yellower *mi* until midnight. Now there's no more than a dozen men, women and children circling the square for leisure. Teen girls like her, in their pink fabric masks, teen boys still taking a selfie or two. Across the square, in the distance, Marapi looms.

Chinna aches for her. For the view, the tree, the far left one, the first in the row of ancient trees lining the far end of the square, with the black balustrades overlooking the city below.

She doesn't dare cross the square. It's virulent, to her mind, the spiked corona thick in the air. Her throbbing brain picks up the smell. Her knees wobble, *danger*.

Yet the nuclear galaxy, the pressure under her skull yearns for her spot. Her pins quiver beneath her. She needs to sit.

After a hesitant moment, she starts circumventing the square, spiralling its perimeter. Walking around, pace by pace, feeling some kind of shelter in her veil, staying as far as she can from anyone. At least she's finally invisible. Passes the myriad, empty entrances of the labyrinth market around the bright new block, still closed, passes the pretty row of little horned shops lining the far end of the square, till she reaches the small raised viewing platform, the row of trees, her old spot, on the edge of the platform. Sinks down, her back against the tree.

She breathes. Her legs shake. Her brain aches. QWERTY—

She closes her eyes. They burn. Tears in her lashes, on her cheeks, tears of sleepless thought and fatigue.

She opens her sore lids and trains her stare on Marapi. The first golden rays of sunset strike across the volcano, teasing out its texture, the ancient lava streams hidden under its verdure.

Minutes pass. Half an hour. Her head, her hands covered with voile.

Her gaze softens. Her breathing. The long song announcing the prayer call starts. Echoes over the city, polyphonic, drifting in and out of phase, from every point on its radius, echoed back by Marapi's green range.

The sky colours, the foot of the mountain lights up with silver little pinpoints, clustered among the deep, emerald stillness. Starry hillside hamlets.

Over Chinna's aching skull, the tree's green sprawl, the ancient crown holds a bright, lime coloured nest of ferns. Lichens, mosses, masses of single-leaved symbionts spiral up along the bark, along the broad branches, like trails of green little ears.

Chinna, for no reason at all, hums the melody of the pre-prayer song. It vibrates in her ribcage, the nape of her neck, all the way up to her scalp and her evolutionary membrane of voile.

Day 53. It rains. If meteorite quantities of water, Chinna thinks, the kind that could fill our current oceans three times over, are your idea of a shower. The deluge hits the corrugated roof like the early Bombardments. Meteorite-sized, and almost equally loud. She loves it.

Lies on the bed. Listening. There is nothing else. Not a sound. Not the traffic or voices, not even the mosque. Every whisper and breath drowned out. It turns the room timeless, boundless.

No wonder people here sleep. The torrential rain is the loudest, most soothing hum in the world.

Even Chinna dozes off, a minute, perhaps two or three, before her brain kicks back in.

Breathe, she thinks. Just be.

But just being, means just being Chinna. Obviously. Which soon feels like a chore.

QWERTY

She gets up. Walks around. All this rain. Loud, insistent. Pungent, hard. Claustrophobic. She can't get out.

And then it's just a downpour, and then a shower, and then rain. And now drizzle, and she's already putting on her long dress. Fixing her face mask. Then gloves, and Muslim socks, and a long hijab. Finally a nylon jacket, which won't stop any rain.

The street is empty. Chinna nearly runs. The town has just been through rain on a Biblical scale. If that hasn't cleared the air, nothing will. The clock tower, the square lie deserted. At the far end, her tree. Steaming, darkly verdant, its contrasting lichens and bird's nest of fern— the leaves like an upright fan of tall, oversized feathers— all sparkling, chartreuse green.

It still drizzles, starts raining harder again. The circular paving spirals and swirls around the clock, as clean as they're going to be. Chinna finally dares cross to the opposite end.

Seeks shelter under the crown. Here, too, all is wet. She takes off her jacket, lays it on the slate step. Sits in her spot, against the old trunk. Very, very wet, still streaming with rain, as are the branches and leaves. It's barely any drier here. Big, steady drops from the crown soak her violet voile, and now her gown.

She doesn't notice. Marapi is almost clear. Ribbons of cloud on the grave, green, motherly shape. For the first time all day, Chinna can breathe. Another thing she doesn't note: for the first time in days, being herself isn't a chore.

Chinna is finally simply being.

ᘐ

The next day, Day 54, it rains again. Going cabin-fevered self-isolating, Elektra sits on the veranda at Lia's. White tiles, a little patch of grass, flowers, the rickety pergola by the garden wall, with bamboo slats for a bench running to the gate in front, the nook in the corner where Chinna likes to sit, hidden from the world. A bright green house across the stairs, and little shacks, shutters, kiosks, most Chinese-owned, all the way down the stairs.

Over two thousand confirmed cases in the country today, two hundred deaths. Most in the Jakarta metropolitan area, with its millions of daily commuters. It still sounds far away. But it won't be for long.

Twenty-five people in quarantine, Lia reported this morning, in this remote little town. Abang's sister works at the hospital. The sister knows, she's seen them. They aren't confirmed, but that's only because the tests had to be sent to Jakarta and haven't yet been returned.

Elektra sits on the porch, in her own corner, on a chair against the wall, watching the rain. Her own battered series 5 has finally given up the ghost, and she's taken to using her daughter's phone. A set of cast iron lanterns has come on. She doesn't know how to tell Chinna. Or how not to let on about the rest of the news. The country still hasn't imposed any form of lockdown. The government isn't about to. There are no dependable tests, burials have gone up fifty per cent, without any cases being confirmed, which means the spread is all under the radar, completely unmapped. From claiming to be virus-free, Indonesia, in thirteen days, has become the worst hit country in Asia. *The Jakarta Post*, on Chinna's phone, just now, quotes estimates of a million undocumented cases across Indonesia before the end of the month. Hundreds of thousands dead.

Elektra tucks the phone in her pocket, away from Chinna.

It rains on. Showers. Downpours, deluges, bucketfuls roaring down the stairs before her. Thunder in the distance. Small intervals, such as now, of mere drizzle. A man passes on the steps, trailing a large sheet of plastic over his head.

From inside, comes Abang's voice, talking to someone, loudly, that hectoring tone she hears in the sermons from the mosque. Napoleon complex, she thinks, cruelly. In a flash, she thinks of the matches thrown into powder kegs of the past, the footage of burned-out kampungs she's seen, the murdered women in the Sixties, the Chinese, her own hounded Indo family—*revenge, bloody revenge*—and stops that line of thinking, immediately.

Two soldiers, in what looks like combat gear, face masks, rush past on the stairs.

She's lost all sense of time. The power dips in and out because of the rain, the lights have sputtered and died, the mosques gone silent. The prayer call is the one thing, she realises, that keeps the country tethered to any sense of communal, daily progression, of time moving on, like vespers, evensong, the medieval *Books of Hours*.

Without the call, it's just the loose sand of its 17,000 islands, the fourth most populous country on earth, the most far-flung, forced together from parts of Siberia, the North pole, all the way down to Antarctica, held together by nothing but continental drift, plate tectonics, all crushing and crunching and sinking, a vortex, an inverted spiral, hot with pushback and centrifugal force, the least coherent country on earth, the most anarchic and least prepared for any kind of centralised effort. At the very heart of the fault lines, the Ring of Fire, the global forces threatening to swallow everyone.

The spread of the virus, underground, hundreds of thousands dead within a month. Elektra can't think about it. Her mortal, see-through, filigree child. She stares ahead, letting each single drop pass her gaze, without singling any one out.

Without the imams, the prayers, the heart-cries of Islam, the country is just this, entire days drowned out by rain, and more rain. Rain, and less rain. And more rain again.

Day 58. The British Embassy urges all British nationals to leave Indonesia, Elektra reads on Chinna's phone. They are pressing commercial airlines, and have made a list of the last available flights.

She spends a day attempting to book any of them on Chinna's little screen. Goes through the Embassy's list. Not a single airline website offers bookable flights. Each time she selects a date, destination or departure time, the whole website crashes.

She starts calling airlines. BA, KLM, Turkish Airways, any commercial flights out of Indonesia. She calls London, Amsterdam. No answer, beyond standard recorded messages.

Finally, she tries Garuda, the local one. She rings one, two, seven times, again and again, fifteen attempts, in all. Chinna's iPhone 11, a computer with the capabilities of what was until pretty recently a Cambridge mainframe, cannot make an Indonesian domestic call.

Elektra goes out, walks around the little main street, then the entire circular road, for hours, trying to find a travel agent, all closed, or even a payphone kiosk. Payphone kiosks, she soon finds out, are a thing of the distant past, together with internet cafes, and backpackers altogether, pretty much, all replaced by mobile devices like her own.

Back home, near tears, she finally knocks Abang's door, asking to use his phone. He appears, spotlessly clean, his small, lopsided body in a starched cream shirt, Javanese style, over a combat print sarong. With his little plastic foldout phone.

No pulsa, he shakes his head. Out of credit.

He takes a look at the iPhone 11. Rose gold. *Why not with yours?*

She shakes her head, tries to explain what she herself does not understand. Chinna's contract doesn't allow it.

He doesn't understand the concept of a contract, it appears, only using pay-as-you-go.

Let me try, he takes Chinna's phone in his hands, studies the interface, dials a number.

It will not connect.

Doesn't work, he agrees. *That was my own number*, he adds, holding up the toy phone. Gives the shiny iPhone back.

Back on the porch, Elektra keeps trying. Still cannot get through to any of the airlines on the list. When she finally gets through to Garuda, every last seat on the very last flight out of Jakarta, the only port left, is taken. There are no more flights planned at all in the coming month.

She goes to her room, lies on the bed. Says nothing.

Chinna sits beside her in bed, spoon in one hand. Avocado in the other.

Elektra holds her breath. Chest raging with feelings, hot, warm. Furious. She will explode, nuclear fallout all over her daughter. Chernobyl.

She exhales.

Radiating heat, light. Energy. Simply refusing to send out any signals of stress.

⑤

In the hall, later, Chinna watches Lia nursing Aafiyah, in her long gown and hijab, barefoot and dancing around, while rapidly talking to Mum.

Mum nodding, smiling, asking questions, while Lia talks and talks, laughing, the baby at her breast, under the veil—Lia's bare, wide cheekbones, her brown eyes and white smile the cleanest, purest things Chinna has seen. Pacing, rocking and nursing the baby, jumping from foot to foot with animation while telling her story, chortling and giggling.

Elektra sits on the floor, arms around her knees, in hijab and a house dress, saying *beranie* repeatedly, the one word Chinna understands, as it's almost the same in Dutch. Cheeky, bold as brass.

Each time Elektra says it, Lia dances harder, laughs more, half embarrassed, half bold all over, giggling like a teenager.

Chinna tries, just an instant, to understand what they're on about. But she cannot get a word.

Gives up. Looks out at the rain. Dancing on the porch.

She longs to go out, is starting to feel locked in.

Merlin, a phrase comes to her. *Meet cute.* Lia is talking about her husband.

She turns back, to Elektra, who is entranced, and Lia, hopping barefoot, blushing, the baby half asleep in her arms.

At some point, abrupt, the call to pray starts, and Lia jumps, looks up, surprised, and still laughing, scurries to her door.

ა

Later that day, Elektra hangs her laundry out to dry among the gowns and hijabs on Lia's lines, when two old men arrive on the porch. One doesn't seem to speak Indonesian, and one Elektra knows from sight, from one of the small houses on the stairs, below.

They call for 'Afin', who, Elektra gathers, must be Abang. There's no answer.

I think he went out to buy credit for his phone, she says.

The men sit to wait on the porch, under the pergola, and smoke.

After ten minutes or so, they get up. They ask Elektra to send greetings to Afin. At least, that's what she hopes they are saying. She also hopes that she guessed right, that

Afin is Abang's actual name. In the confusion, she bows a couple of times, and calls both men *Pak*, Father, many times more. Touching her heart, her mouth. When the whole pantomime is over, the two men shuffle out of the gate, and Elektra is holding, bare handed, some sort of delivery for the family.

A wooden spin top.

੫

Chinna can't find her phone. Mum has been hogging—hiding?—it. Shielding her, perhaps, from the worst of the news. Driven crazy sitting alone inside her room, in the rain, Chinna goes out. She enters the secret little covered market opposite the Great Mosque at the top of the stairs. She no longer dares to go out to her tree, but she aches for its view.

There's the tiny soup stall here, with the tables just at the end in the back, where the roof gives way to the open air, the hilltop panorama, the tiny houses, great whalebone of Pasar Banto's roof below, the paddies, the volcano.

Men smoke at the end of the last table, as always, around the optician's stall, one or two wearing masks, but all playing cards, rubbing elbows, sharing packets of clove cigarettes. Don't they know what social distancing is?

She sits down, alone, at the first table, annoyed. There's a deadly virus around. Why don't they go home?

Chinna orders tea, no sugar, wearing gloves, a mask, staying as far as she can from the men. She tries to take in the view, but the men are in front of it.

She looks at the wall, the table, but this defies the purpose of her trip, making her feel even more locked in. She tries to ignore the men. Simply gaze over, past, their heads.

Now it looks like she's staring at them.

Perhaps she is. Holy Christ, these people have no concept of private space to begin with. They share beds with entire families!

Her tea arrives, politely served at a distance. Everyone does, Chinna notes at last, stay away from *her*. She pulls her veil further down, to cover her hands, anything that might give her away as western. Takes a sip from her tea. *Sweet*. Bloody hell, *no sugar*, she'd gestured, can no one here understand even the most basic order?

But there's something off about all this, she can feel it, though she doesn't know what it is. She sets down the tea, gets up to complain, ask for *unsweetened* tea, for god's sake. She rises from the teal plastic stool, feels people glancing at her.

When it finally hits her. This place is home to the people around her, the secret market's small family. It's where they eat and drink, where they throw in their lot, their fate, with their peers.

It's her, the one with a room of her own, who's intruding, failing to keep her distance.

Chinna, back alone in the room in the rain, undresses, stares at the ceiling.

At the prayer call, *Allahu Akbar*, she pulls on her veil, sits on the bed, wondering what to do. She bows down, rises again, as she's seen Denny's sister do. Holds up her hands, covered under the voile. Opens her mouth. A crackle comes out.

Then a hum, a distant approximation of the tones of the prayer from the mosque. She just follows, sometimes, by chance more than anything else, finds her vocal chords hitting the right note, echoing the prayer, hitting some symbiotic overtone, *polyphony*, and finds her whole body, her throat to her skull, vibrating, resonating, a recollecting, somehow, a remembering—collecting her member parts back together. A feeling older than herself.

ʊ

On the porch, watching the mountain town around her, under its steel-grey cloud, Elektra listens to Lia's husband, Abang, again talking loudly in the hall, to the old man from the corner below, who has returned, alone.

That hectoring tone. She feels it in her throat.

Mulia, Abang is saying, some Muslim term, *haram*, like the Imams. *Corona*. She tries to block out the sound, focus on her breathing, on being, but it still frightens her.

She keeps breathing.

After some time, her ears clear.

She could never understand the Imams, through their microphones, their Indonesian is far too advanced, but Abang's speech now sounds crystalline, even to her. She can't really believe it. She understands every word. Things he's said to her, before, when she thought he spoke broken Indonesian for her sake. But it's just how he talks.

Is this what those Imams where saying, all along?

The clouds keep darkening, in the distance thunder gathers, promising torrents here soon. She listens on. Phrases so simple they break her. *Hati bersih.*

A clean heart.

Hati senang.

Happy.

Hati puas.

Contented.

Hati sehat.

A healthy heart.

ʊ

The next day, Day 59, and all over the world, over-booked, lone, final flights take off, while terminals close.

Lia wakes to the strangest sound. Her first thought is, papaya leaf. She needs to go to the market. But the thought was not what woke her. It takes her awhile, on her batik sheet, to figure out what it is. The baby sleeping against her chest. Her husband with his light little snore, on his back, open-mouthed, his sarong wrapped tight around him from his upright feet, like a shroud. Their hot little bundle, Aafiyah, holding the spin top, between them. Everything looks normal. The rains have stopped. There's the usual predawn ticking of the iron roof, always shrinking with the nightly drops in temperature, from hot middays to cold mountainous mornings. The light zing of stridulating insects. A lone car somewhere in the distance. Tooting, for some reason, in the dark. But that isn't it, the strangeness. The strangeness is deeper, more strange. More unsettling, ominous. Ghostly. It's an absence. No sound at all.

There's no *tahrim*, the preamble to the prayer call.

And then she remembers. The mosques have closed. All day yesterday, the day had been silent. The long melodious song, winding its way through her daily hours, giving shape to her existence, giving rise to her actions and thoughts, gently leading her towards surrender and meditation, reflection, joy, had stopped. The actual call to prayer had kept falling upon her like a judgement, out of nowhere, out of the clear blue sky like thunder, and she'd had to stop collecting the washing from the line, drop her cooking, or a story she was in the middle of telling Elektra, and scramble into her prayer clothes.

Lying in bed in the dark, listening to the breath of her children, her husband, she jumps. Here it is again.

Allahu Akbar!

She sits up. Damn. It's hard to be in the mood without any notice at all. But she sighs, climbs from the bed, gets into her gown. Yawns. The mood will usually come.

An hour or so later, Chinna too wakes. Elektra still sleeps, turns to cough, sleeps on. Chinna watches her. Mum looks hot, fevered perhaps. Chinna cuts that thought, kills it right here. Her brain will not go there.

Mum is fine. She's strong anyway, and still young. Not old, in any case. Has great lungs, never smoked, or not since Chinna came along.

Elektra, muttering something, rolls onto her side, exposing Chinna's iPhone, tucked under her pillow. So that's where it lives.

Chinna reaches for it, careful not to wake Mum.

News at last.

But now that she holds it in her hands, she feels weird.

Opens the screen. A message from Dad.

Trying to book the last seats from Jakarta. Come to Medan as soon as you can.

Chinna leaves the message for Mum, wants to check her newsfeeds but feels herself putting the phone down. The thing somehow no longer feels like an extension of her, like her own limbs and fingertips. She feels less… wired.

Gives her pause for thought.

But then she's sure it will pass. Once all this is over. Once she's back in Merlin's class. In her virtual lab.

Elektra wakes ten minutes later, slips Chinna's phone into her pocket, gets up and sits at the little wrought-iron table. Chinna eats an avocado in bed.

Elektra stares out the window. Dawn. Lia's fraying blue nylon laundry lines. Haphazard is the word to describe everything in this corner of the world. Make-do, can-do. The stairway alley, flanked by the high walls of rooftops on top of roofs.

Over one of those walls, two small heads, one stationary, one rotating slowly. Children. One head going in circles, like a ghost, moving continuously, without any jerks from walking, a spectre, a ghost-head rotating over the wall.

Schoolboys, stuck at home, bored, one steering a bike around.

You getting bored? Elektra turns to Chinna on the bed.

Who shakes her head.

Silence. Even the mosque has gone quiet, the sermons, the rants. The crickets are waiting for the sun to come out, for the heat.

Elektra half-longs for Chinna's manic rave on the bus, the travelling salesman problem, the virus, genotypes, some double DNA in her womb. It had been chatter at least. Her daughter's voice.

But she shivers at the memory. Even mute, Chinna looks less ill.

That horrible fever, that urgency, rush.

A rush she knows well in herself. This slight fever of the mind she feels even now. Her own rush always, of chasing things, securing things, safety, knowledge, bonds. Even here, with Chinna. Securing connection.

Yet what has it brought? Lethal forces lock her daughter and her into this single room, like tectonic plates: yet even compressed here under volcanic pressure, in the middle of a pandemic vortex, they remain in utterly separate worlds.

She coughs, feeling her mind rush. Hot.

Either Chinna, or she, will yield. To the forces, the virus. If she has any agency at all, any power or will left to fight, it will be her, Elektra.

That bloody spin top. Straight from China. *In her bare hands.* Touching her face, her mouth.

How could she be so dumb?

Another cough.

A million undocumented cases, before the end of the month. And she acts like a fuzzy hare-brained thing, like a kitten.

She looks at Chinna's phone. They could go to Medan, as Nova wants. Not that he'll get those seats. But Elektra could self-isolate in Sofia's room, at least.

Leaving the lounge to her in-laws. Her daughter.

It's the best thing to do. The only reasonable thing. All at once, she longs for that room, for Sophia's bed, those four airless walls, where it all began with Chinna. Sophia's hand-stitched mosquito-net, the whale-sized indentation on her mattress.

Like a sick cat, Elektra craves being be alone, suddenly,

craves isolation, keeping Chinna safely away from her.

Better hurry.

She looks out the window again, where the boys hold still for a moment. Two stationary heads, above a wall. Then the second boy starts spinning.

They've taken turns.

It's a sign. The boys, switching places. A signal. Her life for her daughter's. A command, Abraham's sacrifice in reverse. Could not be clearer. Do it today. While there's still a chance in hell to even get to Medan, before things go in lockdown altogether, even in Bukittinggi, and Chinna is saddled here with her.

Now that she has decided, at last, has a plan, Elektra already feels better. The pain, the deep, corrosive vein in her body—the ache of wanting her daughter, of just for one second hearing her talk, hear her voice, that life-giving, gorgeous hum that she loves above anything else in the world—is almost gone. She can live without Chinna's voice, without her scent, the damp aroma of the nape of her neck. The warm skin of her body. She can do without, live or die without. Die alone.

Now.

Peace descends. She's already doing it. Simply getting up, towards the phone, making the call.

And so, it's Day 59, and my timekeeper's account, my timeline, my Chronicle, comes to an end.

My young self is watching my mother, who looks fevered, and ill. I lie and watch, and picture her alone in Medan, in Sophia's room, burning with fever and pain, alone in the scorching furnace of those walls, and even then I had the eye I have now. And I was as chronological then as I am now, child, but I had no voice.

And even now, what preceded this loss has no home in my body, my memory, no place on my timeline, no fixed abode—

My chronology breaking—

The thing I can't remember is the thing I can't forget, Poppet, and it can only happen to me in flashback—

In the present, happening forever more—

Only here, only now, this minute—

As soon as I stop thinking about the virus, about spirals and pure maths and DNA, as soon as I start feeling, I'm back in the lab again—

Day 14, that Saturday morning, after my first flush with Merlin. *By stimulating the mycelium*, Adam says, *we could input data into the mycelial computer—*

He's inserting electrodes into oyster mushrooms, setting out stimuli, the vial of acid, the burner. Wiry hair in his ears—

And I felt—I feel—I think—I thought—

The next day—Day 15, Sunday—I stand—stood—crying at Merlin's door—

In front of his home—

He's in a dressing gown, the door only part open.

We're nowhere near biocomputing yet, he is saying, patient, kind. *Yes, you've shown that mycelium can be electrically sensitive, but you haven't proved you can link a stimulus to a response—*

He shrugs his tall, delicate shoulders.

It's like you stuck a pin in your toe, detected the nerve impulse that travelled through your body, but haven't been able to measure your reaction to the pain.

I'm breaking down further—Searching his blue eyes, his dimples, for some sign of recognition, some sign that what I'm feeling is real, that he feels what I felt—what I feel—what I felt—This flesh of my flesh. If all flesh is fungus—I thought—I think—I thought—

Is this love?

Day 59, still barely past dawn. Back home, after the market, there's little for Lia to do but go back to bed. Her husband and child still sleep. It's not yet seven. It occurs to her, with a start, that the market may soon be closed.

But no. Impossible.

There's no way to stop this city from teeming, from growing and fruiting and trading. How will anyone live? Even Afin, fast asleep, and she, could never close their doors, have no income apart from their boarders, students, travelling salesmen, coming and going.

She returns her thoughts to her family.

The baby, so peaceful. Still clutching the spin top. Clean as a button, the toy, smelling of Chinese formaldehyde or Lysol or whatever it is, that brand her mother in law loves, but has run out of, Great Panda. She sniffs again, lightly—when taken in neat, the stuff will rattle your teeth. The spin top must be the most sanitised thing ever flown out of China.

She gazes past the toy, at the pillow beside hers. Her husband dreaming, probably, of Elektra's handphone. He saw it last night, when Elektra struggled to make a call to her embassy, and asked Afin for help.

Oh, Afin and handphones. She recalls how he used to come to the shop where she once had a job for a month, Toko Song. He worked in a stall selling handphones, downstairs in the same block. Rahmi, her colleague, had pointed him out. Salesman himself, travelled around. Now he uses his little knockoff Nokia, lies there dreaming of Elektra's iPhone, so miraculously handsome and smooth.

That's how he'd appeared to her. Picking out shirts in Toko Song. Handsome, smooth. With his girlfriends everywhere, in every city and town, his bright, wide, light chocolate eyes. His wider smile.

She'd not hesitated, when he came to her counter to pay. She was the cashier, taking his money. Not just his money, that day. Sell yourself dear, her mother, her friends always said. Value yourself. Price yourself high, you are precious, *mahal*.

She'd tallied his purchases, charged him alright, taken his money. The handsome handphone man. But she'd taken more, while ignoring her mother, the lady from the large longhouse: gave for free what they told her to price.

She'd taken the number of his handphone. Simply asked for it. Just like that. Bold as could be. Never done it before, never did it again. It had been someone other than she, some primal echo or alter ego almost. That same night, alone in her boarding house room, in the attic, right under the roof creaking with heat, she had called.

She rolls over in bed to face him. Handsome and smooth. Even now. Dreaming of iPhones, in rose gold. So humble. He will speak to Elektra in the morning, she's sure. About how much an iPhone costs in the West, if there's any chance they might be cheap there, not like here, second-hand at best, refurbished, without war-ranties or a box and still the price of a house. But in his heart he will know they are yet *more* expensive there.

She looks at his sleeping face, his brow. Smooth. Not a wrinkle or ripple or frown. None of it is disturbing his dream, Lia knows, it simply enhances it, makes the iPhone, remote, out of reach, even more rose gold, even more worthy of his dream.

This is why she'd chased him, that day, asked for his number, this is why she'd been utterly bold faced and called. Even scaled Mount Kartini, Oma, her awesome mother-in-law. This gift of his, to value not the having of things, not the chasing, but the patient waiting, the contented hopes, faith in fate. The humble, peaceful joy of his dreams.

Just a few rooms away, under Lia's roof, Elektra straightens her spine. The schoolboy's head still swirling away behind his wall on his bike, Elektra, by the window, has made up her mind. They're going to Medan. They'll get a taxi somehow, drive the 400 miles, she in front with the driver, her daughter safely alone, in the back. She picks up Chinna's phone, scrapes her chair.

The silence breaks. The bird outside, the cricket, the critter, whatever it is, strikes up. That piercing, stridulant voice. Insistent, like a singing saw, zig-zagging louder and louder.

Other crickets or creatures respond. What's that word Chinna uses, polyphony. A choir, a chorus.

She pauses, listens, hallucinating now for sure, hearing strange echoes—*You're not the only one*—in the strident, singing saw.

The Women of Mycenae? It's *her*, not Chinna, who's going crazy—*You show less restraint*—being locked in this room for so long—*Do you not see how by your own actions*—distancing even from her daughter—*Self-inflicted ills*—

But something tells her to stop acting, just one instant, stop deciding, stop furiously securing her fate.

I have an idea, Elektra gets up, sits on the bed. Discards the phone.

Stretches out, lies down.

Holds her daughter.

There it is again, the chorus. Outside: the creatures. Screeching. Inside, echoes twenty-five million years old, *syncytins*—cells with two different, discrete genomes, reverberating in her body, her womb, where its retroviral DNA prepared the way for her child—a choir, voices. Singing in her perineum, where she ruptured, end to end, giving birth. Where her daughter's stem cells healed her wounds, and still make up her tissue today. In her brain, where too Chinna is alive and well, with her own DNA, still active, where she still makes new connections, rewiring Elektra's logic gates. Emergent, polyphonic song. Emergent form.

Explain it to me, Elektra says. *Hyper-dimensionality. Geno-type networks, change. How it all works. Evolutionary algorithm.*

She pauses, only an instant.

We have all the time in the world.

And I, I have no voice. Only thoughts, because if I stop to feel—

I'll be back in the lab—and I couldn't, not here, not now, so close to the end—a minute to midnight—

Or could I—

All the time in the world—

And then I felt—I feel—I think—I thought—over and over, happening only now, only here—where I have my mother's ear—And it has to be *this now*.

Day 14, Cambridge. Back at the lab, the day before I break down at Merlin's door—Adam and I insert electrodes into the oyster mushrooms that I, she, young Chinna has grown, sprouting in clusters from mycelium on blocks she's pampered with coffee grinds, has watered and fed all month.

The electrodes all in place, the pale, velvet flesh connected to their various action potential detectors, all in turn wired to the data-collecting hardware and software, Adam probes the network with the stimuli he's prepared.

They have, as Adam describes it at his laptop, *detected spontaneous waves of electrical activity.*

When Adam brings the Bunsen burner to the mushroom, the others within the cluster, he points at the graph on his screen, *respond with a sharp electrical spike.*

The oyster mushroom communicates the stimulus to its peers. A signal travels the network.

Towards [A] Fungal Computer, Adam gestures as he sits at his keyboard, hands in the air bracketing the disputable, single indefinite article. He likes that pun.

Sipping coffee again, thinking of how to present the data, how to write his paper. *We could input data by stimulating the mycelium...,* he begins. Not exactly dictating, just thinking out loud, typing QWERTY, for something to do. *For example, he goes on, articulating, with a chemical or a flame.*

Chinna does not see or understand at that moment, only feels how her body responds—responded—responds— Her neural ends, her fingertips, those sensitive skins, with their action potential—A sharp tingle—A sign that the mycelial computer is already here—

She spikes—

Pain travels her neural network, the Bunsen burner

scorching her Root-Brain—burning—*flame*—searing her hyphae—

Her pale, velvet skin *screams*, at her pale velvet peers—*we are not you and we are not me*—We are in PAIN—

We have to run—escape—from these insentient beings—this human flesh with its acid and flames—with its singular, murderous minds—its self-isolating thought—its mental cages—solipsistic skulls—its boneheaded brains—THIS ISN'T LOVE—

The biocomputer is me.

All the time in the world...

Elektra is holding her child, arms around her sharp shoulders; entangled life.

Chinna still cannot speak, cannot explain. How Merlin is flesh of her flesh, but does not understand her root-brain, her first-flush love—how everything is connected, the fungal computer, complexity, genotype networks, evolution, algorithm. There's the book she brought with her, the Swiss scientist's, with the pretty birds. Darwin's finches. She still cannot read—hasn't been able to, since running from the Bunsen burner that day, escaping the lab—still isn't able to eat or to speak—

QWERTY—No.

She's safe in Mum's arms. Slowly, the scorching abates. In Elektra's embrace, Chinna's sensing skin—her velvet membrane, contained in the larger membrane of her mother—is finally cooling. The burning, the pain.

Mum is listening, waiting still. *Explain it to me…*

Evolutionary algorithm is like prayer, perhaps, part of Chinna wants to say. But she could never bring herself to use those words. Data, numbers, logic are her realm.

And yet. Something resonates in her. Pale, velvet flesh. Entangled life.

Flesh of her flesh, yes, despite it all. Merlin Sheldrake, with his innate, golden psilocybin flush—Yes: *love!*—

Rupert Sheldrake, Merlin's father, with his psychic cats and dogs—Morphic resonance—the *habits* of nature, not natural laws—genes as *receptors* of nature's habits of form, of its cosmic song, the platonic shapes underlying us all.

Jill Purce, Merlin's mum. *More Ways Than One:*

Surely these forms go right through all the different levels of nature, and also through the levels of our own consciousness— And this is why we actually see them? Our minds structure what we see and are structured by the overall order—it's a recognition, of what we already are.

Chinna's thoughts are interrupted—without any pre-ambles, without the long and winding preparation of song —by a sharp creak of the speakers next door.

She jumps, holds on to Mum. *Allahu Akbar.*

In addressing the overall order, Chinna is thinking—whatever we call it, fate, the Big Bang's original *om*—you can change every word, every sound, every gesture, every detail: without losing the song underlying your *own* consciousness' order.

Like rewiring logic gates.

She gazes at Darwin's finches, their pretty beaks.

DNA is the same. Complexity begets robustness, which in turn begets astronomical numbers, the realm of pure order and form. You can spiral all the way around that spectrum, a genotype network, mutate almost every gene, without losing the phenotype, the function, the overall structure with which you'd begun. Change is robust, an armed spiral, a habit, a hum much deeper, older, more stable, sustaining, and ingrained than we. Undersong.

It sounds very simple suddenly, even to her. Zeros and ones.

Mum, I begin.

A first word, once more.

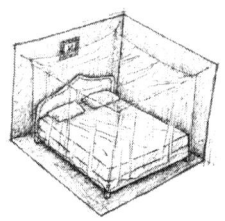

And it is not yet dawn, and outside the earth is empty and void. Row after row. And waving crowns, trees, breathing leaves, there are none.

And yet we breathe. And we hum and move on the soil, on the waters travelling the underworld, the tangles and swirls underground, feeding a lone seedling's first leaf, still furled, held tight in its coil.

And we breathe on the woman waking inside, and you open your eyes, Elektra. And you hear us not, and your eyes see us not.

And you feel alone, in the house on the scorched, viral earth, and outside there is row after row. And you turn to the window, breathing for green, and there is none. And you lie in the bed that you share with your loved ones, your husband, your mother in law, your daughter yet unborn. And you lie with your child yet unborn, of whom until your clock strikes midnight, all you will know is her smile.

And you will yet know her face, today, as it will come to you in your dream, and your child yet unborn will appear to you as a girl. And your child will smile, and your child is happy and smiles at the world.

And all will be well, and we tell you that all will be well, and that all things will be well.

And yet you hear us not, and you know not what your day and your time of labour will bring. And still we sing, and we sing to you all manner of things.

You are not the only one…

And you don't know who you yet are, Elektra, and you don't know how to yet do this, how to be broken and cleaved and opened to the earth enough to give birth.

And yet you will do it. You will tear, sunder, rupture from end to end.

And your child, carried full term, has thrived on the backwards viruses that entered your blood, and it thrives on the one of your fate, the virus wedged into your womb. And its genome thrives in your cells and will thrive in your child, as it will in all children from woman born.

And you will rupture from end to end, beginning to beginning, and your child's cells will enter your blood, and your child will heal your wounds. And your child will live on in you, the days of your life, and you will live on in her all the days of her life.

And you are it, Elektra, the riddle, and you are the spiral, and you are the algorithm. And you must grow like the spiral, and you must grow at the mythic rate that brings life to your child. And if you grow too slow, you will yet lose her. And if you rage and pace and cycle your mind, your furl will grow too tight. And if your furl is too tight, your daughter will not thrive. And your daughter yet will die. And as you furl and shield your child, you shall shield all manner of things. You shall furl the earth and the soil and the rocks and the sea and all manner of being.

And you are we and we are you, no end, no beginning. And so it is.

See: At the stroke, the om of midnight, your time will come.

And there is no end, only this, your big day, this viral earth, the sun already zinging, the crickets at dawn, the call from the mosque, your husband and mother-in-law rising to pray, the end in itself, the beginning of everything.

Acknowledgements

This book is the work of many. Huge thanks to Merlin Sheldrake, Jill Purce and Rupert Sheldrake for graciously lending their voices. Books by Andreas Wagner, David Quammen, Carl Zimmer provided evolutionary history, Jane Allison's the novel's structure. Debi Alper and Katy Whitehead helped crystallise its ideas. Sophie Lambert was, as always, an all-round star. Thanks to Adrian Cooper at Little Toller for early support. Lois Hambleton read early drafts. Thanks to Jill Dawson. My dear nieces, Rahmi and Afiyaa, offered their home and their love. Jamie McGarry at Lendal threw in his lot. My editor, Paige Henderson, did all the hard work. She's the smartest girl in the room. The title is hers. Illustration of Sophia's room by Sazli. Artwork by Ananda Kupfer. My sister Janneke paid 25 million rupiah to fly me back home to him. My first reader, as always. He is the point.

About the Author

Nada Holland was born in 1968 in the Hague, boomeranged everywhere from the Dutch polders to Nigeria, until she found herself waiting tables at a series of Portuguese beachfront cafes by fifteen. Deciding she'd like to interview rock stars instead, and ended up reporting from San Francisco and New York for a leading Dutch newspaper. She met her son's father on an island off the coast of Bali, got married in Jakarta, and fell in love with green, volcanic Sumatra.

Living with her child in a snug cabin under Redwood trees in Santa Cruz, Nada volunteered at a Tibetan Buddhist experimental school, while writing short stories, before settling in London, where she lives on the eleventh floor of an East London tower block with her son and a cast of tropical plants. *Motherborn* is her first novel.